"Dylan, " Rommie said a

For all his faith in the
that several hundred Vipers could do Andromeda some real
damage.

"Beka, increase speed. Let's shake these little—"

A concussive wave interrupted his insult, rocking the
Command.

"Return fire," Dylan commanded.

"Firing," Rommie replied. In his tactical viewscreen Dylan saw missiles streaking across the strip of blackness that
separated Andromeda from the front wave of Vipers, and
then the explosions as those missiles found their targets.

"They're still firing," Rommie reported.

"Enough of this cat-and-mouse, Dylan." Tyr said through
clenched teeth. "I recommend that you hit them with something more meaningful."

"Something big won't necessarily do the job," Dylan argued.
"There are just so many of them, and they're so spread out, we
pretty much have to target them one by one . . . Rommie, take
them out."

She flashed him a brief smile. "I'll do my best," she
agreed.

The Andromeda Ascendant's best, as Dylan knew, was
pretty damn good.

GENE RODDENBERRY'S
Andromeda™

NOVELS FROM TOR BOOKS

BOOKS BY JEFF MARIOTTE

GENE RODDENBERRY'S
Andromeda™

THE ATTITUDE OF SILENCE

JEFF MARIOTTE

A TOM DOHERTY ASSOCIATES BOOK
NEW YORK TOR®

GENE RODDENBERRY'S ANDROMEDA: THE ATTITUDE OF SILENCE

Edited by James Frenkel

A Tor Book
Published by Tom Doherty Associates, LLC
175 Fifth Avenue
New York, NY 10010

www.tor.com

Tor® is a registered trademark of Tom Doherty Associates, LLC.

ISBN 0-765-34411-4
EAN 978-0-765-34411-3

First edition: May 2005
First mass market edition: October 2005

Printed in the United States of America

0 9 8 7 6 5 4 3 2 1

For David,
who did the math,
and Holly,
who keeps me grounded

ACKNOWLEDGMENTS

Sincere thanks to Gene Roddenberry and the show's writers, producers, and brilliant cast for creating such a terrific canvas. Thanks also to Jim Frenkel—it's been a long time coming, hasn't it? And deepest appreciation to Cindy, Tara, Howard, Erin, and the gang. And Maryelizabeth, of course, for giving me the space and time to write about time and space.

Freedom is like silence, shattered by the sound of a gun, embraced only with a peaceful heart.
—SUPREME HIGH GUARD COMMANDER SANI NAX RIFATI,
"PERSUASIONS AND EXHORTATIONS," CY 4279

In the attitude of silence the soul finds the path in a clearer light, and what is elusive and deceptive resolves itself into crystal clearness. Our life is a long and arduous quest after Truth.
—MAHATMA GANDHI,
SYSTEMS UNIVERSITY ARCHIVES

GENE RODDENBERRY'S

Andromeda™

THE ATTITUDE OF SILENCE

ONE

> "Welcome to Caernaevon Drift. Now go home!"
>
> —GRAFFITI

The residents of Caernaevon Drift didn't like strangers.

There was just no other way to say it. Some folks were shy about meeting people they didn't know, and hid away or built big walls. Others were polite, even outgoing—they enjoyed the novelty of fresh faces, new ideas, and the opportunity to make new friends.

Still others—like those on Caernaevon Drift—just loosed their dogs. Or pointed guns. Or both. In the case of Caernaevon Drift, the dogs were metaphorical—in fact, what they sent winging toward *Andromeda Ascendant* were not dogs, but an entire fleet of Vipers— small, fast, two-person fighters, heavily armed and Slip-capable.

Not truly dogs at all.

But the guns? Those were real.

And everyone on *Andromeda*'s Command Deck was looking at them. "We can take these clowns," Seamus Harper insisted. "Rom-doll could do it with her eyes closed." He paused a moment. "I mean, if she even needed her eyes to do stuff like that, she could."

"She could," Captain Dylan Hunt agreed confidently. "But should she?"

Beka Valentine arched an eyebrow at Dylan. "Dylan," she said. "Can I just point something out? They *are* attacking us."

A slow smile crossed Dylan's face as he regarded Beka. Her concern was real—and quite possibly warranted—but he found it oddly amusing just the same.

After a moment, she seemed to realize she was providing Dylan with some private merriment. "Is there something we should know, Captain Hunt?" she asked him. She generally used the formal address only when she was truly ticked. "Some kind of secret you haven't shared?"

"No secret," Dylan replied. "It's just that we don't really have any urgent business here anyway. Caernaevon Drift isn't going to join the Commonwealth. We could use some hydrogen, and they dealt in it, once upon a time. They also deal in smuggling, and I guess they've prioritized that over more legitimate businesses these days. Anyway, we're not desperate enough to get into a fight over it. I guess I just thought it was kind of entertaining that you guys are so ready to mix it up with them for absolutely no reason. They just want us out of here, and since we don't have any pressing need to stick around, why not just go?"

Tyr Anasazi gave him a sidelong glance. As usual, of the small crew who had joined Dylan on his mission, Tyr was the most difficult to read. "Sometimes you surprise me, Dylan," Tyr said. "I would have expected you to consider it a matter of principle or something. Instead, you are taking the pragmatic, survival-oriented approach. I approve."

Harper interrupted Dylan's chuckle. "I'm glad you're enjoying yourself, Boss, but those things are gettin' closer. A single mosquito can be annoying, but a thousand of 'em can kill somebody."

"Nobody's getting killed today," Dylan assured the young engineer. "Certainly not by those bugs." He gripped his captain's console and braced himself. "Get us out of here, Beka. Sometimes discretion is the better part of valor," he said. "And sometimes it just saves ammo."

"So we're just going to cut and run?" Beka asked.

"I don't know about the cutting part," Dylan said. "And not so much run as Slipstream. There's a Slip point nearby. Let's use it."

He was putting a good face on things, but the fact was, Harper was right. *Andromeda Ascendant* probably could take the Vipers—at least, a lot of them. But they continued to swarm from the Drift— not yet the thousand Harper had mentioned, but at least a couple hundred, and counting. They were small, but they were fierce. And as the engineer had pointed out, an overwhelming number of opponents—even little ones—could be real trouble. Dylan wasn't a guy who would run from a fight, as long as there was a compelling reason for it.

But in this case, there wasn't. *Andromeda* ran on hydrogen and antiprotons, both of which allegedly could be had on Caernaevon Drift, but from the looks of things the Drift had become pretty possessive of what they had since Dylan's last trip here— which, admittedly, had been about three hundred eleven years earlier. Dylan was willing to pay any fair price, but blood was too high.

Just as the first of the Vipers swung into weapons range, Beka accelerated into a Slip portal. A flare of light filled the main viewscreen, followed by the tangled, knotted strings that always made Dylan feel like a blood cell traveling through a circulatory system. Then he gave up on metaphorical thinking altogether and watched his pilot guide the huge warship.

Beka was strapped into her seat, which rocked and swiveled as she kept up with the dizzying twists and spins of Slip navigation. She'd done it a thousand times, but each Slip journey presented its own challenges. Locks of blond hair fell in her face and her bright eyes focused rigidly on the screen ahead of her. Only humans could effectively navigate Slipstream, and since faster-than-light propulsion remained in the realm of the purely theoretical, only the Slipstream lanes allowed transit between the galaxies.

Dylan didn't imagine the Vipers would give chase, since their goal had been achieved. *If they do,* he thought, *well then, they'll learn just what a Glorious Heritage Class starship is capable of.*

Trouble is, most people who learn that because they're on the receiving end of her weaponry never take the lesson home to share with others.

A few gut-wrenching moments later, they transited out of the 'stream into a planetary system where he knew he could acquire fuel, and which he'd been wanting to visit anyway. The relative smoothness of linear space was always a vast relief after the stomach-churning motion of Slipstream, and the appearance in the main viewscreen of a huge green planet, like a jade ball resting on the rhinestoned velvet backdrop of space, was a welcome sight.

"Welcome to Festival," Dylan announced.

Rommie's face appeared on screens all around them, and there was an anxious edge in her reply. "Dylan," the ship's avatar said, "Vipers are dropping out of Slipstream behind us."

Dylan checked a secondary viewscreen, and saw that she was—as usual—correct. Small, pointed ships filled the space behind *Andromeda* like so many angry wasps.

"I thought they just wanted us to get out of their neighborhood," Harper whined.

"Apparently they also want to make sure we don't come back," Beka opined.

Now Dylan was angry. The Caernaevon Drift stop had simply been one of convenience. It would have been profitable for the Drift's residents, too, assuming they'd marked up the price on their hydrogen supplies fairly. But Festival was his real next destination, and he wouldn't be chased from here by a bunch of little gnats. "Maintain course," he ordered. "We're going to Festival."

"Dylan," Rommie said again. "They're firing."

For all his faith in the big ship's weaponry, Dylan knew that several hundred small ships could do *Andromeda* some real damage.

"Mr. Anasazi, deploy ECM fans and point defense lasers, and ready defensive missiles," he commanded. "And Beka, increase speed. Let's shake these little—"

A concussive wave interrupted his insult. *Andromeda* had been hit, somewhere astern, and Command rocked from the impact. Harper, not actually holding onto anything at that moment, was thrown to the deck. Trance Gemini looped her tail around a handhold just in time to catch herself. Tyr hadn't been holding on either, but it took more than a little explosion to make the Nietzschean lose his balance. He took a quick half step but maintained his footing.

"Return fire," Dylan commanded.

"Firing," Rommie replied. In his tactical viewscreen Dylan saw missiles streaking across the strip of blackness that separated *Andromeda* from the front wave of Vipers, and then the explosions as those missiles found their targets. Whether the Vipers hit were the ones that had fired made little difference—the other pilots would quickly understand that their weapons wouldn't take out *Andromeda* easily, but their own much smaller ships were no match for the big warship's armaments.

He was about to comment when he spotted another half dozen tracers closing on them.

"They're still firing," Rommie reported. A moment later a much bigger shock wave battered the deck. Everyone was ready for it this time, but even holding on or strapped in, the impact was jarring.

"Enough of this cat-and-mouse, Dylan," Tyr said through clenched teeth. "I recommend that you hit them with something meaningful."

"Something big won't necessarily do the job," Dylan argued. "There are just so many of them, and they're so spread out, we pretty much have to target them one by one."

Rommie stood by Dylan's side. He thought he could see a slight distraction in her eyes, which would not have been surprising considering that she was operating all of the ship's systems, including, at this moment, weaponry, and probably tabulating damages at the same time. But usually she didn't show the strain of that much activity, so he figured he was probably just projecting.

"Rommie, take them out," he commanded.

She flashed him a momentary smile. "I'll do my best," she agreed.

The *Andromeda Ascendant*'s best, Dylan knew, was pretty damn good. Officially designated the Shining Path to Truth and Knowledge AI model GRA 112, serial number XMC-10-182, she had been built for the Systems Commonwealth's High Guard in the Newport News Orbital Shipyards, high above Earth, in the year CY 9768. The ship, with Dylan on it, had been trapped near the accretion disk of a black hole—stuck out of time for three hundred years, during which virtually everyone Dylan had ever known had aged and died. Beka Valentine and the crew of her salvage ship, the *Eureka Maru*, had rescued them from the black hole's rim. The universe had changed drastically in that time, but one thing had not changed: then or now, *Andromeda Ascendant* was one of the finest fighting vessels anywhere.

Dylan took comfort in the view he had of the little needle-nosed ships exploding right and left. But that comfort was minimized somewhat by the fact that they were right and left, and up and down, and virtually everywhere else, filling every viewscreen. The hits were coming harder and faster now, each one shaking the Command Deck again. *Andromeda* fired back, and gave as good as she got, but this unceasing barrage was going to take a toll.

"Dylan—" Tyr began, but his words were cut off by a loud boom and a flash of light. That one had hit very close by, Dylan knew. Another shot like that and they'd be blessed with the familiar Roman candle effect, sparks blasting out of control panels. Harper, who'd have to get down behind the panels with his tools, would be in a foul mood until he'd repaired the damage.

The big Magog, who had stood silently on the Command

Deck's upper tier, finally spoke. "The Divine prescribes retreat rather than intentionally inflicting harm, when possible," Reverend Behemiel Far-Traveler growled. His tone wasn't angry or upset; it was just that every utterance from the furry, clawed Rev Bem sounded like a growl.

"We're not retreating!" Dylan shot back. Under his breath, he added, "I hope."

Another blast rattled the deck, and alarm Klaxons began to whoop. Dylan frowned. It wasn't as if he needed those to know that his ship was taking a beating.

"Dylan," Rommie said.

He cut her off. "I know! And you can turn off those Klaxons any time. I know we're in trouble."

"That wasn't what I was going to say, Dylan. Please take a look out your tactical viewscreen."

Dylan did as she suggested. What he saw surprised him: yet another fleet of ships, but these were good-sized warships. Not as big as *Andromeda*, but each one far larger than the Vipers of Caernaevon Drift. And they were approaching quickly.

"They left the orbit of Festival several minutes ago," Rommie reported. "On an interception course with us."

"I'm gonna have to go with the Rev on this one, Dylan," Harper put in. "Gettin' the hell out of Dodge seems like a really good idea right now."

Dylan glanced over at Tyr. Tyr nodded once, calmly. Dylan couldn't remember Tyr Anasazi, out of Victoria by Barbarossa, last of the Kodiak Pride, ever willingly running from a fight. *First time for everything*, Dylan thought. *That's the old saying, right?*

Dylan told Beka to scan for Slip points, where they could dive into the 'stream if it became necessary. The Festival fleet drew nearer, their big ships already appearing far larger on *Andromeda*'s screens than the tiny Vipers did.

"Dylan, the new ships are firing," Rommie warned.

"Stand by for evasive action."

But the missiles fired by the Festival ships bypassed *Andromeda* and sailed into their targets—more of the seemingly innumerable Vipers. Satisfying bursts of light and flame filled the screens.

"Hey, they're on our side!" Harper exclaimed. "All right!"

Rev Bem looked toward the ceiling. "Thank you," he uttered softly.

Even Tyr managed a brief smile.

Once the Festival ships got into the mix, the battle was short and lopsided. The remaining Vipers darted back into Slipstream, within minutes the skies were quiet again. Harper breathed a loud sigh of relief, and Dylan figured everyone else felt pretty much the same way.

Andromeda's virtual face appeared on one of the viewscreens. "Incoming transmission, Dylan," she said. "From the Festival Fleet."

"Put it through."

A moment later, the screen flickered and a friendly-looking, apparently human face came into view. The face was of a male, dark-haired, with large, inquisitive brown eyes, a straight nose, and a firm jaw. His mouth was turned up in a pleasant smile. He wore a dark blue uniform, trimmed in red at the neck and cuffs. On his shoulder were three narrow red stripes that Dylan thought probably indicated rank.

"This is Admiral Parnett Havil of the Festival System Command," he said. "Do I have the honor of addressing Captain Dylan Hunt of the New Systems Commonwealth?"

"You do indeed," Dylan replied. "And thanks for the assist, Admiral Havil."

"Not at all," Admiral Havil said. "We were happy to do it. And happier still to welcome *Andromeda Ascendant* and the New Systems Commonwealth to the Festival System. If you'll follow us in, we are very much looking forward to getting acquainted with you."

"Lead the way," Dylan said. The admiral nodded once and broke off the transmission.

"Hey, Captain," Harper said. "You're famous here!"

Dylan couldn't help chuckling. "So it would appear, Mr. Harper. So it would appear."

TWO

"In the future, everyone will be world-famous for fifteen minutes."

—ANDY WARHOL, CE 1968

When the *Eureka Maru* docked on Festival's orbital platform, a welcoming party was already underway. The vast docking bay was festooned with streamers in every color of Festival's rainbow, which included a couple that Dylan had never seen before and couldn't really describe: something between a green and a gray, and another that he could only liken to red, but a red that had been turned inside out and mixed with blue and brown. A band played music on instruments he didn't recognize, the melody sweetly stirring, but with discordant bass notes and a percussion section that seemed off by itself, or playing another song altogether.

The welcoming committee was all uniformed military, including the musicians and the support crew working the docks. *Andromeda*'s crew gathered in the *Maru*'s flight deck so they could all emerge together. Only Rev Bem wasn't there; the Wayist Magog had refused to come planetside, announcing that Festival was "a spiritual wasteland, a party planet that has completely forsaken the Divine, a den of iniquity and vice that reeks of sin and degradation. I will remain on *Andromeda* and continue to work on my memoirs," he had added. He had decided, sometime in the past couple of weeks, that the story of his journey from flesh-eater to spiritual leader merited recording for posterity. "Not to satisfy my own ego," he had declared, "but to help those who follow find their true path."

"Sin and degradation? Sounds like it's not half bad, for a mudball," Beka had said in response to Rev Bem's description of the planet. Born and raised on spacecraft, Beka "Booster Rocket" Valentine had a deep-seated distrust of planets. "Maybe I'll enjoy it after all. At least briefly."

She looked like she was ready for it. She'd dressed in a tight off-the-shoulder black top, dark leggings, black boots, with only a force lance strapped to her thigh for a sidearm. Dylan couldn't help admiring her powerful physique. Her blond hair was tied back into a ponytail, her lips were red and full, and her blue eyes sparkled like a mountain creek Dylan had once seen on Hamilton's Reach.

Dylan himself wore a dress uniform, black leather with a maroon trim, bib-fronted, a row of magnetic metal buckles running up the diagonal hem. He too had a force lance at his hip. Tyr looked impressive in a loosely woven mail shirt and tight dark pants, with a Gauss pistol that some might mistake for a cannon strapped to his side. Rommie had gone for elegant minimalism: a black sheath dress with a hint of a military cut to it. Harper was casual in a Hawaiian shirt, red with colorful surfboards on it, and white pants. And Trance wore her typical purple bodysuit, a few shades darker than her skin.

Heading down in the *Maru*, Harper had barely been able to contain his glee at the coming planetfall. "It's been so long since I've had solid ground under my feet," he said excitedly. "Especially solid ground where the fun never ends. The way I hear it, the ladies on Festival not only don't know how to say no, but even if they did they wouldn't understand why anyone would ever want to."

"And won't it be good to know that they like you for yourself?" Tyr teased.

"Hey, I don't care *why* they like me, just as long as they do," Harper fired back, running a hand through his spiky blond hair. "Did you mistake me for someone who was picky?"

Tyr offered a single dry chuckle, which was about as close as he got to falling-down hilarity.

Dylan was glad to see the crew in high spirits—if you didn't count Rev Bem, which he didn't—because he was feeling pretty good about this trip himself. The beginning of the journey had been inauspicious, what with the nest of Vipers crawling up their tail, but it looked like things would go better from here. Festival's warm welcome was heartening. Dylan had been a firm believer in the original Systems Commonwealth. Though it had fallen apart during the Long Night following the civil war—and Dylan's long sleep, which had seemed like only moments to him—he was working hard on bringing about a New Commonwealth.

Dylan's goal was the restoration of the Commonwealth's values: peace, cooperation, self-determination, and individual rights. The *Eureka Maru*'s crew—and Tyr, not a member of their crew but a surprise guest on the salvage mission that had brought them to *Andromeda*—had joined him on his quest. Festival was, Dylan knew, the dominant world in the Festival System, and if he could swing it on board, he could add a dozen planets to the six already signed up, all in one fell swoop. Still a far cry from the million-plus worlds that had belonged to the original Commonwealth, but one had to start somewhere.

He had been unsure of the reception his idea would get here, but from the reception so far, he felt very encouraged. His tendency, optimist that he was, had always been to trust first, then take appropriate measures if that trust was betrayed. Which, in fact, it had been on enough occasions to make him wonder if the whole trusting thing was really the way to go. His best friend, Geheris Rhade, who was to have been best man at his wedding, had betrayed him—and the entire Systems Commonwealth—to the Nietzschean forces that had launched the civil war so long ago. When Dylan realized what Geheris had done, that had soured him on the trust thing to some extent.

But his faith had been restored by Beka and the crew of the *Maru*—people he had learned that he could count on to watch his back, no matter what. He smiled at his minimal crew, and at his nod, Beka opened the hatch. The six of them exited the *Maru*, Dylan and Rommie in front, and were greeted by a roar of applause from the assembled troops.

A uniformed woman, lanky and tall, with short, brown hair barely peeking out from under her cap and an amiable grin on her face, strode toward them. Behind her were several dozen soldiers, while the band stood off to one side. All around were ships, all of them bearing military markings. "Welcome," the woman announced with a polite bow. "I am Captain Lancaster Wylx, Captain Hunt. I'll be your attaché while you're here enjoying our system."

Dylan returned the bow, not certain if that was customary here, but assuming that it was. *Andromeda*'s database didn't contain much information on Festival's manners and customs, and what it did have was three hundred years out of date.

But Captain Wylx grinned as if Dylan were an old family friend, so he guessed he'd done it right. "Thank you for the kind welcome," Dylan said. "We're happy to be here."

"We hope that you'll stay for a long visit," Captain Wylx offered. "Most who come to Festival find they never want to leave it again."

Dylan chuckled. "We have a lot of space to cover," he said. "But we'll stay as long as we can."

"That's all we can ask," Captain Wylx said. Behind her, the assembled ranks parted, making a passageway. She gestured for the *Andromeda*'s crew to precede her through the opening.

As they went, Beka sidled up to Dylan's side. "I don't see a party," she whispered uneasily. "I just see a bunch of uniforms." Beka was, by nature, a bit of a rebel, and by trade she was not always on the right side of the law, so he understood how uniforms might make her nervous.

"Maybe the party begins planetside," he suggested.

"Let's hope," she said. "Or else we were seriously misinformed."

Beyond the gathered spacecraft and the uniformed soldiers, a door slid open. "Our space elevator module," Captain Wylx told them. "It will carry us down to the surface. We don't allow spacecraft on the planetary surface for purposes other than law enforcement."

Dylan raised an eyebrow at the captain's comment, but didn't ask any further questions. They'd be down on the planet itself soon enough, he figured, and everything would be made clear. Once there, he would bring all his diplomatic skill to bear to try to bring Festival into the restored Commonwealth.

The six of them were accompanied by Captain Wylx and what seemed like—but certainly wasn't—a random assortment of other Festival System officers. All of their uniforms were the same dark blue with red trim that Admiral Havil had worn, and they carried themselves with appropriately military rigidity.

Once they were all on board the module, the door whooshed closed. The walls inside were covered with images of Festival's surface—mostly natural images, meadows and forests and rivers. Festival's cities might as well not have existed, if one were to judge by the images surrounding the group. As the descent began, Captain Wylx approached Dylan. "I hope your trip here was not too contentious," she said.

"A little unexpected turbulence near Caernaevon Drift," he replied. "But your Admiral Havil helped calm that."

"I've heard stories," Captain Wylx said. "Caernaevon Drift has never been what you'd call friendly. But lately they seem to have become even less so. They're cutting themselves off from trade, from engagement with anyone else. I don't see how it can be good for them."

"I don't either, Captain Wylx," Dylan agreed. "But then, I tend to think it's a good idea to be involved with others, interdependent. That's why I promote the Commonwealth."

"And why Festival hopes to join it," the captain said. "But please, call me Lancaster."

"Very well, Lancaster," Dylan said. "I'm Dylan."

"It's a great pleasure to make the acquaintance of the famous Dylan Hunt," Lancaster said. "And of his crew."

Dylan introduced Beka, Rommie, Harper, Trance, and Tyr. The trip to the surface was amazingly fast and smooth, and after a few minutes of small talk, they had come to a halt. The door opened and bright light washed in.

"Your first taste of Festival life," Lancaster said. "I hope you enjoy your stay."

The point of egress for the space elevator's module had obviously been chosen for maximum impact. Dylan and the others disembarked onto a platform positioned high up in one of Festival's cities. It was sunset here, an extended period, since Festival had two suns. What must have been a million lights glittered from sleek high-rise towers against a backdrop of golds and indigos. Some of the towers were simply cylindrical, but others took greater architectural risks. Dylan saw unexpected cutaways, arching bridges between towers, even an inverted pyramid that seemed to balance on its tiny point, far below.

"It's gorgeous," Trance said, sounding almost awestruck by the sight. "For a city."

"Thank you, Trance," Lancaster replied. "I'm glad you like it. This is Gala, our capital city." With a nod of her head she indicated a procession of what were evidently dignitaries approaching them. "And that is Efreld sur Havasu, Festival's Supreme Regent, exalted commander of the Festival System armed forces, and your host—along with his Council of Ministers. I know you aren't familiar with our customs, Dylan, but you're doing fine. A simple bow like the one you so graciously offered me is the preferred greeting, and the proper form of address is 'Your Regency.'"

"Your Regency?" Dylan echoed.

"It may not be standard Common usage, but it's our way," Lancaster whispered. The Supreme Regent and his advisors were almost close enough to hear.

Dylan suppressed a shrug. He had learned long ago that it wasn't a good idea to quibble with how people in positions of power chose to be addressed. He pasted a smile on his face. "Do I go forward to greet him?" he whispered through the smile. "Or wait here?"

"You're our honored guest," Lancaster assured him. "You wait. His Regency will come to you."

Dylan waited. As he did, he studied His Regency, Efreld sur Havasu. Somewhat surprisingly—especially for the ruler of such a big world—he was a young man. *Well*, Dylan corrected himself, *he looks young, anyway*. Looks could be deceiving, he knew. He didn't look 342 years old himself, for that matter. The Supreme Regent was tall and powerfully built, with thick blond hair and a ruddy complexion. His suit was an unstructured rich red, somewhere between crimson and salmon, made of a soft, flowing fabric. Beneath the jacket was a buttery shirt. He carried himself as if he were in a formal situation, but Dylan couldn't tell if the suit itself was formal or not.

He stopped six paces from Dylan and regarded him with a friendly smile. Dylan bowed, as Lancaster had advised. When he was finished, Havasu returned the bow, then stepped closer. "It is a pleasure to meet you and to welcome you to Festival, Captain Hunt," he said. "Your esteemed reputation precedes you."

And you let us land anyway, Dylan thought. He kept the grin plastered to his face. "I'm honored, Your Regency. I trust that our visit will be mutually satisfactory."

"I have no doubt," Havasu said. "Your Restored Commonwealth holds great interest for me, and for many of my ministers as well. I hope that your presence here will serve to convince the others, and that the entire Planetary Assembly of the Festival System comes on board."

"Then our goals are compatible," Dylan said. So far, this looked like it would be an easy sell. He had been around the proverbial block enough times to know that the easier things looked, the harder they often were. But still, he remained guardedly optimistic about the Commonwealth's chances here. At least the world's most powerful individual had not only heard of him, but approved of his mission.

"Indeed," Havasu agreed. "I know you've had an eventful day, Captain Hunt. Captain Wylx will show you and your crew to some rooms in the Hall of Regency that I trust you'll find quite comfortable. A bit later, we will have a banquet in your honor. There I will introduce you to the rest of the Council of Ministers, and we'll discuss how best to proceed."

"That sounds good to me," Dylan said, relieved that he didn't have to try to be charming immediately. It had, in fact, been a long day. Maybe in a few hours he could master charming. Right now, all he wanted was to put his feet up for a while.

THREE

"Free food is almost invariably overpriced."
—SINITA SKLIF SIVINITA, "THE GOURMET'S GOURMAND,
OR, LESSONS FROM A HEAVY EATER," CY 7212

The rooms were, as promised, quite comfortable. Dylan's had a remarkable view of the cityscape and a vast bed, at least double the size of the one he had on *Andromeda*. The walls and carpet were a soft cream, but hanging artwork and scattered, deeply cushioned furniture provided accents in a variety of bright colors, like confetti scattered on sand. A second, smaller room provided bathing and toilet facilities. Lancaster Wylx and her staff took Dylan and the others to the rooms, explaining on the way how security would be provided by trusted members of her own personal guard.

Tyr took advantage of a quiet moment to stand close to Dylan. "Does it sound to you like we're guests, or prisoners?" he asked softly.

"Maybe a little of both," Dylan admitted. The same thought had occurred to him. They were in a strange place, which none of them had ever visited. But instead of explaining, for instance, how the shower might work or how to order a meal, all they had been told was that there would be armed soldiers outside their rooms at all hours. "Stay alert," he suggested. "Chances are they really are concerned about our safety. But don't let your guard down, just in case."

"I never do," the Nietzschean said.

Dylan knew that was true. Before he could say anything to the others, though, Lancaster and her soldiers had caught up. Lancaster held a hand up to her ear, her brow furrowed. After a moment, she said, "Understood, thank you." Then she faced Dylan, focusing on him. "I've just downloaded your schedule," she said. "We'll retrieve you in two hours for the banquet. You, Dylan, will be seated with His Regency."

"I'd like Rommie there with me," Dylan said. "And the others, if they'd like to be."

Harper spoke up first. "You bet, Boss."

"Me too," Beka said. Tyr and Trance added their affirmatives.

"Of course, anyone you wish. Afterward, anybody who so desires can explore the city. We'll provide guides, of course, so no one gets lost. It can be a frightfully big and confusing place for first-time visitors."

"I'm sure that would be greatly appreciated," Dylan told her.

A few minutes later, he was alone in the room. He glanced out the window at the impressive view, then turned to explore the rest of the room. He was absolutely certain that he was under some kind of surveillance; he was trusting, but not naive. He couldn't see any lenses or microphones, but such things could be at the nanoscopic level, and without investigating every apparent speck of dust on every surface in the big room, he likely wouldn't find it.

His initial optimism about Festival was rapidly being overshadowed by a new concern. The constant presence of the military surprised him a little. He was a military man himself, and as such he understood why highly valued visitors might be kept under the watchful eye of a security detail. But he would expect a civilian presence in addition to the military, and so far he had not seen that here. The Council of Ministers was presumably civilian, but the Supreme Regent was also commander-in-chief of the armed forces. What he had heard of Festival made him expect someplace a little looser and less martial than what he was seeing so far.

He also knew it was a mistake to jump to conclusions, though. The day would bring what it would bring, and there was no point overanalyzing things right off the bat. Heedless of any unseen on-lookers, he began to strip off his uniform for a quick shower.

Beka didn't like Festival at all so far. Of course, she hadn't expected to in the first place, except maybe for the amusements Rev Bem had warned of. Drifts were okay—they were small, they offered distractions hard to find in deep space, and they could be left behind easily. Planets, especially big ones like Festival, freaked her out. Leaving the *Maru* behind and traveling to the surface in an elevator freaked her out more. She didn't like to be more than a few minutes from a quick exit. Long experience had taught her the wisdom of her particular lifestyle choice. She had found, more than once, that a hasty escape saved her from years of unwanted planetary life, usually as a guest of the state. The only thing worse than getting stuck on a planet would be getting stuck in a planetary prison.

Her unease was made worse by the fact that the crew had been separated without having had an opportunity to consult beforehand. She wasn't worried about being attacked; Beka Valentine could take care of herself. But she would have been more comfortable if she had been able to compare notes with Dylan, or Tyr, or even Harper.

Maybe worst of all was the idea of a formal banquet: sitting with a bunch of strangers—and likely uniformed strangers at that—trying to be pleasant while wondering which of them, if any, read their intergalactic law enforcement bulletins. Maybe Rev Bem had had the right idea after all.

She plopped down on one of the big overstuffed chairs in her room, watching the sky darken outside and wondering what kind of fun there was to be had out there. Whatever people were doing outside, it was certainly more entertaining than her evening would be.

Tyr Anasazi slept.

He felt perfectly safe. He and the others from Andromeda were honored guests—and more than that, high-profile guests. It didn't matter for the moment whether or not they were also prisoners. No escape attempt would be made before the banquet, and no banquet would have been planned for visitors who were to be executed instead of fed. Since there were guards outside the door to keep anyone who might wish to forestall the banquet from attacking, and since those same guards would not pose any immediate threat, he took advantage of the situation to rest. Later, he might need to be functioning at full capacity. Nietzscheans refused to function at anything less. So a quick nap, when possible, was always something to be prized.

Hands crossed over his chest—knowing that the slightest sound, the barest hint of motion in the room would wake him instantly—he slumbered.

Seamus Zelazny Harper paced in front of the floor-to-ceiling windows. He tried to look down at the street below—at least, the street he *assumed* was down there—but he couldn't see it. They had been led to believe that the space elevator had brought them to the vicinity of Festival's surface, but for all he could tell they might still have been miles above it.

Which wasn't necessarily a bad thing in itself. But he had been looking forward to the streets. He had heard stories of Festival's streets for years. The phrase "seamy underbelly" had been bandied about quite a bit, he remembered. And he thought he recalled something about "sin-choked alleyways." He had visions of women strolling about down there, dressed in little if anything at all, just looking for men who might enjoy such a thing.

And I'm that guy, he thought. *I'm exactly the demographic they want. Young, male, energetic, mammalian. I don't know, that last might not be a prerequisite, but still . . . I'm what they need.*

But they were way down there, presumably, and he was up here, high in the Hall of Regency, with soldiers between him and them. Soldiers, and who knew how many stories of whatever building this was, and a banquet that would no doubt be a real snooze-fest, full of long-winded speeches and endless toasts.

He pressed his hands up against the glass, put his face to the window, and tried to look down.

Rommie was simply the avatar of the ship. She didn't need to rest or clean up, and she certainly didn't need whatever local delicacies would be served at the banquet. What she needed was to talk to Dylan. She was pretty sure he had already figured out that the hospitality they were being shown was not unlike that afforded a condemned prisoner getting his last meal—at least that was her assumption. Dylan was smart and perceptive. But then again, he only had the one brain, and it was about the size of both his fists put together. Hers was somewhere around 880,000 times as big, and it processed much more rapidly.

She was, however, smart enough to know that if she made a scene about trying to get to him, it would only interfere with his diplomatic efforts. And she had to admit that even she was not infallible. The possibility existed that she was reading the whole situation wrong. Dylan had been pretty casual about going into his room when it was shown to him, with just a cheerful "see you later" to Rommie and the others. And the diplomatic mission, the New Commonwealth, was the most important thing, so she didn't want to take a chance of screwing it up.

With nothing else to occupy her, she sat on the edge of the bed she had been given and allowed herself to slip into standby mode.

Trance bounced on the huge bed, watching the sky change colors outside the equally huge windows, and calculated the odds that she would still be bouncing on the bed when she was fetched for dinner. About 97.754 percent, she figured. But she kept bouncing—the bed was *really* springy—and as she did she amended her calculations.

Now 98.126 percent.

She bounced. The sky grew darker, the lights of the city burned brighter.

. . . 99.539 percent.

A tap at the door.

One hundred percent.

The banquet hall was enormous. Dylan, standing at its front, could hardly see the back wall. Even as big as the space was, though, it was full. Apparently the Supreme Regent knew how to draw a crowd. Dylan didn't know if all these people had come because this was a command appearance for them, or if perhaps they had paid something to be here—a fund-raiser, as it were. Or maybe they were all just hungry, and this was a chance at some free chow. But he figured asking his host would be borderline rude. He and his friends had been brought in through a private door, while everyone else filed through entrances on the far end of the hall, so he didn't get a chance to find out.

Dylan and the crew found themselves seated at a big rectangular table at the front of the room, facing all the other diners, who were seated at equally large tables facing the front. "Guess we can't talk with our mouths open," Harper noted.

"Unless maybe that's some kind of local custom," Beka added.

"Let's try not to," Dylan suggested. "Unless His Regency does it first." He didn't bother to point out that since His Regency was supposed to be seated with them, facing the hall like the others, only those sitting directly on either side of him would be able to see how he ate.

When the room was completely full, with every seat, as far as Dylan could tell, at every table occupied by one of the congregated thousands, a hush fell over the room as if at some prearranged signal that he hadn't caught. As one, the entire body rose. Dylan glanced at Lancaster, who indicated with a tilting of her head that he and his crew should do likewise. Dylan stood, nudging Beka, who had been seated to his left. Rommie, on his right, didn't need the nudge.

Through the same doorway that *Andromeda*'s crew had used, His Regency entered, accompanied by a small entourage. He had a woman hanging on each arm: two absolutely stunning redheads, each wearing a low-cut white gown that left little to the imagination that they so pointedly stirred. Havasu himself had changed into a white suit, as unstructured as the one he'd been wearing earlier, but with a chocolate brown shirt with collar high and stiff around his neck. He walked across the floor, nodding from time to time at the guests who still stood silently beside their chairs, and then stopped across the table from Dylan.

"Captain Hunt," he said with a broad smile. "I am honored by your presence at my table."

"As am I, at the invitation," Dylan replied. "I look forward to becoming better acquainted."

Havasu nodded as if he agreed that it would be a pleasure for someone else to get to know him better. "This," he said, raising his right arm slightly to indicate the redhead standing there—the long-haired one, Dylan noted—"is Ashala."

Dylan bowed deeply. "It's a pleasure to meet you, Ashala," he said.

She returned the bow, but Havasu was already elevating his left arm, which made Ashala's bow more than a little awkward. "And this," he said, "is Valunta."

Dylan bowed again. "And an equal pleasure to meet you, Valunta."

"When I made the seating arrangements, I wasn't sure which

two were your women," Havasu said. "The purple one looks amusing, but not quite fitting for a man as serious and powerful as yourself, so I guessed these two." He indicated Beka and Rommie. Dylan felt Beka tense beside him. *Don't go off on him*, he thought urgently. "I hope I was correct."

"Actually," Dylan replied, "Beka here is our pilot, and Rommie is the ship's avatar—not actually a person at all. Neither one is my . . . 'woman.'"

The two redheads giggled, and Dylan thought that Havasu blushed a little, but with his rosy complexion it was hard to tell. "I hope I haven't offended any of you," he said. "An honest mistake, as you'll see when you get to know our culture a little better."

"No problem," Beka said through clenched teeth. Dylan appreciated the effort—and appreciated the fact that she would probably have rather incinerated His Regency with a force lance than be polite at that precise moment.

"I'm sure we both have much to learn," Dylan said graciously.

"Well, then," Havasu suggested. "What do you say we put this little faux pas behind us and have some dinner? I think you'll find the menu quite delightful."

That, Dylan agreed to.

FOUR

> "The shortest meeting ever held was longer than somebody's
> lifetime."
>
> —ABNER KLUM, "FUNDAMENTALS OF BUSINESS
> PRACTICES," 23RD EDITION, REVISED, CY 8290

Formal dinners gave Beka a headache. *It's all that smiling and nodding*, she thought. *It's unnatural.* By the end of the meal she
thought her jaw would splinter and her eyes would explode from
all the tension in her head.

And after the banquet—after Havasu's forty-minute speech,
which several bouts of "spontaneous" and prolonged applause had
transformed into a fifty-minute ordeal—His Regency had invited
Dylan and the others into a smaller, more intimate salon to discuss Dylan's mission on Festival. Dylan had kindly allowed the rest
of the crew to choose whether or not to join in the discussion.
Rommie—*of course*, Beka thought—stayed with Dylan, but Beka,
Harper, and Trance all wanted to go out on the town. Tyr had
chosen to go back to his room. Captain Wylx arranged an escort of
six soldiers for the three friends, and off they went.

The elevator ride down to the street took longer than the space elevator down from the orbital platform had. But then, this elevator wasn't nonstop, and at least fifty people—well, people and other beings, Festival having a large nonhuman population as well—had gotten on or off during the trip. But finally they had reached the ground floor and left the building through a cavernous, elegant lobby.

Lieutenant Patterson sur Blehm led their little protective coterie. The lieutenant was a muscular woman, taller than Beka, with a physique that would have made a Nietzschean proud. Her shoulder-length hair was green, and her manner casual in spite of the uniform she wore and the Gauss gun she carried. "What do you guys want to do?" she asked when they reached the street. A constant flow of pedestrian traffic ran in both directions; humanoids and others, in every kind of physical condition, wearing every kind of clothing imaginable, thronged the street. They seemed to be primarily civilians, but there were a number of military personnel mixed among them as well.

Beka shrugged. "Word is that Festival is party central," she said. "Are there any bars or clubs around?"

Harper was staring at the sky. Buildings glittered above them as far as the eye could see, festooned with brilliantly-lit signs advertising everything from personal hygiene products to Sparky Cola to apparel. "Yeah," he said distractedly. "Clubs."

"Seventeen million," Trance said.

"Excuse me?" Patterson asked.

"Seventeen million. I'm guessing there are seventeen million residents in Gala."

"Just based on what you've seen today?"

"That's right," Trance said. Beka knew that Trance's calculations were never "just" based on any single observation, but short, purple, and mysterious was less than forthcoming about her nature and background, so Beka had no idea what really went on in that strange head of hers.

"Lee," Patterson called to one of the other soldiers. The one named Lee turned around.

"Yes?"

"What's the population of Gala?"

"Hang on." Lee put a hand over his ear and muttered something. In a moment, he lowered his hand. "Sixteen million, nine hundred and seventy-eight thousand, eight hundred and forty-two. Not including our six visitors from the *Andromeda*."

When Patterson looked at Trance again, Beka thought she could see something like amazement in the woman's green eyes. "That's very impressive," she said.

Trance just smiled. "It's something I do."

"We don't get used to her either," Beka said. "So don't think that you will."

Patterson caught Beka's gaze and shook her head. "How about those clubs?" she asked.

"Good idea," Beka agreed.

"Maybe one with a lot of hot women?" Harper pleaded.

"Mr. Harper," Lee promised, "we wouldn't dare take you to any other kind."

As they negotiated the crowded boulevards, the soldiers mostly talked among themselves while Beka, Harper, and even Trance were stunned into contemplative silence by the sheer mass of the city. Beka tried to look past the buildings, hoping to see her beloved stars out in the distance, but it was impossible. All she saw was more construction, and more, and more. Directly overhead, the buildings seemed to converge on one another, and the wash of light blotted out any sky. The enormity of the city's population bore down on her, until she felt hemmed in, trapped, by it all.

At ground level, the buildings were occupied by innumerable shops, restaurants, and bars. Every one of them seemed to be open and crowded. Along the way, they passed several clubs with raucous music pouring out and throngs of people spilling onto the street. Each time, Trance, Harper, and Beka looked in expectantly. "What about that one?" someone would ask.

"No," one of the soldiers said. "We're going someplace way better than that."

After twenty minutes or so they had woven their way into a less populous neighborhood. Here, most of the buildings fronted the street with blank doorways. The streets weren't limited to pedestrian traffic, and commercial vehicles rumbled along them or sat silently to the side, waiting for morning. On the main avenues people had tended to congregate in groups, or at least couples, but here they were just as likely to be out on their own, hurrying down the quiet streets, leaning on walls, sitting on steps watching the occasional traffic.

"I'm getting a little freaked out here," Beka whispered to Harper. "You think they're taking us somewhere to rob us?"

"You got anything worth stealing?" Harper countered. "Because I sure don't."

"What, then? Kill us?"

"Seems like a bad idea at the same time they're applying for membership in the Commonwealth," Harper pointed out.

"I know," Beka agreed. "But why take us to the middle of nowhere when we've already passed at least two dozen clubs?"

Harper shrugged. "They're soldiers. Would you go to Dylan for a club recommendation?"

"Good point," Beka admitted. "He's a great guy, and he's saved all our skins a dozen times. But he's kind of a stiff when it comes to fun."

"Yeah, he's probably perfectly happy sitting in a room with all those monkey-suited ministers, talking about public works projects or something."

"Here we go," Patterson called out, interrupting them.

She stood in front of an unmarked door that looked like the entrance to a warehouse. Beka felt a momentary shudder. She knew she could handle whatever came up, but still, voluntarily going into a quiet building like this with armed soldiers at her back was a little disconcerting.

"This doesn't look like much," Trance pointed out.

"It's not supposed to, from here," Patterson said. "Just wait till we get inside." She pushed the door open and stepped inside. The other soldiers ushered Beka, Harper, and Trance in ahead of them, then brought up the rear.

Inside, they found a wide, plain stairway with a simple metal railing, leading down, lit by glowing disks set into the otherwise undecorated walls. Something seemed to vibrate the railing and even the concrete stairs, as if with a deep electrical hum. As they descended floor by floor, the hum grew more intense, until Beka could feel it in her teeth.

"What *is* that?" she asked after a few flights.

"You'll see," Patterson promised. At the bottom of the staircase she stopped before a steel double door. Beside the door, a glowing box, about twenty centimeters square, was mounted on the wall. Patterson pressed her hand against the box and waited.

Thirty seconds later the doors opened up and a deafening wall of sound erupted. From inside, as the doors swung wide, Beka could see flashing lights and moving bodies through a thick haze of smoke. On a faraway stage a group of alien musicians banged away on instruments she didn't recognize, creating a wall of sound not unlike her late-twentieth-century Sex Pistols CDs, but more jarring.

And *much* louder than any sound system she had ever owned could approximate.

"This is an underground club!" Patterson shouted, her mouth close to Beka's ear. "In more senses than the obvious! It's officially banned, but we only enforce the ban when we have to! In return we get to come whenever we want!"

"Why is it banned?!" Beka shouted back.

"It tends to get a little rowdy!" Patterson yelled. "You up for it?!"

"Let's go!" Beka called. Patterson smiled, nodded, and led the way.

Andromeda, with everyone else away, was a remarkably quiet and peaceful place in which to write. The ship maintained her own orbit around Festival, so Rev Bem didn't have to worry about piloting it. Festival's fleet was guarding it so he didn't have to keep an eye out for a return of those annoying Vipers, or, he assumed, anyone else. He was free to focus on his newest project, his as yet untitled memoirs.

As yet untitled and unstarted, for that matter. He'd had several false beginnings, dictating to one of *Andromeda*'s data recorders, but he hadn't been really happy with the way any of it had turned out, and so far he had deleted everything he'd begun.

He wasn't concerned about turning out any kind of literary masterpiece. He simply wanted to set down his experiences, in case they might prove helpful to anyone who might be considering following the People of the Way in the future. He still met individuals from time to time who didn't believe that a Magog could be a spiritual being—even though The Anointed, founder of the People of the Way, had himself been a Magog. People were just closed-minded sometimes, unwilling or unable to look beyond their own prejudices, and he couldn't help hoping that his memoirs might help open some minds and hearts.

But he hadn't been able to figure out just where to start it, and that was the reason for all the deleted attempts. His initial impulse had been to begin with the events that had triggered his own spiritual transformation: his introduction to the Divine. When he tried that approach, however, he quickly realized that it lacked impact because he had not established who he was before his enlightenment. Without knowing what he had come from, the destination he had reached seemed somehow pale.

And with the rest of the crew around—even though it was easy on a ship made for four thousand, but with a crew of six, to find privacy—he was a little shy about detailing his early life out loud.

They were gone now, though. Just him and Andromeda on board, and though she remembered everything, she could be counted on not to repeat what she heard without his permission. In fact, it was her memory banks he would be using to compose the book.

Rev Bem paced, clenching and unclenching his clawed fists nervously. *Where to begin?*

Finally, he made up his mind. At the beginning, of course.

"*Andromeda*, please record," he requested.

"Recording," the ship's voice replied.

"When I was hatched, my name was Redplague, and I ate my way out of my host in just hours. That host—whose identity I never knew, although I had flashes of her memory for my first seventeen years—was my first victim. In the years since, I have killed a hundred and seventy-two more that I know of. Vedrans, Than, Perseids, Nietzscheans—my lust for blood was unquenchable. I killed to eat, I killed to procreate, and I killed for pleasure.

"But that was then . . ."

Dylan sat with Havasu's Council of Ministers in a comfortable, intimate room not far from the ballroom where the banquet had been held. The ministers were mostly male, but not exclusively—out of eleven, there were four women and one unknown—a buglike alien who might have been more akin to a Than than a human, except that its carapace was a brilliant rainbow of colors, like an oil slick, its face broad and multieyed, and its voice a low rumble that reminded Dylan of thunder. Its name was something unpronounceable—Dylan had settled on Gert, because it was somewhere in the right neighborhood, and the androgynous bug-thing seemed willing to accept it.

Havasu's two redheads had been excluded from the room, leading Dylan to believe that he had been brought in here for a serious discussion, and that whatever else Havasu kept the women around for, serious discussion wasn't part of it. Drinks had been brought in, potent clear blue beverages that Dylan was afraid to more than sip from. At least they had the fringe benefit of washing the taste of dinner out of his mouth. The meal had been an assortment of local delicacies, animal and vegetable, that Dylan had barely been able to choke down.

Havasu himself led the conversation, though the other ministers felt comfortable interrupting or interjecting as they saw fit. After dancing around the topic of the Restored Commonwealth for a while, Havasu honed right in on it. "We think the new Commonwealth is a fabulous idea, Dylan," he said. They had graduated to first name basis—or at least, Havasu had. "Its benefits are numerous and self-evident. Increased trade opportunities, mutual protection from Magog invasion, better prospects for peace and prosperity throughout our system overall. We weren't part of the original Systems Commonwealth—I expect we were a little too backwater at the time to be of much interest—but we have grown up over these past centuries, and we clearly see the dividends of inclusion."

Dylan found himself smiling and nodding along. This was exactly what he had hoped for when he'd begun this crusade. To him, the payoff was obvious. Any world could improve its lot by cooperation with other planets, whereas trying to remain isolated and independent would always result in stagnation, or worse. "That's it exactly," he agreed. "We are all stronger together than any one of us separately."

"As you may or may not be aware, my dominion over Festival itself is virtually total. Oh, there are a few naysayers; there always are. A handful of parties who dispute or disapprove of my leadership. But this world, far and away the largest and most powerful in the Festival system, is largely within the control of those of us in this room. If we say we're joining the Commonwealth, then we *are* joining the Commonwealth."

"I would, of course, feel more comfortable if any such decision were to reflect the will of the people," Dylan pointed out. "And not just a small handful of the powerful."

"Of course, of course." Havasu showed yellow teeth in an approximation of a smile that didn't seem to rest comfortably on his face. "I'm only saying that the people will choose to follow my lead. They generally do. The people of Festival like having strong leadership, they like being told which direction to go in."

"Is your position one which they voted you into?" Dylan asked. There might certainly have been a more diplomatic way to phrase the question, but he felt like the guy was campaigning for his vote now, and he wanted to get it out of the way.

"Well, in a manner of speaking," Havasu dodged. "We'll explain our electoral system—a sort of representative democracy, in a way—at some other time. It's all more complex than is absolutely necessary to go into just now, with so many more pressing demands on our time."

"Okay," Dylan agreed. "And do you speak for all of Festival?"

"Again, complicated," Havasu replied. "There are independent nations on our world, as there are on many of the other planets throughout our system. But they are independent in name only. Their heads of state report to me, and they take direction from me. Gala is the capital of Festival, and Festival is a nation, a world, and a solar system.

"The point is, I can persuade the people of Festival," Havasu went on. "But what we would like to see—and I think what you would like too, Dylan—is for the entire Festival system to join at once. A dozen populated worlds. Billions upon billions of inhabitants."

His Regency had it pegged. This was what Dylan needed to convince the rest of the known universe that the New Commonwealth had legs. A major announcement, a tripling of the worlds that had signed on already. "That sounds good to me. How do we accomplish that?"

"As I said, Festival has a great deal of influence throughout the system. But it isn't as complete everywhere as it is here on our own planet. I think what we should do is to have you give a speech which will be broadcast throughout the system, to all of our worlds."

"A speech?" Dylan echoed, hoping he had misunderstood.

"A speech. A glorious speech, full of pomp and emotion. Explain to our worlds what you're about, what you see as the future of the Systems Commonwealth, and why everyone should join up. I will follow up your speech with individual meetings with the governments of each world—each nation, on those planets that aren't as unified as we are here. But I think that you should lay the groundwork, the foundation, as it were, for the effort. You can certainly speak to the issues far more eloquently than I. After all, you are a survivor of the first Commonwealth, right? You know better than anyone else what can be achieved, if we only try."

Dylan wasn't crazy about making speeches. His training was built more around shooting people than persuading them with high-flown words. But he understood Havasu's point, and the way the man stared at him, leaning forward, his beefy hands on his knees, silently pleading for Dylan to pick up the gauntlet that had been placed before him—Dylan couldn't bring himself to say no.

He looked around the room at the other ministers. They all seemed to be saying the same thing with their body language. "All right," he said finally. "I'll make the speech."

"Excellent," Havasu said, relaxing his posture. "It's all set for tomorrow morning. Now let's get to work on what you're going to say."

FIVE

"Imagine the best that could happen. It won't. Now imagine the worst that could happen. That's what to expect."

—WALCEDUS BIERT, IN HIS CONCESSION SPEECH AFTER
LOSING A RACE FOR THE POST OF SUPREME AUTARCH
OF THE WESTERN REACHES, AVERY'S HOLE, CY 9112

Harper's intention had been to meet a woman.

Instead, he met a man.

True, the club was dark, smoky, and loud, and the flashing lights made it hard to see. Even with those handicaps, though, he spotted plenty of women who were, in fact, women. Some of them were absolutely stunning. Some were friendly. Some were willing to dance with him, or to allow him to spend a few guilders buying them drinks. Most were, like him, there to have a good time, and maybe to find some companionship.

It should have been heaven.

But there were too many factors working against him to successfully close a deal. Most of the women spoke Common, but with a local accent he couldn't always understand. The blasting music from the stage interfered. Conversations had to be shouted at full volume, and that didn't help the accent situation any. And he couldn't read the body language well. They didn't move like any women he was used to. He thought he was picking up a go-for-it signal from one, and wound up getting a slap that rattled his teeth.

Eventually, the man approached Harper after seeing a couple of hotties walk away from him. "Not having any luck?" the man shouted.

Harper shrugged. The guy looked harmless enough—about Harper's height, a little heavier, a little more muscled. Black hair that hung to his jaw, a plain face, violet eyes. He wore a black shirt and tan pants tucked into heavy black boots. Harper didn't know enough about local fashion to know if the guy was cool, or a hope-less geek. But he had struck out enough times to suspect that he himself had fallen into the latter category, even if just because these women weren't taking the time to get to know him.

"It's because the women here are so conceited!" the guy yelled.

You're not kidding, Harper thought, glad to have his dawning sus-picion confirmed by a local. "Is that what it is?"

"Definitely!" the man shouted. He cocked his head toward an exit. Harper looked around for his military escort, but the crowd, bad lighting, and smoke had made their task more difficult too, and they seemed to have lost track of Harper for the moment. That didn't bother Harper any—he was a little put off by having soldiers trailing him around anyway. For all he knew, that was part of why he'd been striking out—who would want to get busy with a guy who came with his own audience?

Well, he realized, *there are always some with exhibitionistic tenden-cies. But they're usually in the minority.*

He followed the guy to the exit. They passed through a thick door, like the ones through which Harper had entered, except this one was a single door, and it led to a darker, more narrow staircase.

As soon as the door was closed, the music was muffled to a point that Harper thought his ears might someday recover. Not immedi-ately—he was pretty sure they'd be ringing for a while, until he could get some nanotechnological relief. He shook his head violently. "Man, that's freakin' loud."

"It can be a fun place," the stranger said. "But it is loud, and it's not a good place to meet women unless you have a lot of money to spend. They're spoiled here."

Harper tried to remember if he had asked to be taken someplace where he could *meet* hot women, or just someplace where hot women would *be*. If it had been the latter, then those soldiers hadn't lied. But simply window-shopping hadn't been exactly what he'd had in mind. What was the point of coming to a choice spot like Festival if you weren't going to sample the local cuisine? And he didn't mean the cuisine they were serving at that banquet, most of which had remained uneaten on his plate.

"I had a feeling that was the case," Harper said. "My name's Seamus Harper."

"I'm Fujiko Ellston," the man said. "You're not from around here."

"I'm from Earth."

"It's a pleasure to meet you, Harper from Earth," Fujiko said. "Are you interested in discovering where the friendlier women are? The ones who don't require a man to have wealth and prestige before they will spend some time with him?"

"You got that right," Harper said.

"Very well, Harper. Gala is full of flesh and fun if one knows where to look. Let's go find it."

Trance was only inside the club for five minutes when she estimated that there were six hundred people in there, and that the chances that the six soldiers assigned to them would be able to keep track of everyone were about one in two thousand seventeen.

That was okay with her. She was a free spirit, and having armed men and women flanking her all the time was anathema to her. She hadn't especially expected to have a good time here on the surface, but those natural images that had been projected on the space elevator had raised her hopes. Despite the undeniable joys of the ship's hydroponic garden, she missed living green things, and the thick, verdant forests promised by those pictures had seemed like places she would love to spend time. But the fact was, the planet, at least, that part of it that she had seen, was completely paved over and built up. She had tried to conceal her disappointment, though, and had gone out with her friends in hope that everyone else would have a good time while she pretended to for their benefit.

But while maybe Beka and Harper were enjoying the loud music and strobing lights and the crush and odor of sweaty bodies, it had all been a bit too much for her. At the first opportunity, she danced her way out of sight of the soldiers and found a door that led to a small office area. From there she slipped down a corridor cramped with electronic equipment, boxes, and old furniture, until she found an exit door.

The staircase she took to the street opened into a dark alley. She stepped out quietly and walked to the end of the alley. The street they had come in on was almost silent now, but a few uniformed soldiers patrolled it, looking grim and intent on their task. The contrast to just a short time before was marked, and Trance wondered if maybe there was a curfew here. That might be one reason the authorities had insisted they have a military escort when they went out.

She went back to the door from which she had come and tugged on it. Locked up tight. She shrugged. As she'd expected. No way back in now, not through this door.

So now she had slipped the guards, and she was on her own in a gigantic city that might just have a military-enforced curfew. She had studied the probability paths and knew this would be the likeliest result of her action. But it was still preferable to spending another minute inside that club.

Instead of going back to the street she knew was patrolled, she went the other way down the alley, toward the cross street on the other side. She knew there was a high probability that that street would also have soldiers on it.

When she got to the end of the alley she stayed in the shadows and peered out onto the street. This one was narrower than the one she had been led down by Patterson and the other soldiers: more of a neighborhood lane than a main transit road, she thought. For the moment, it appeared empty.

Trance had an exceptionally good sense of direction, and though she hadn't been paying particularly close attention to how they had arrived at the club—assuming, of course, they'd have guides take them back to their rooms—she still wasn't worried about being able to find her way. Now that she had ditched those guides to get away from the oppressive atmosphere of the club, she had a couple of choices.

She could give up on this and go back around to the front door, which she assumed would still be open, down the stairs, and try to get back into the club that way—although she wasn't sure if the glowing box Patterson had pressed her hand against had been a sensor of some kind, reading Patterson's palm print or DNA. And she knew that street was patrolled, so she would have to risk being spotted by those other soldiers, and having to explain why she was away from her guides in the first place.

The other alternative was to make her way back to the Hall of Regency, and then explain that she'd lost track of the guides so had returned to the only place she knew.

There were a number of uncertainties with either approach. It was unlikely—though of course not impossible—that any potential curfew would be enforced with a shoot-first-ask-questions-later order. Of course, if there was a curfew imposed, then the soldiers she had seen around the outside of the building wouldn't be the only ones out and about, and chances were that security would be even tighter in front of the Hall of Regency.

On balance, Trance was almost sorry she hadn't just sucked it up and stayed inside with the noise and smoke and crowd of the club.

Almost, but not quite. Because out here, while she ran the risk of being arrested or shot—at least she could breathe, and she didn't feel like her ears were being violently assaulted with pointed sticks. She examined the probability paths, but all the available alternatives had more or less equal prospects of success. Her first choice out of all those options would have been "none of the above."

Because she had to try, in spite of the minimal chance of success, she touched her neck to activate her subdermal comm unit and tried to hail Beka.

No dice. The units were routed through *Andromeda*'s communications system, and the ship was too far away—or blocked by the sheer mass of the city, or perhaps intentionally jammed—to reach.

With the odds being what they were, she decided she would try to get back to the government building unmolested. She stayed in the shadows, watching her back as well as the road ahead. When she was close enough to it she would let some soldiers find her, feign innocence and ignorance—which she could do to devastating effect when she wanted to—and allow herself to be led back into custody.

The fact that the streets were essentially vacant made the task somewhat easier than it might have been. She recognized the possibility that security cams might have been watching her the whole time, but if that was the case there wasn't much she could do about it. She made quick progress, though, moving down blocks that roughly paralleled the course she thought they had taken getting to the club. The buildings all looked different from this angle, and when she could look down toward the blocks she thought they had taken earlier, the shops and restaurants were all closed, so they didn't look the same either.

Still, she was reasonably certain that, mazelike as the streets might seem, she was headed in the right direction. She had been at it for almost fifteen minutes when she saw a squad of soldiers turn onto the street and start in her direction.

Trance froze where she was. The eight soldiers headed toward her were heavily armed, but their demeanor seemed casual—their voices were loud, and they were joking and laughing with one another. They didn't appear to be on a search-and-destroy mission of any kind, but were either on patrol or just going someplace.

If they saw her, though, their attitude would probably change fast.

She had passed another alleyway, just about ten paces back. Without taking her eyes off the soldiers down the street, she backed up a step, and then another, a third. They hadn't noticed a thing yet. She kept going, back, back, eyes front so she would know if they spotted her.

Another couple of steps back and she was there, the mouth of the dark alley yawning beside her. Holding her breath, she spun around the corner into the darkness. At the last moment, as she was being engulfed by the shadows, she heard the soldiers down the street raise the alarm.

"Down there!" one of them called. Others shouted, and then she heard the clatter of booted feet breaking the silence. She broke into a run.

Trance was about halfway down the alley, hoping the road on the other side of it was clear, when a powerful arm grabbed her around the waist and hoisted her into the air. "Hey!" she started to shriek, but a big hand clamped brutally down over her mouth. She could barely see anything at all, what with the dense shadows and the arm across her face, but she could tell that she was being drawn in through an open window, and the soldiers ran past, down the alley below, without seeing where she had gone.

She knew there was every likelihood that she had simply exchanged one potential danger for another—but at least whoever had her now wasn't shooting at her.

Yet.

SIX

"It is easier to neglect your friends than it is your enemies. But at the end of your life, it is the friends you'll remember. So think twice about that neglecting business."

—KELEDON BOYD, CY 8788

Cam Prezennetti had been waiting years for an occasion such as this.

He had proven his skills many times over. It had been his campaign, after all, that had sold seventy-three million, two hundred fifty thousand—and counting—Sticky Bars to the people of Gala since their introduction six months before. And not only did Sticky Bars taste terrible, but their sugar content was high enough to start eroding teeth before they were even unwrapped, and they had no known nutritional value whatsoever.

And they were . . . well, they were *sticky*.

It had been Cam's idea to capitalize on that drawback by putting it into the name. Anyone eating a Sticky Bar would have to wash his or her hands afterward, or else endure a period of time in which anything touched would adhere to the hands. And they stuck to the teeth, too. But Gala's government owned a piece of the company, so they wanted a lot of Sticky Bars sold, and Cam had done it for them.

They owed him this one.

Advertising and marketing were big business on Festival, where the enormous population made for an equally enormous number of potential consumers for any given product. Because the population was concentrated in a few giant urban areas, competition was especially keen there in Cam's chosen field. Gala, capital city and by far the biggest, was where careers were really made, and where only the very best got to play for long. Cam was near the top of the game.

Which wasn't good enough. Cam wanted to *be* the top: undisputed king of the sales world. He had sacrificed much to get where he was. Three failed marriages trailed in his wake, ex-wives who saw what he was and had loved him anyway, only to find that he couldn't love them back, had only really taken up with them to prove he could sell himself to a succession of ever younger and lovelier ladies. He once had friends, who had been used, then abandoned, like rungs on a cheap ladder.

One way, going up.

Cam had seen others, ones who went before him but on round-trip tickets. And going down was never pretty. Their careers ruined, these women and men had been broken and battered, and they found that the way back down was even harder because everyone who had been betrayed on the way up now had the chance for petty revenge.

Cam never wanted to be one of those. He was at the brink, on the precipice, and from here he could either claw his way to the summit or fall down. Falling wasn't in his game plan. He would reach the pinnacle and stay there, and if ever he felt his hold slipping, he would leave the game altogether. There was no point in staying in it if he couldn't remain the best there was.

Part of playing it well was making the right contacts, and Cam had always been successful at that. He was handsome, well dressed, well spoken. He had made it a point to court Havasu and a few of his more influential ministers, and it had paid off, landing him the Sticky Bar account. Sticky Bars had paved the way to tonight's opportunity. It would be up to Cam to make the best of it, and he had every intention of doing so.

While Captain Hunt met with His Regency and his ministers, Cam was relegated to a side room, awaiting the moment he would be fetched and escorted into Havasu's presence. In the meantime, he paced, he planned, he plotted, and he checked out the two sexy redheads—Havasu's current paramours, he was led to believe—who were parked in the room with him. The one with short hair was pretty but not really his type. She was tiny, like some kind of a sprite or elf, and even though her clothing revealed a body that he was sure could be put to amazingly good use, it was her taller, long-haired friend who caught Cam's attention.

The longer he watched them—and the wait was becoming interminable—the more he came to the conclusion that they weren't really friends at all. They were both friends, or playmates, of Havasu, but beyond that they didn't seem to be very connected to one another. Cam was good at reading people that way: sizing them up quickly, figuring out how they were wired, determining how best to meet whatever needs they might have in the most profitable fashion possible.

What he saw in this one was a woman who was bored, who felt alone even in the midst of what were probably the most exciting events of her life. She may have come from one of the smaller cities of Festival, or possibly a poor neighborhood of Gala, and somehow caught Havasu's eye. Now she found herself surrounded by royalty, living in undreamed-of luxury, but there was no one around whom she could really call a friend. She sat, very occasionally speaking with the elfin one, but only a few words now and again. She roamed around the big room, occasionally gazed out the window, helped herself to a drink from the bar. Once in a while she turned to Cam and smiled; more often she glanced at the two guards who sat stone-faced near the door.

Finally, when he thought he had the pattern figured out, he went and fixed himself a drink, then accidentally managed to be heading for the window at the same time she was.

"Oh, excuse me, lady," he said politely. "I didn't mean—"

"No, that's all right," she replied. "I mean . . . we're both kind of trapped in here, aren't we?"

"It looks that way," he agreed, trying on a warm smile. "At least until His Regency is ready for me."

She chuckled. "I know how that feels," she said quietly.

"I can imagine." He allowed himself a long look at her, toe to head, knowing that she understood he was enjoying the vast amount of exposed flesh. "I would think he'd be ready a lot." He knew he was treading on dangerous ground—if she chose to, she could repeat a line like that to Havasu and he'd find himself strung up from Gala's tallest tower by morning.

But he had a feeling she wouldn't repeat the line. She blushed, which he had expected, but she locked eyes with him and gave him back a smile. "You might be surprised," she said.

That was when he knew he had her.

But he didn't have a chance to press his advantage, because the door opened and three soldiers entered the room. The guards by the door snapped to attention. "Mr. Prezennetti," one of the soldiers said. "His Regency requires your presence now."

"Good luck," the woman whispered before he left.

He wouldn't need luck, though. He was Cam Prezennetti, and he made his own chances.

"Captain Hunt," he said effusively, when he had reached the private meeting room and met the spacefarer. "What an honor it is to meet you."

"Mr. Prezennetti," the captain said. "My pleasure."

"Please, call me Cam," Cam begged him. "My friends are working people, too busy to say Prezennetti, and those people of leisure who can take their time with it are so seldom worth the effort."

"Um . . . okay," Captain Hunt said. "Call me Dylan."

"Dylan, very well. It's . . . well, I already said it's an honor. I mean that. Your reputation precedes you, and it's the kind of reputation that most people—decent people, you know, like those here in this room—wish we had as well."

"I just fly a ship," Dylan protested.

"And modest, too," Cam said with a chuckle. He could already see that Dylan would be a handful. If his modesty was real, it would be hard to appeal to his ego. If it was false, then his ego was already so swelled that he would simply expect the accolades of strangers. He decided to try a different approach—*one thing about Cam Prezennetti*, he mused, *is that he can think on his feet.*

"We have invited Cam," Havasu interrupted, "to help us . . . let us just say . . . shape your message."

"That's right," Cam said. "That's what I'm good at. I may not be good for much, but I am good at messages. Can you step over here to the window, Captain Hunt? Dylan?"

Dylan did as he was asked. That was a good sign, at least. Maybe he'd be malleable, easy to work with. He looked the part: attractive, decent, honorable, a man of action—which was a good thing. Cam didn't have time for all the reconstructive surgery that would have been necessary to make some bloated bureaucrat look like a leader worth following.

Standing by the window, Cam pointed out toward several of the glowing promotional signs visible from here. "Do you see that?" he asked. "The sign that says 'SAV-IT Security—because your neighbor has one too'? That's one of mine. That campaign has moved fourteen million home security systems." He paused for a moment, then dropped the other shoe. "This month."

"Home security systems?" Dylan asked.

"It's a fancy lock," Cam admitted. "Opens only to your precise DNA coding. Doesn't matter what it is, really. What matters is that people didn't know they needed it until I told them they did."

"I see," Dylan said. He didn't sound convinced yet.

"And there," Cam said, directing Dylan's attention toward a

Sticky Bars sign that read "Sticky Bars. You can't put them down!"
"That's one of my big ones."

"Sticky Bars have been extremely successful," Havasu confirmed.

"They're hideous," one of the ministers said. "Absolutely the
worst snack food ever. Especially the rockfish-flavored ones."

"But profitable," Gert added.

"Monumentally profitable," Cam amplified. "Dylan, the point
is, I know these people. I know what they respond to. I know what
they don't respond to, but can be sold anyway. And that's really
what's important, right? Selling people what they want is child's
play. Selling them what they would never buy in a million years—
that's art."

"I wasn't really expecting to sell them anything," Dylan said.

The guy was a schmuck, that was the only way to look at it. Cam
hated clients like this, clients who thought what they had to offer
was so freaking precious that all they had to do was put it out there
at a fair price and those who wanted it would lay down their
money. But the world didn't work that way. Fortunately for losers
like that, Cam knew how it did work.

He also knew that this account was the one that would push him
to the top, if he made it work. And if he didn't, then he was on the
downslope, which would mean quitting the business. He had to
play this guy right, schmuck or not.

"Of course you're selling them something," Cam argued. "We
all sell, every day. I'm selling you, right now. Doesn't mean I expect
you to put money in my hands. I wouldn't object if you wanted to,
but that's not the point here. The point is that you have a message
to deliver, and you want your message to spur a certain action.
That's selling. The other point is that you're a stranger here. You
don't really know your audience, your potential customer pool. I
do. That's expertise. With my expertise and your product, we can
do some selling. So how about it?"

"Well, I—"

"Dylan," Havasu interrupted again. "I would not have brought

Cam here if I did not believe that he could be of great service to us both, and to our effort to persuade our system's worlds to join us in the new Commonwealth. The goal is important enough to be worth allowing some new ideas, some new insights, to cross our path, yes?"

"Of course," Dylan said.

"Well, then, I'm your man," Cam insisted. "Nobody's better at this kind of thing, believe you me."

"Oh, I have no trouble believing that," Dylan answered.

Cam thought maybe he was being gently mocked. That was okay. He didn't mind if a schmuck didn't understand what he was about. Just as long as the space captain did what he was told and smiled that toothy grin when the rubes were watching, everything would be just fine.

Beka figured maybe her social skills were a little rusty, having spent so much time on the *Andromeda* in the company of a tiny handful of crew mates. That was the only way she could explain the fact that it took nearly an hour for her to fend off the advances of the men in whom she was not interested and yet manage to attract the attention of one of the few in the big room in whom she might be.

The guy she eventually set her sights on fell squarely into the tall, dark, and handsome category. Maybe a little overlap with the dangerous bad boy category, but hey, she figured, the boundary lines were fuzzy, and she'd never minded a little bad with her boy. He wore dark clothes that matched his hair and goatee, and the scrollwork of an intricate tattoo curled up out of his shirt and around his powerful neck. His sleeves were cut high and showed muscular, cut arms.

She thought for a moment that he might be a Nietzschean, but then she watched him down a drink and turn to survey the room. Despite his obvious self-confidence—and mixed in with that, more than a little narcissism—he didn't have that Nietzschean swagger, that "the rest of you are just *kludges* who are barely worth my notice" posture that was so common to the breed. He also didn't have the bone blades in his forearms, which, frankly, was a relief.

No, this was just a guy who had worked on his body and was proud of the result. That, Beka could understand. And if his body performed half as nicely as it looked, he might be an entertaining way to spend some time.

She put down her drink and approached him—not looking directly at him, but not letting anyone block her path, either. When his gaze landed on her she felt it, and when it hadn't gone away for about thirty seconds, she slowly brought her eyes up to meet his.

His eyes were dark, smoldering, almost black. His teeth, when he smiled at Beka, were white and even. Dimples carved themselves in his cheeks when he grinned—not those cute, youthful ones, but deep crags. He crossed his arms over his impressive span of chest and waited for her to reach him.

"Hello," he said when she had. His Common was unaccented, his voice deep and rich, full enough to be heard over the music. "I'm Fyodor Tennyson."

"Beka Valentine." She bowed as she had seen others do on Festival, and he returned the gesture.

"I noticed you when you came in," he claimed.

That has to be a line, Beka thought. *A room this big, with the smoke and the uneven lighting?* She could barely even remember where the door was. She was about to say so when he interrupted her. "You were with some soldiers," he said. "And a couple of other guys, civilians."

"You *did* see me," she said, shocked.

"Of course. I said I did. Anyway, I'm a pilot. We have to be observant."

Beka found herself nodding. "I'm a pilot too," she said. "Who do you fly for?"

"Myself," Tennyson answered with a sly grin. She took that to mean he was a smuggler, or did some other less than savory form of business. That was okay. She'd been there herself, once or twice, to understate things just a bit. "You?"

She laughed, bit her lower lip. "I have my own ship," she said. "But I've also signed on with a Commonwealth warship."

Tennyson's eyes widened. "There is no Commonwealth. Is there?"

That kind of thing drove Dylan nuts, Beka knew. He wanted to believe everyone had heard about his cause. "There didn't used to be. Well, there was, and then there wasn't. Now there is again."

"Hmmm," he said. "A new Commonwealth. And they need pilots? Do they pay well?"

Beka pulled out a stool and sat down at the bar. Tennyson turned, tugged a stool underneath him, and joined her. "That's the thing," Beka said. "It's more or less kind of a volunteer gig. For now, anyway."

Tennyson laughed again. "Volunteer? You surprise me, Beka Valentine."

She ordered a drink: same thing she had left behind a few minutes ago, except this time Fyodor Tennyson would be paying for it. "I do?" she said after she'd placed her order. "You've only known me for about forty-five seconds. You can't have formed too many opinions about me yet."

"A few," he admitted. "You value your body and you like it when others do too. You have quick reflexes, excellent vision, good decision-making skills. You are honest, but not to a fault. And sometimes you're dishonest, but not to a fault."

"Pretty fair assessment," Beka admitted. "But are you talking about me, or looking in a mirror?"

"If I were looking into a mirror I would have complimented your goatee," Tennyson said with a grin.

"It is a nice one."

"Those soldiers you came in with . . ."

"What about them?"

"Are you a prisoner? An honored guest?"

"Is there a difference?

"On Festival, not much of one." Tennyson paused, as if deciding how much he wanted to reveal. "Where are they now?"

"Dancing, I think," Beka said. "I haven't seen any of them for a little while. I think they all thought someone else was watching us."

"And your friends? Where are they?"

"Oh, crap." Beka realized it had been a long time since she had seen Harper or Trance. Surely they were just lost in the crowd somewhere. "I'm sure they're around."

"But not with the soldiers?"

"I don't know," Beka admitted. "They could be. I guess."

"Because if they're not, I'm afraid their situation might be a dicey one."

"What do you mean?" she asked.

Tennyson rested his elbows on the bar and put his fingers to his chin. Beka was certain he knew how that popped his biceps. She admired them silently and let him continue. "How much do you know of Festival's politics?" he asked.

"Even less than I know about you."

"I thought as much. Here's the thing. If your friends are under guard, which is the same thing here as having an escort, and they have somehow shaken those guards, then they are as guilty as if they had been convicted of crimes and escaped from prison. You are, too, for that matter, except that if you haven't left the general area in which you last saw your guards, then chances are you'll be okay because the first guard back to that spot will realize he shouldn't have left you alone there in the first place."

"But—we haven't done anything wrong here. We haven't broken any laws."

"Just being without your escort is a violation of the law," Tennyson explained.

Beka swept a hand around, encompassing the whole room. "But surely not all of these people are under guard."

"A few have safe conduct passes—the result of having clean records, or buying off the right people. Most of the others will stay here until morning," Tennyson said. "At which time the curfew will be lifted, so they can go home, or to work. And most of them didn't come here under military escort, so as long as they're not out on the streets they're not breaking the laws. Except, of course, the laws against this place existing in the first place."

"Which are rarely enforced," Beka offered.

"That's right. But *curfew* laws are rigorously enforced. As are the laws against escaping from military custody."

"This place . . . this place sucks!" Beka said. Suddenly anxious to warn the others, she tried her subdermal comm unit, but to no avail.

"Indeed it does," Tennyson agreed. "That's why I spend as much time as I can offworld."

"I've got to find them!"

"Did the soldiers leave you waiting at the bar?"

"Yes," she answered.

"Then you can't leave the bar, or you're guilty too."

"But . . ." She didn't even know how to phrase her next question.

"I'll look for them," Tennyson suggested. "You stay put, and if the soldiers come back, just pretend your friends are out dancing. That's probably where they are anyway. I'll track them down and bring them back to where you are."

"You don't even know what they look like," Beka retorted.

"I knew what you looked like," Tennyson reminded her with a mischievous grin. "If they're still in here, I'll find them."

"You would do that for me?"

"I would. I'll extract my payment later."

Beka returned his sly smile with one of her own. "You were probably gonna get that anyway."

"I know," Tennyson said. "But I like to feel that I've earned it."

He vanished into the crowd. Beka waited, biting the inside of her cheek and trying to restrain the urge to hit something. She wasn't particularly a fan of rules, especially when she thought they were stupid ones. Which, frankly, were most of them except those she made up. But she was *able* to follow them when she chose to— if she knew what they were beforehand. Those soldiers should have warned them what the score was. Now she had to count on a complete stranger to find Harper and Trance and persuade them to come back to the bar with him.

And of course, there was always the chance that Tennyson was full of it, and would be back in a few minutes, unsuccessful but willing to console her for her loss.

Either way, she would find Harper and Trance, and once she had, she was going to haul them both back to where they had left Dylan. It was apparent that Dylan saw the Festival System as an opportunity, and maybe as a challenge. Beka had quickly changed her opinion of it, though—or maybe just affirmed what she had suspected from the beginning, although she'd tried to keep an open mind.

Mudballs weren't for her.

At the first opportunity, she'd be hitching a ride back to the *Maru*. Maybe she'd even hang with the Rev on *Andromeda* while Dylan finished pressing the flesh down here.

When she saw Tennyson again, an anxious look marred his handsome face. "Have you seen the soldiers yet?" he asked.

"Not yet."

"Good. I saw them fanning out through the crowd, looking nervous—I think they've realized that they've blown their assignment. But your friends are nowhere."

"What do you mean, nowhere?" Beka demanded.

"Gone," Tennyson said. "I covered every inch of the club. I told you, I'm a pilot—eyes like a hawk. If I say they're not here—"

"Then they're not here," Beka completed. "How many ways are there out of here?"

"This is an illicit underground club, Beka," he reminded her. "There's only one way in, but there are at least half a dozen ways out."

At first Beka was going to point out how little sense that made, but then she gave it a few moments to sink in and realized that it was logical, in a twisted fashion. One way in, to control access and to be warned of possible raids. Many ways out, in case a raid actually happened.

The realization chilled Beka to the bone. If Harper and Trance had really left—without knowing what the score was, as she had not—then they were outside, maybe lost and quite possibly in serious trouble.

Having half of his crew members on the planet arrested on their first night here would probably reflect poorly on Dylan's judgment, and perhaps even jeopardize his mission. She didn't want that to happen. And besides, the captain of the *Eureka Maru* took care of her own.

She grabbed Tennyson's muscular right arm and gave him her most flirtatious smile. "You've got to help me find them," she said. "Before we all get in trouble."

"I'm sorry, Beka," he said simply. "Did I give you some reason to believe that I want to spend the next ten years in jail?"

"Is that all?" she replied. She pressed herself against him. "I'm worth twenty, easy."

SEVEN

> "If you lose a phalange, you forfeit the game—unless you get
> two of your opponent's on your next turn."
>
> —W. E. DIXON ON SKIN THE SHARK, IN "DIXON'S
> OFFICIAL RULES OF GAMES," CY 5944

Easily accepting the logic behind the guards, Tyr had invited in
the one stationed outside his room, and before long the two were
involved in a friendly local game called Skin the Shark. It was
played with a deck of wedge-shaped cards which the guard, Tartagus Nels Swinniten, just happened to have on him. He revealed
that it could also be spiced up with knives—the winner of each
hand got to throw a knife into the floor as close as possible to the
loser's foot. If he came within ten centimeters he took an extra ten
percent of the pot from the loser, but if he nicked the other's foot
then he had to pay back double. "I won't make you play that way,
though," Tartagus had said. "Not till you've got some experience,
at any rate."

"Is there something about me that makes you think I'm not a
fast learner?" Tyr had asked.

So it was that Tyr Anasazi had a hefty blade in his hand, and

Tartagus stood with his feet spread on the floor, his knees shaking a little. The floor where he stood had already suffered multiple gouges. Tyr planned to sleep on the floor—the bed was far too soft for his comfort—but these cuts wouldn't disturb him, and if this world had any civilization at all, after he had gone nanobots would repair the damage before anyone else stayed in the room.

Tyr balanced the knife across his fingers, then quickly flipped it into the air, caught the very point, and hurled it toward Tartagus's feet. It *thwock*ed into the floor and vibrated there, three centimeters from the soldier's left foot.

"I think you've got the hang of the game," Tartagus said. "Maybe we should put the cards away for a while." He picked up the knife and put it on the table, where Tyr was already helping himself to his extra ten percent. So far he had taken the equivalent of fifteen thrones from the soldier in local currency, if Tartagus's description of the exchange rate could be believed.

"If you're tired of playing," he allowed.

"I'm just not sure how it would look, you know. I'm supposed to be guarding you, not playing games."

"I understand," Tyr said. He watched Tartagus pocket his last few remaining coins.

"Thanks."

"Tell me something, Tartagus," Tyr said, when the man had put away what little money he had left. "Just what is the function of the military in Festival society? So far I have not been without a military presence since I arrived here."

He sat on a comfortable chair, with a gesture inviting Tartagus to do the same. Tartagus took a seat, but remained rigid, keeping one eye on the open door. "The military?" he repeated. "It's everything. Well, not everything. But all-powerful, I guess. We control law enforcement, taxation, the press, public opinion. We are well paid, respected, feared."

"Feared?" Tyr echoed.

"You know, most folks—those who aren't in the military—lock

their doors at night. Quadruple locks, most of them. And then in the morning, if no soldiers have knocked on their doors, they count themselves among the lucky ones and open them up again."

"Why should a soldier knock upon their door?"

Tartagus shrugged. "Keeping the peace. Checking for criminals. Search and seizure."

"It all sounds rather oppressive," Tyr opined.

"I guess, from the outside," Tartagus said. "But if you lived here you'd know it's not like that. This is a dangerous world, with a lot of crime. We just try to keep people safe."

"By keeping them locked up."

"If that's what it takes."

Tyr shrugged.

"Do you think that's wrong?" Tartagus asked.

"I have no problem with it," Tyr replied. "Someone has to maintain order. Better a trained and well armed military force than utter anarchy."

"That's the way I see it. I'm glad you agree. You're obviously a pretty smart guy."

Tyr didn't bother to answer that. Not only was the truth evident, but it had been directly stated. He simply lounged in the chair, fascinated to hear more about life on Festival.

"What kind of crime do you have to deal with here?"

Tartagus considered this for a moment. "Well, there are a lot of people who don't accept the laws that His Regency hands down, you know. A lot of folks who like to think that they have better ways of doing things. And then, you know, theft and murder and so on, but not so much of those."

"So mostly political crimes, thought crimes?"

"Yeah," Tartagus said. "A lot of that."

"Do you deal with many threats from without? War? Raiders?"

"No . . . most people know our reputation and leave us alone, I guess."

"And you are treated well, by your superiors?"

"Oh, we make out fine," Tartagus assured him. "I wouldn't give up this job for anything."

"I see," Tyr said. He was about to say something else when Tartagus put a hand over his ear, as if he'd had a sudden earache. After a moment, he lowered his hand and looked at Tyr.

"It's your friends," he said, an expression just short of panic showing on his face. "They've disappeared."

"Well, find them," Tyr said. A simple enough solution, it seemed to him.

"We're working on it," Tartagus replied. "But the thing is, by slipping away from their guards, they've broken the law. They're criminals now—when they're found, it's possible they might be injured or killed."

"They had better not be. Has Captain Hunt been notified?"

"He's in a meeting with His Regency," Tartagus said. "Which is not to be disturbed."

Tyr stood up. "Come on, then. We are not leaving my shipmates at the mercy of your soldiers."

"But . . . Tyr, we're supposed to wait—"

"You have been ordered to guard me, right?"

"Yes, of course, but—"

"You cannot guard me in here, if I am out there. Are you coming, or staying?"

Tartagus came up out of his chair with a worried look. "Coming, coming. I'm coming."

Finally, Dylan could stifle his yawns no longer. His eyes were bleary and he was having trouble following Havasu's lofty flights of long-winded rhetoric, not to mention Cam's slick salesman's patter. He was afraid his eyes would have to close, his head nod, and a string of drool reach to his chest before Havasu got the hint and called the meeting to a close.

But Rommie—as she so often did—came to his rescue. "Captain, if you're going to speak to a large assembly tomorrow, you should get some rest tonight," she suggested.

"Good point," Dylan agreed immediately. "I think we've covered everything pretty thoroughly." *In ridiculous detail*, he wanted to add. Havasu, his ministers, and Cam Prezennetti had essentially spent the last few hours rehearsing the "extemporaneous" speech they wanted Dylan to give. If they kept drilling him, not only would he be too exhausted to see straight, but he would give a robotic performance, simply reciting the talking points they had provided—probably exactly what they wanted, but not what Dylan had in mind.

"If you're sure, Dylan," Havasu said. "I only want you to be fully prepared for such an important address."

"Rommie's right, Your Regency. If I don't get my shut-eye, I'm worthless."

"Very well, Dylan," Havasu said. He started to stand, and his ministers, in unison, did likewise. Cam kept his seat, but tossed Dylan a friendly, casual wave. "You'll be shown back to your quarters, and summoned when it's time for you to appear. If there's anything, anything at all, you would like in the interim, you have only to ask."

"A good night's sleep and maybe some breakfast," Dylan replied. "I'm a pretty simple guy, when you get right down to it."

"Don't think you can make me underestimate you, Captain Hunt," Havasu said with a friendly smile. "Because that will not happen."

Excused from the royal presence, Dylan and Rommie were led back to their rooms by different soldiers than the ones who had brought them to the banquet. Passing the rooms occupied by Trance, Tyr, Beka, and Harper, Dylan nodded to the soldiers standing guard. "They all asleep?" he asked.

"That's right," one of the soldiers answered firmly.

Dylan caught Rommie's eye. "Lucky them," he said.

The soldiers took them to their rooms, opened the door, and made a quick security sweep of each one. "It's all clear," the one checking Dylan's room said.

Dylan bade Rommie good night and went in. His crew had the right idea—might as well get in some good sleep time while they had solid ground beneath them and were in a safe and secure environment. Rommie had a disappointed look on her face, as if maybe she wanted to talk privately for a while, but Dylan figured whatever it was would wait. There would be plenty of time in the morning.

EIGHT

"The difference between 'honest work' and any other kind is
invariably determined by someone who's never done either one."
—BETTINA VOLE, CY 7792

It turned out that Fujiko Ellston had a different sort of thing in
mind than Harper did. Harper's intent had been to meet a lady
who might be inclined to spend some time with him. Fujiko envi-
sioned more of a professional/client relationship, an exchange of
currency for services rendered.

By the time Harper figured that out, though, Fujiko had already
scared the bejeezus out of him. That had started as soon as they hit
the street outside the club, when Fujiko started scanning for soldiers or voybots, which he explained were miniaturized voyeur ro-
bots the authorities used to patrol the city and enforce curfew.
Fortunately, Fujiko said, even the voybots couldn't be everywhere,
and the underground sex trades were grudgingly tolerated—on the
assumption that if they weren't, they would only become more
popular—so there were select neighborhoods that no one patrolled.

"So what we're doing is against the law?" Harper asked anxiously, walking fast to keep up with Fujiko's pace.

"You've never broken the law before?"

"I didn't say that," Harper shot back defiantly. "I just like to know when I'm doing it. I also like to have a ship handy to get away from any unintended consequences, whenever possible."

"That's not going to work here," Fujiko reminded him. "No civilian ships. But don't worry, chances are good that no one will spot us before we get to the red zone, and even if they do they probably won't shoot first."

"Oh, I feel a whole lot better now," Harper answered, hoping his utter lack of sincerity was plainly evident.

The "red zone," as it happened, was only a few blocks from the underground club. Harper knew when they reached it because Fujiko slowed to a more leisurely pace, and because the sterile, blank facades of the buildings gave way to garishly lit storefronts with signs and pictures advertising the sorts of activities that took place inside.

Also because suddenly there were women on the street—*females* might have been more accurate, actually, because some of them weren't humanoid in the least—and most of them wore less fabric over their bodies than went into one of Harper's socks. Males too, for that matter, again of a startling variety of species. Individuals of both genders, and possibly some indeterminate others, beckoned and called to Harper and Fujiko.

"Ignore them," Fujiko whispered. "We're heading for the good ones."

Good ones? If prostitutes had been what Harper was interested in, he had already seen four or five, just in the red zone's first block, whom he would have categorized as good ones. Stunning faces, bodies that were curved and full in all the places he liked them to be, firm and flat in the others. Harper appreciated good design and quality engineering, and many of these women had both.

But Fujiko had a specific destination in mind, and he urged

Harper to keep going, not to meet the eyes of any of the professionals on the street. Harper had already realized that what Fujiko was looking for wasn't the way he had wanted to spend the evening, but he was along for the ride now, and what with the warnings about patrols and voybots and shooting first, he figured sticking close to his guide was for the best. He would hang with Fujiko for an hour or so, let the guy get his jollies, and then demand to be taken back to the club where he could reunite with Beka and Trance.

The place Fujiko was headed was in the next block. A tall, muscular woman stood at the door beneath a glowing holographic sign that promised the "Best Show in Gala." Behind her was a small windowed booth, inside which a rodentlike alien sat.

"Ten guilders, my friend," Fujiko told Harper. "They accept Common currency or credit chits here. And it's well worth the price."

"Ten guilders?" Harper echoed. He hated to part with that kind of dough simply to keep Fujiko entertained. It didn't look like he had much choice, though. Instead of waiting around to discuss it, Fujiko was already approaching the big woman at the door.

"Hello, Mara," he said.

"Evening, Ellston," she replied with a welcoming smile. *If the bouncer knows him,* Harper thought, *I guess he's a regular.* "Come on in. I see you brought a friend."

"That's Harper," Fujiko said. He waved Harper over to them. "This is Mara. She owns the joint."

"Welcome, Harper," Mara said, bestowing the same smile on him. "I hope you have a good time, whatever your tastes are."

"He will," Fujiko promised before Harper could even reply. "You pay over here, Harper." Fujiko went to the window and handed over a credit chit. Harper reluctantly fished a chit of his own out of his pocket and followed suit.

Once they had both paid, the front door swung open automatically. "Mara likes to be her own security force," Fujiko whispered as they went in. "Nobody messes with her, and her performers know they're well taken care of."

"Are there a lot of . . . um . . . professionals in Gala?" Harper asked.

"The red zone goes on for about ten more blocks," Fujiko said. "Day and night. So maybe fifty thousand, in all. It's a living."

Harper was about to ask another question, but they passed through the door and suddenly music almost as loud as that back at the club blasted them. Easy conversation was a thing of the past. Instead of talking, he concentrated on following close behind Fujiko so as not to lose him in the dark maze they entered. Walls and doors appeared seemingly out of nowhere, and Harper had no idea what was what, or where.

"Do you prefer humanoid or non, my friend?" Fujiko shouted into Harper's ear. "It doesn't make any difference to me."

Harper still wasn't sure what exactly the nature of the "Best Show in Gala" might be, but he had some guesses, and he figured humanoid would be the least objectionable. Besides, if the women on the street—and Fujiko's easy dismissal of them in favor of the "good ones"—had been any indication, then the ones in this place must be truly spectacular. He figured he might as well see the best of what the city had to offer, rather than indulging any minor curiosities about other species.

Besides, there were always flexis to indulge those curiosities, if he'd been so inclined. He had peeked from time to time, but his tastes ran along more familiar lines.

"Let's stick with human," Harper replied.

"Got it." Fujiko led the way with an easy, practiced stride. A few moments later they had entered an auditorium with a couple dozen rows of wide, comfortable seats, occupied by a scattering of individuals, some human, some not. On the stage, moving and grinding in classic strip show fashion, was one of the most amazing women Harper had ever seen.

She's no Rommie, Harper thought, comparing her—as he did

most women—with the avatar android he had built for *Andromeda Ascendant*. But she was, nonetheless, virtually flawless. Her tresses were thick and luxuriant, cascading down around her shoulders like a golden waterfall. Even in the dim, red-tinted light, her wide blue eyes sparkled with wit and intelligence. Her nose was small and precisely carved, her cheekbones high, jaw firm and defined. Her mouth was a masterpiece of sculpture, lips full and perfectly shaped, teeth even and white. Her pale skin was without blemish or imperfection. Harper couldn't shake the feeling that he was looking at a heavily retouched flexi, except that she was right there in front of him—a dozen feet away, if that—and she appeared to be entirely real.

Fujiko led him to a seat a few rows back from the stage. Harper could barely look away from the dancer up there, but he managed to get his butt in the chair. Onstage, the woman was peeling away a thin layer of fabric that could barely contain the full, heavy breasts that strained against it. He had to admit that although he had not anticipated spending the evening as a spectator, the dancer was so stunning, and her smile as she gyrated and moved to the music so genuine-looking, he could not be entirely sorry he was here to watch her.

Someone else loomed at the edge of his vision, and Harper brought his feet closer to the chair, believing that someone was trying to slip past him to a seat farther down the row. But a hand on his shoulder—a firm, seductive grip—told him that his initial impression was mistaken. Almost grudgingly, he looked away from the stage.

Leaning toward him was another magnificent example of feminine pulchritude, wearing only a skimpy fluorescent green wrap about her hips. This one had dark hair and green eyes and was a few pounds heavier than the dancer on stage, most of those pounds contained in the enormous expanse of bosom that dangled before his eyes like fruit ripe for the picking. She favored him with a brilliant smile. "Would you like some company?" she asked. "There's no pressure; I just thought you were awfully handsome when you came in, and I'd like to sit with you if you want."

"I . . . uhh . . ." Harper was at a loss for words, a truly uncommon circumstance for him. Did she expect some kind of payment? Of course she would. But just for sitting? He wasn't about to do anything with her beyond that, even if she was offering, which he wasn't at all sure was the case. If he said no, would she take it personally? Because suddenly the idea of spending some time with such a woman was incredibly appealing.

He glanced over at Fujiko, sitting beside him. But Fujiko had already accepted a similar invitation, and had his arms wrapped around yet another lovely lady. One thing in this guy's favor—when he had promised the "good ones," he hadn't been joking around.

When Harper looked back at the woman, waiting patiently for an answer, there was the slightest hint of a pout on her impossibly luscious lips, as if she was afraid he was going to turn her down. He couldn't bear to see her pout. Anyway, the big seats were easily large enough for two—had been designed, he was sure, specifically for that purpose. "Sure," he said. "Have a seat."

Her face brightened again, and she extended a hand toward him. "I'm Abundant," she said cheerily.

"You sure are," Harper agreed, giving her hand a squeeze.

"I mean, that's my name," she said, giggling a little. "Abundant Mercy."

"Seamus Harper," he said. "Somehow that seems a little nondescript at the moment."

"I like it," Abundant said. She squeezed in beside him. Her flesh was warm and soft and when she sat, Harper was enveloped in a cloud of perfume that smelled like fresh flowers and exotic spices. He found that he was suddenly very hungry.

Or something.

———

Trance struggled against the powerful arms that held her, but couldn't break free—at least not without making enough of a ruckus to give her location away to the soldiers who had chased her into the alley.

Inside the room, other hands gripped her. After a few anxious moments, she stopped fighting, knowing that it was useless. A face pressed close to hers—even in the dark she could see that it was broad and bearded, with rough, unrefined features. "Are you going to be quiet? You almost got us all killed," the man said.

"I did?" she asked when the hand was removed from her mouth. "What did I do?"

"You were leading them right to us."

"I didn't even know you were here." Which was not entirely true. Trance was very difficult to take completely by surprise. But it was the story she was going with, for now. At least she was out of sight of the soldiers, which was the important part.

"That has nothing to do with it," he said. "Whether you knew or not is beside the point. If they had grabbed you before we all got inside, they'd have spotted us too."

"I don't see how I can be held responsible," Trance argued. "Anyway, they're gone by now, I'm sure, so if you don't mind I'll just be on my way."

"You're joking, right?" the man responded. "Now they're looking for you. And we don't even know who you are or what you're doing here. You might go out there and tell them we're in here, just to take the heat off yourself."

Trance felt anger building up in her, and it was not a feeling she enjoyed. "A couple of problems with that theory," she declared, ticking them off on her fingers. "One, I don't know who you are either. Two, I don't know who *they* are. Three, I don't know *where* we are. And four, there is no heat *on* me. I guess a couple is two, so that's more than a couple, but you get the idea."

Now she could see that there were six of them, all men. They stared at her as if she had lost her mind, which maybe wasn't so far from the truth. "Guess again," the one who had done all the talking so far said. "We're in the middle of a job here, and you are staying with us until we're done."

"What kind of job?" Trance asked, the very picture of naivete. "You guys are, like, carpenters or something?"

"Something," the guy said. "Now you just keep your mouth shut and stay out of our way and you'll be fine."

"You might even learn a little something," another one added. They were inside someone's home, Trance realized. An expensive home, at that, with beautiful works of art on the walls and scattered on the furniture. One of the men opened a big cloth bag and snagged a statue that Trance recognized as sculpted from Triluvian crystal—grown only in a few square kilometers of that world's dense forest, highly prized for its beauty as well as its healing attributes. He dropped the statue into the bag and continued casting about for more. The other men—except for the one assigned to keep an eye on Trance, the burly one who had first grabbed her—peeled off to search the rest of the home.

"You . . . you're burglars!" Trance objected. "Criminals!"

"Are you really that slow?" the man asked. "How do you function in society?" He fixed her with a suspicious gaze. "What are you, anyway? Where are you from?"

"No place you would know," Trance retorted. "And I'm not slow. I function just fine." Although to be perfectly honest—which she always was to herself, even though she wouldn't be to these men—she was kind of clumsy sometimes. Falling in with these guys was just one more in a long series of accidents. Usually they were happy accidents; fortuitous events that led to good results were her specialty. So far, she was having a hard time seeing how this one qualified. Maybe it didn't.

She tried to get a handle on the probability paths, to see where this was all leading. But with the fear, the physical violence that had occurred and the potential for more, she couldn't focus on them. She was tense, her tail curled up and around and gripped so tightly in her fist that she was afraid she would squeeze the tip off.

She would get away from these men soon, she was sure.

She just hadn't quite figured out how.

The guy left to keep an eye on her watched her with unblinking intensity. Around them, she heard the sounds of the hurried gathering of objects, followed by footsteps rushing back toward them. When the men reappeared, their bags bulged with the take. They were fast and efficient, and Trance hadn't even begun to think of a plan yet.

"Let's move out," one of them whispered urgently. "There's someone home upstairs."

"Home?" the one who had been watching Trance repeated angrily. "There wasn't supposed to be anyone home!"

"Jock screwed up," the man said with a shrug.

A man who must have been Jock, a small, wiry guy with short blue dreadlocks, glared at the speaker with knitted brows and a furious gleam in his eyes. "I didn't—well, let's just get out of here!"

Trance's mood began to brighten. The man who had grabbed her had said that she could leave when they did. She had—as she so often did—fallen into something, in this case a situation rather than a potted plant or a hole in the deck. But now it looked as if extraction was only moments away. Which was good, because spending the night with a bunch of home invaders wasn't exactly how she had been hoping to spend her time on Festival.

"Getting out is a good idea," she put in. "A really good idea. The faster the better."

"We're getting," her captor told her, an unfriendly snarl on his face. "And you're going with us. We can't risk having you alert the patrols until we're done."

Which she had, of course, known was the likeliest outcome. But hope couldn't be abandoned, ever, and in this particular case she had been hoping that she'd be proven wrong.

"Oh," she said. "I guess I see your point. I wouldn't do that, though. I'd be in as much trouble as you."

"I don't think so," the man argued. "Unless you've already killed a couple of people tonight, I don't think you'd be in nearly as much trouble."

NINE

Beka wasn't going to just stand around the club while her crew faced dangers of which they might not even be aware. Sure, she had willingly yielded command of the overall mission to Dylan Hunt, and allowed the *Eureka Maru* to become a support vessel to the *Andromeda Ascendant*. But she had been a captain and she still felt a ship's officer's responsibility for those who willingly served under her. Fyodor Tennyson could help. That wasn't all he could do for Beka, she was convinced, but the other stuff was now secondary. Finding Harper and Trance took precedence.

"If we're leaving," Tennyson urged, "we should do it now. The soldiers will be back here any second looking for you."

"Do you know how to get out?" Beka asked.

"I've skipped out of better joints than this," Tennyson replied with a rakish grin. "Come on."

He quickly led Beka down the length of the bar and through a pressure-activated irising door at the end of it. This doorway led into a narrow kitchen area where a handful of cooks worked preparing snacks and hors d'oeuvres for the customers. They looked up at Beka and Tennyson with curiosity but not outright surprise, making Beka think this exit path was not an especially uncommon one.

"Have you seen a guy in a tropical shirt and a purple girl with a tail?" she asked the cooks.

They just looked at her for a moment, and then one of them shook his head sadly. "You're on your way out, right? Because if not, I'm going to tell the barkeep to cut you off. Sounds like you've had a few too many."

"She's just joking," Tennyson assured them. He tugged on Beka's hand. "Come on, Jane."

When they were on the staircase heading up to street level from the kitchen door, Beka wrenched her hand free. "Jane? What kind of name is that?"

"One that doesn't sound like Beka," Tennyson explained. "You already made an impression on them. When the soldiers ask them—which they will—those cooks are going to remember you. Best not to give them your real name to go with the description."

He had a point. Beka had assumed different names and identities from time to time during her career, when it had seemed judicious to do so. She just usually liked to put a little more thought into it. Once, for a couple of weeks, she had been Glorious Sun Rising in the West Wilson. At the end, that con had blown up in her face, and she had walked away from it—well, Slipstreamed away, to be more accurate—without a single guilder for her efforts, so on further reflection maybe Jane wasn't so bad.

"Okay, Jane it is," she relented. "And I have another question."

"What?" he asked. He stopped in front of a door that she guessed would lead outside, and waited.

"Keeping in mind just how gigantamous this city is, how are we going to find Trance and Harper in it?"

"Lady, they're your friends," Tennyson replied. "I was hoping you had an idea." He pushed the door open cautiously, cracking it first and peering through to make sure no one waited for them outside. When he had decided it was clear he opened it the rest of the way and they both stepped out.

"Well, Harper's pretty basic," Beka admitted. "He likes to tinker with machines and engines and gizmos. He likes women. He likes Sparky Cola. He likes . . . well, that's about the full range."

"And the other one? Trance?"

"Trance is harder to pin down," Beka said. "She could be pretty much anywhere, doing pretty much anything."

"That will make her harder to find. Maybe we should start with Harper. Any chance Trance would be with him?"

"Anything's possible, with her. But if she is, then Harper isn't having the kind of fun he'd like to be having."

"Let's start with the red zone," Tennyson suggested. "I don't know where there are any all-night machine shops or Sparky Cola bars. But if he likes women, he could definitely find some there." He started down the street, and Beka stuck close behind him. She worried about her friends. If they'd had any idea that the laws here were so strict and enforced so harshly, they would never have taken off. Their own ignorance could cost them dearly.

She would have a few things to tell Dylan about this place—assuming she survived the night and found her way back to him.

None of them would be favorable.

Tartagus took Tyr to a central surveillance post on a lower floor of the Hall of Regency. The walls were covered with flatscreens, in front of which sat uniformed soldiers, noting every movement they saw. Live images from voybots all over Gala were projected onto the screens, Tartagus said. A secondary set of screens could replay images from earlier, so they could speedscan and see if his friends had been spotted anywhere.

The way it appeared to Tyr, if Beka, Harper, and Trance had

been spotted, they would have been dealt with immediately—and not gently. Most of the flatscreens showed empty streets, but as he watched, a voybot signal came through showing a couple of men rushing down a shadowed road. The soldier monitoring that particular screen barked out coordinates, and the closest foot patrol responded. Just minutes later, another nearby voybot picked up the men, and the patrol as it closed on them. The men were ordered to stop, but they didn't. Instead, they broke into what looked to Tyr like a terrified sprint. The soldiers on patrol opened fire with energy weapons that flared brightly on the flatscreen. When the screen came into focus again, the men were down, the soldiers picking through their remains to find out just whom they had killed.

"Decisive action," Tyr acknowledged.

"Curfew is not taken lightly in Gala," Tartagus agreed. "Which is why I wouldn't let you go off by yourself. Bad enough that your friends are out there somewhere. Heads are going to roll for that."

"Literally?"

"We're not so big on decapitation here," one of the other soldiers answered. He didn't take his eyes off the set of screens he monitored. "Creates a solid waste problem. We tend to go in more for incineration."

On the flatscreen where the patrol had brought down the violators, Tyr saw what the soldier meant. Having identified the two men, the soldiers on patrol aimed their energy weapons at the corpses. The screen burned once more with a brilliant light, and when Tyr could make out shapes on it again, the two bodies were only charred impressions on the pavement.

Tartagus beckoned Tyr over to the secondary screens. "Let's see if we can spot them," he suggested.

"They had better not have been treated like those people we just saw," Tyr said firmly. "Not if your government wants entry into the Commonwealth. And wants not to make enemies of Dylan Hunt and myself."

"We won't know until we see what we see." Tartagus spoke a command. On a set of six flatscreens, images began to flit past, starting much earlier in the evening, when there were still people on the streets. Soon enough it grew dark and the streets emptied out. Only the occasional brave soul risked exposure on them, and a few of those met with the same treatment Tyr had just observed. Others, whom Tyr assumed were beyond the immediate reach of foot patrols, were allowed to go unchallenged.

When they had speedscanned up to the present, they started over with input from a different set of voybots. Tyr began to grow impatient. The whole process was eating up valuable time during which Beka, Trance, and Harper were in danger. Tyr had not exaggerated the ferocity of Dylan's reaction to this; if anything, he had probably understated it. If his crew members were killed, these people would be lucky if he didn't fire a Nova bomb into their sun.

Finally, he spotted a familiar, colorful shirt. "Stop there!" he commanded. Tartagus paused the image. It clearly showed Harper, in the company of a man Tyr had never seen. They had been walking quickly and with evident purpose.

"How long ago was that?" Tyr wanted to know.

"A bit less than two hours," Tartagus said.

"And what happened to them?"

Tartagus continued the transmission. The two walked off the screen and were not seen again. "It looks like they were headed into the red zone," he explained. "We wouldn't have bothered with them if they were near enough to its boundaries."

"What is the red zone?"

"Allowable vices," Tartagus said. "Prostitution, controlled substances, entertainment for adults. All carefully monitored and regulated. Keeps the locals happy and feeling like they're getting away with something."

"I see," Tyr said. "If they had come out of the red zone, would they have been picked up by one of your surveillance cameras?"

"The voybots keep a pretty close eye on the red zone's fringes," Tartagus answered. "They don't go in, but they do watch the perimeter. So chances are, yes."

"Then that should be our destination," Tyr declared. "Now. One of these others can scan for Trance—a tailed, purple woman will be easy enough to recognize, no?"

"I'll see that it's taken care of," Tartagus promised. He spoke a few quiet words to one of the soldiers and then led Tyr outside. A small patrol had been hurriedly organized to accompany them on their search.

"Remember," Tyr said, addressing the group of ten. "If we see them, no shooting. Let me take the lead."

"Yes, sir," several of the soldiers said. There were both men and women in the unit, all with military bearing, fully equipped for any circumstance that might arise.

They headed out on foot, walking briskly toward their destination. Tartagus had explained that the only aircraft allowed in Gala were those used for official military or law enforcement purposes, and while taking one now would save a few minutes, the reaction inside the red zone would be swift. Doors would disappear, lights would turn off, and anyone inside would become much harder to find. Better to go in on foot, he said, and not create a furor. Tyr understood his reasoning, and agreed that the few minutes saved would probably not be worth it.

But when they were a little more than halfway there, it turned out that their few minutes would stretch into a longer delay.

Tartagus listened intently to a voice Tyr couldn't hear, even with his enhanced Nietzschean hearing. Tartagus had his hand cupped over his ear, and an unhappy look crossed his face. He acknowledged the message and lowered his hand. "Change of plans," he announced to the patrol.

"No change," Tyr said.

"It won't take long, Tyr," Tartagus insisted. "But I'm afraid it has to be. There's a gang of criminals—we've been after them for some time—and they've been observed in the area. We're the nearest patrol. We've got to take them down, and then we'll be on our way."

"That does not take precedence," Tyr objected.

"Maybe not to you," Tartagus argued. "But these people are murderers and thieves. Your friend Harper is likely enjoying himself considerably at this moment, so it's a safe bet he won't mind if we delay briefly."

"Very briefly," Tyr allowed.

"How many are there?" another soldier asked.

"Possibly six or seven," Tartagus replied. "They managed to dodge the voybots for the most part, but one caught them from almost a kilometer away. When the image was enhanced Sekta Myandoc was identified by his gait. The voybot only got a glimpse, though, so they aren't certain how many are in the group."

"Myandoc," a third soldier repeated. "He is a bad one."

"He's evaded us for months," Tartagus said, starting off at double time toward the coordinates he'd been given. "We've got to stop him if there's a chance."

Tyr fell into a jog with the other soldiers. "This seems like a law enforcement operation," he said. "I know you told me, Tartagus, that Festival's military handles law enforcement as well. But I find it strange that there do not seem to be separate units for each. It seems that you spend most of your energy battling crime."

"Not as much as there would be if we didn't enforce our laws so strictly," Tartagus explained. "Believe me, this is a fairly new thing, in the last decade or so. Before that, crime was rampant."

"Why?" Tyr wondered.

No one answered immediately. "Surely there is speculation, if nothing else," Tyr went on. "Some reason for so much crime, if it really is a problem. Or was."

"I guess . . . well, there's a lot of poverty," Tartagus said. "A lot of people getting by on very little, and others who have a lot. Not much in the middle, though. So I guess the people who don't have much try to even things out by stealing what they can."

"In my experience, that usually means those who have a lot stole it first," Tyr suggested. "And they are better at keeping it."

He half expected someone to object to his implicit characterization of their society, but no one did. Soldiers, he knew, tended not to be the most political or opinionated of people. They were usually content to do as they were told, rather than worrying about the whys and wherefores of policy-making. Still, he realized as he ran alongside these brothers-and-sisters-at-arms that there was a camaraderie among military people that he enjoyed, and had missed since his pride had been destroyed and he had signed on with Gerentex, the Nightsider in whose employ he had first boarded *Andromeda*. Soldiers knew what to expect from one another. They had each other's backs and they knew about the same things: about weapons and combat and the price of life. By facing death on a daily basis they learned to value life, and that knowledge, rarely spoken of or acknowledged, informed everything else that they did.

In response to another voybot's report, Tartagus changed the patrol's course slightly. Reaching the end of a block, he came to a sudden halt, raising a hand to signal those behind him to stop as well. The soldiers gathered behind him, preparing Gauss rifles for combat. Tyr freed his force lance from its holster. The soldiers waited in absolute silence while Tartagus quickly laid out the battle plan with additional hand signals. At his command, they broke around the corner, spreading out, training their weapons down the block.

Tyr joined them, seeing the targets as soon as he cleared the corner. There were seven of them, three women, three men, the seventh a stocky porcine alien of a sort that Tyr didn't immediately recognize, with pointed, steel-tipped tusks jutting from either side of a wide mouth. At the sight of the soldiers, the criminals opened fire with their energy weapons.

The soldiers did the same.

Outnumbered and outgunned, the criminals fell quickly. The only one who dodged the initial burst of fire from the soldiers was the piglike alien, who rushed the patrol with his head lowered. One of the soldiers was sighting down his Gauss rifle and failed to look up in time to see the alien bear down on him. The alien brought his head up at the last second and his tusks caught the young soldier in the collarbone, tearing him open. Blood flew in the air and coated the steel tips of his tusks.

The alien avoided another plasma blast, fired once with his own gun, and charged another soldier. Tyr exploded into action. He ran two steps and then hurled himself into the air, sailing over the soldier who was only now realizing that he was in the path of those killing tusks and landing in front of the alien. With a snap of Tyr's wrist, his force lance extended to quarterstaff mode. He thrust its end between the pig-thing's legs, entangling them. The alien stumbled forward. Tyr dealt it two swift, hard blows, and with a soft grunt the creature fell into unconsciousness.

"You might want to interrogate it later," Tyr said.

Tartagus nodded, clearly impressed. "We might at that," he said, though the surprise in his voice made Tyr think the concept had never occurred to him. "Maybe you'd consider enlisting. We could use some like you."

Tyr suspected the offer was half-hearted, a spur-of-the-moment gesture rather than a serious request. But he decided not to answer right now anyway. The idea had some merit on the face of it, and he was not one to let an opportunity slip past lightly, without giving it appropriate consideration. "We have a mission to accomplish," he reminded Tartagus.

Tartagus nodded, as if to show that it had not slipped his mind in the heat of the moment. He ordered a couple of his soldiers to take the alien into custody, and they continued on toward the red zone.

TEN

"Prostitutes, unlike politicians, seldom make promises they can't keep."

—TARUDEN ABSHAW, CY 9002

Abundant Mercy turned out to be the best thing about the red zone, as far as Harper was concerned. She was pleasant, sweet-natured, and had a biting sense of humor that took Harper by surprise. She was also, as it turned out, brutally honest about herself and her life.

"I work here because there's decent money in it," she admitted at one point. "I don't always like all the things I do to earn it—or all the people I do to earn it, I guess. They're not all as cute as you are, not by a long shot. But I definitely do earn it. I work hard and I provide good service for a fair price."

"I have no doubt about that. But if you don't like it, there have got to be other jobs you could get," Harper suggested. "You're smart, personable, attractive." She was still sitting with him in the chair, their bodies mashed together in a way that was enjoyable and stimulating. She rubbed his leg with her left hand while they talked.

"You'd be surprised," she said. "A city as big as Gala, right? But the rich folks keep the good jobs for themselves, and the other jobs don't pay for crap. Taxes are high so we can keep Festival's military strong—they tell us it's necessary because there's so much danger out there. It's never really clear where 'out there' is, and I don't really see them doing much except around here.

"Anyway, the result is that the poor stay poor, no matter what. By doing what I do, I make more than twice what my parents made doing more traditional jobs."

She had already told him that she was well educated by Festival standards, and although at first he had assumed that she was simply trying to play up a stereotype—the whole naughty coed thing—he was beginning to believe that she had told the truth. "Sounds like a rough place to live," he admitted.

"It is," Abundant agreed. "If you want to get ahead you've got to be born to the right parents, or exceptionally skilled at crime. I'm not willing to do that, but I am willing to work hard at my trade to try to get somewhere. At least keep food on my table and a roof over my head, you know?"

"I understand," Harper said. He was about to add something when Fujiko Ellston came in from some other room. Harper realized he hadn't seen his companion for at least an hour.

"Harper, my friend, you've got to come with me now," Fujiko insisted. "You've spent enough time with the lovely lady. We've got so much more to do and experience."

Abundant frowned. Harper wanted to believe it was because she would miss his scintillating companionship, but he suspected the fact that he'd been sitting with her for so long while parting with so little coinage had something to do with it. "So soon?" she asked.

"Yes, so soon," Fujiko replied. He tugged on Harper's shirt. "Come, Harper. A world of pleasure awaits."

Harper reluctantly left with Fujiko, though he would rather

have stayed with Abundant if it had been up to him. He still needed Fujiko to get him back to the club, however, and he intended to bring that up in a little while.

"I could see that you were just sitting with her," Fujiko said when they had left Abundant Mercy behind. "So I guessed that she wasn't your type. I've found us something a little more exotic."

"Exotic" wasn't the word Harper would have chosen to describe the rest of the entertainment Fujiko had lined up. He had led Harper to another section of Mara's "Best Show in Gala" complex, where a live sex act, between corpulent, tentacled aliens who required five parties for procreation, was taking place. It was over before Harper had fully parsed out what parts belonged to whom, but that may have been because he spent much of the time looking at the floor or covering his eyes with his hands. Fujiko took it all in enthusiastically, though, and then insisted they go see something *truly* exotic.

Five stops later—after Harper had turned down an even dozen unwanted offers from a wide variety of species—he finally put his foot down. Fujiko seemed intent on finding ever more repulsive and degrading displays, and Harper would have been much happier chatting with Abundant while Fujiko got his fill. "That's it," he said, ignoring the mating display on stage and the nearly naked, gender-indeterminate alien crowding their table with three palms out for donations. "Fujiko, I appreciate your informed and, may I say, eager enthusiasm for all this stuff, but we've long since passed out of my range of interests. Can you guide me back to the club so I can hook up with my friends?"

Fujiko's face fell. "Surely that can wait until morning? When it's daylight the curfew will be lifted and you can travel the streets unmolested. Until then, there's still plenty to do in the red zone."

"I'm sure there's just tons to be done here," Harper countered. "But I'm not on that menu, and I'm just plain tuckered out. Let's go."

Fujiko shrugged sadly. "You can go, my friend," he said. "But I'm not finished here."

"Fujiko," Harper said with exasperation. He turned to the alien, who continued to lean in toward them and had begun to massage Harper's shoulder. "Look, not now, okay? *My friend* and I are having a discussion."

"Fine, whatever," the alien said. He, she, or it spoke as if gargling with wet cement, but whatever it was waddled away, searching for another customer in the dark, sparsely populated room.

"Fujiko, you said you'd take me back there."

"And I will, come morning," Fujiko replied. "The patrols don't much care if people come toward the red zone at night. That's why it's here. But they aren't very understanding about people moving about the rest of the city. We didn't get caught the first time, which I personally count as fortunate. I don't know that we'd be as fortunate again."

"My friends are there," Harper complained. "Waiting for me. What happens if I don't show up? They're probably already worried."

"In which case waiting until morning won't make much of a difference."

"It will to me."

Fujiko waved his hands dismissively. "Harper, it's almost morning already. You should feel free to do whatever you want. There's a piece of delicious Dilivian tail—and I do mean tail—waiting for me in the next room, and I'm not leaving here until I've sampled it."

"You're not talking about a breakfast buffet, are you?" Harper asked.

"Not in the sense you mean."

Harper shuddered. Fujiko's appetites were far beyond Harper's comfort level. "Didn't think so." Without thanking Fujiko for the tour of Gala's fleshpots, he left the man to his Dilivian treat and found his way back out to the red zone's main drag.

Fujiko had been right. The sky was already lightening. Either the nights were particularly short on Festival, or the time had flown much faster than Harper had realized at the time. He could see how the latter might be true—even though much of what he had witnessed during the night had been light years away from being his personal cup of Sparky Cola, there had been a disturbingly fascinating aspect to some of it. And Abundant Mercy had been a genuine delight, so the time spent with her had passed quickly.

But now it was almost morning, and his friends were probably frantic. Fujiko's tour of the red zone's most debauched spots had taken them several blocks down its main drag, so even though he wasn't lost here, he had plenty of ground to cover.

It wasn't until he got out of the red zone that he would be lost. On the way over Fujiko had been leading the way, and on the assumption that they'd be returning together as well, Harper hadn't bothered to memorize the route. Now he'd have to wing it as best he could.

He was almost to the border of the red zone—even at this hour, with the sky turning pale as one of the big planet's suns rose, it was much busier than the streets around it—when he heard someone call his name.

Turning, he saw Beka running toward him from somewhere deeper within the red zone. He felt a moment's embarrassment. *Yeah, Beka's a big girl and she's been around the block a few times*, he thought. *But if she saw some of the stuff I did tonight, I don't want to know about it.*

"Hey, Beka," he said, with as much casualness as he could muster. "I was just gonna look for you."

"I've been looking for you for hours," she said. A tall, dark-haired man came up behind her with a devil-may-care grin on his face. "This must be Mr. Harper," he said.

"That's him. You okay, Harper?"

"Yeah, fine. I'm fine. What about you?"

She ignored the question. "Have you seen Trance?"

"I thought she was with you."

"I think she left around the same time you did," Beka said. "But since neither of you bothered to tell me you were going, I don't know for sure. Do you know what kind of danger you were in?"

"I do now," Harper admitted. "But I had no idea when I took off." He glanced around as if to see who night be listening. "This place freakin' *sucks*."

"Nobody here is going to argue with that, Mr. Harper," the man said.

Beka jerked her thumb at him. "That's Tennyson. He's been helping me look for you."

"Not exactly how I hoped to spend my night, but there you go," Tennyson admitted.

"Hey, you're not alone there," Harper said. "This has been the longest short night of my life. And I just realized I'm starving."

"I don't know," Beka put in. "Looks like there might have been plenty around here to keep you entertained."

"Don't even go there," Harper said. "I've seen things tonight that made me want to burn my eyes out of their sockets with a welding torch."

"I don't think there's much Harper can't do with a welding torch," Beka told Tennyson. "Although he might have a hard time getting the second eye, unless he left some healing time between them." Then she turned back to Harper, and all the humor had drained from her face. "We've got to find Trance," she insisted. "We figured you'd be somewhere around this district, but who knows, with Trance?"

"Who knows anything with Trance?" Harper agreed. "Do you have the first idea where to look?"

Tennyson shrugged. "It's a big city."

"Sun's coming up," Beka observed. "She may well have found her way back to wherever that place was we were staying. And if not, she could be on her way there now."

"Or in police custody, or shot, or—"

"That wouldn't happen," Tennyson interrupted.

"What, they wouldn't shoot her?"

"There's no such thing as police custody here. She might possibly be in *military* custody, but it would be much more likely that she'd have been shot."

Harper wasn't exactly uplifted by that news. "So how do we go about this? How can we find her?"

"Well, splitting up's out of the question," Beka answered. "I'm not letting you out of my sight again. I say we work back toward the Hall of Regency. If we don't see her on the way and she's not there when we get there, then we alert Dylan and Tyr and the military and we turn the city upside down until we find her."

"Makes sense to me," Harper agreed. "Man, Dylan is gonna be so pissed."

Trance still couldn't see how her adventure was going to turn out, but she was sure of one thing: the longer she stayed with the men who were holding her, the less likely were her chances of surviving the night.

On the bright side, death was not as big an issue for her as it was for most. She had come back from it before, and no doubt would again. On the other hand, it was not a lot of fun, and it hurt. She would always avoid it if at all possible.

Her break came as the sky was beginning to lighten and the criminals made ready to go into hiding for the day. With her in tow, they had hit four other homes, making off with easily carried and expensive items. In spite of their veiled threat, she had not seen them commit or attempt violence against anyone, if you didn't count grabbing her and yanking her bodily through an open window. If they had tried anything more than that, she would have had to stop them. As it was, going along with them and refusing to be a problem had seemed the wisest course of action. They were hungry and desperate men, she had decided, stealing not out of malicious intent but because they had families and expenses and they had run out of other options.

Or they thought they had. Trance knew, better than most, that there were always other options. Closing down all probabilities except one was so rare it might almost be considered impossible. Either way, the result was the same—they had given up on things like jobs or military service and turned to crime, and they felt that the ills they had suffered at the disembodied hands of society justified the decision.

So when they were ready to split up, they had a difficult decision to make about her. If they had been truly evil, there would have been no argument—they'd have killed her and been done with it. As it was, the one who had been assigned to watch Trance most of the night—whom she had learned was called Karit, though he refused to say if that was a real name, or what his full name was—argued for releasing her.

"She doesn't know who we are," he pointed out. "Or how to find us again. We didn't want her to call a patrol while we were still at it, but we're done now. She can scream all she wants."

"But we've still got the goods on us," another one said. The others had been more careful about not letting her hear their names at all, but this one was the biggest of them, probably even taller than Tyr, though not as muscled. He had thick black hair, uncombed and wild, and a perpetual sneer on his face. "If she alerts a patrol before we get it hidden away we're as good as dead."

"I won't," Trance promised. "Why would I?"

"We don't know what you'd do," the big one said.

"But she wouldn't have any reason to say anything," Karit argued.

"That's right," Trance agreed. "I was in all those places too. I'd be considered just as guilty as you!"

"She's right," Karit said.

One of the other men weighed in. "We've just got to kill her," he said. "It's the only safe thing to do."

"Killing me isn't safe," Trance argued, pretty sure the claims they had made earlier, about murdering people, had been so much hot air. "Not at all. Killing is just about always a bad idea in this kind of situation. It, you know, raises the stakes, makes whatever else you've done that much worse."

"How much worse could it get?" another one asked.

"It could get pretty bad," she opined.

"It will get bad if we don't get out of here," Karit said. "Let's get moving, just forget her. You guys are idiots if you think she's going to be a problem."

The idiot word was all it took to escalate a disagreement into an argument. The men lost control of their tempers and suddenly were in each other's faces, snarling, clenching fists, acting for all the world like a pack of Guvidrian warthogs scrapping over something they had found crippled next to a water hole. Trance thought they would come to blows.

She didn't really care if they did. The good part was that as long as they were focused on each other, no one was watching her. She had fallen into this situation by accident, and now it looked like she could get out the same way.

She didn't try the old sneak-away-and-hope-they-don't-notice thing, though. That almost never worked. Instead, she took advantage of the confusion to take a couple of steps away from the circle and then she launched herself into an all-out sprint, her tail bobbing behind her for balance. They noticed by the time she had gone a few paces, but the head start was enough. Trance was fast, and the men were all too close together, too entangled. By the time they'd extricated themselves from one another, Trance had reached the closest main street. The sun was just spilling its rays through the deep canyons of the city, but there were already people out. Curfew was over, and if the men followed they risked calling attention to themselves. She heard a few half-hearted shouts from the alley, but they died quickly. Trance didn't slow down, even though pedestrians were stopping to stare at her as she raced past them.

She was used to being stared at. There were worse things.

She had just avoided one of them.

ELEVEN

> "When you have nothing to say, say it loudly. When each word
> is vital, whisper."
>
> —ELDOUS TERN, "NOTES FROM A RESTLESS LIFE,"
> CY 7786

Dylan woke early the next morning. Light streamed through his room's big window, and he snapped to attention immediately. Dressing quickly, he went to the door of his room and opened it. The guard outside turned at the sound. "Captain Hunt," she said politely. This was not the same guard who had been there the night before, but a young woman with short copper hair and a serious expression. "Is there something you require?"

"I'd like some breakfast," Dylan said. "And I'd like to eat with my crew."

The guard looked quickly at the floor, then back at Dylan. The look on her face went from businesslike to uncomfortable, almost frightened, and her green eyes wouldn't meet his. "About that," she said. "I'm afraid your crew has stepped out."

"Define 'out,'" Dylan instructed.

"I'm not sure where they are, sir. They went out last night and haven't come back. A patrol is looking for them now."

"All right, define 'crew.'"

"The one called Andromeda is still in her quarters. The Nietzschean is with our patrol. The other three are still missing."

"Bring Andromeda to me," Dylan ordered. "Now. And I want a status report on the search."

"Yes, sir." The guard stepped crisply away from Dylan's door, but only a couple of paces. She spoke in hushed tones with the guard in front of Rommie's door, and returned a few moments later.

"Andromeda will be over momentarily," she said. "The patrol has not yet reported back on the search results. Captain Wylx promises to keep you updated."

"Surely the patrol's in contact with somebody," Dylan suggested. "Find out where they are and what they've learned." If anything had happened to any of his people . . . well, he didn't even know what the end of that sentence would be. But he was pretty sure the authorities on Festival wouldn't want to find out.

He went back into the room and waited for Rommie, who showed up just moments before a breakfast for two was delivered. She had a worried look on her pretty face, which Dylan figured probably came pretty close to mirroring whatever expression he wore. As he looked at the breakfast—unrecognizable items he assumed were food—and sniffed it, he realized he wasn't all that hungry after all. His stomach churned with worry for his friends, and anxiety about the big speech he was supposed to deliver in a very short while.

"I hear there's a problem, Dylan," Rommie said. She took a seat across from him: a mere politeness, given that she had no actual need to rest her legs. She looked crisp and professional in her uniform-cut black dress.

"There's a big problem," Dylan replied. "Trance, Beka, and Harper are missing. Tyr's gone out to look for them."

"How could they be missing?" Rommie asked. "Weren't they under guard—oh."

"Not like they all haven't escaped custody before, at one time or another," Dylan observed. "And I'm sure they're probably fine. But that doesn't keep me from being worried."

"Do you want to go out and look for them?"

"I would, but I have that speech," Dylan reminded her. Not that she would have forgotten. "I really have to get ready for that. I haven't even written it yet."

"Then I guess you're giving it off the cuff," Rommie pointed out. "You're on in thirty minutes."

Dylan glanced at the sky outside. "How can that be? It's only—"

"An hour here is only forty-three Common minutes," Rommie told him.

"So the four hours I managed to sleep—"

"A little over two and a half."

Dylan considered this news for a moment. "On the bright side, I guess, it means they haven't been missing for as long as I thought they had."

"However, it also means you'll have to give your speech earlier than you expected to. Unless there's a way to delay it."

"You were there last night," Dylan said. "You heard what they said: broadcast live, via subspace particle beams, to all the worlds in the Festival system. I don't know a whole lot about their technology but I'd guess that postponing would be difficult at this point, and would reflect badly on the Restored Commonwealth."

"Do you want to go ahead, though, without knowing what's become of Beka, Harper, and Trance?"

"It's not the ideal situation," Dylan acknowledged, "but I don't see that I have much choice."

He picked at the breakfast. Some of it tasted better than it looked, while other parts were every bit as bad as they smelled. After ten minutes they came to fetch him for the speech.

———

Dylan guessed the audience was mostly for show. They were probably hand-picked by His Regency, and ordered to respond enthusiastically to Dylan's every word, so that the broadcast audience would be swayed by his speech. The idea didn't bother him in the least. In his pantheon of pleasures, speechmaking ranked somewhere around being the guest of honor at a Magog dinner party, and not having to worry about his delivery was a bonus.

Even with the audience's thunderous applause and warm welcome, though, Dylan was anxious. About the speech, but mostly about his missing crew members. Postponing the speech would have been his preferred solution, but his guess had been correct—delaying it was virtually impossible, and would reflect so badly on both the Commonwealth and Festival's leadership that he agreed to go on as scheduled. Havasu promised that every effort was being made to locate the missing parties and gave his assurance that they would be found safe and sound. Dylan took scant comfort from the pledge, but he had agreed to go forward, so he did.

Which was how he found himself standing on a balcony looking out at the sea of faces filling a huge public square. Buildings surrounded the square, jutting into the sky like cliffs. The crowd was strangely silent until Minister Bet Na introduced him, at which time they delivered an explosive ovation.

He waited until the noise died down. "Be modest," Rommie had urged him. "Ask for their help. Don't lecture them." He tried to remember those things, as well as all the pointers Cam had pressed upon him last night, which had little to do with modesty, as he waited, and then he took a step toward the edge of the balcony.

"Thank you," he said. Cam had written a few jokes for him to open with, all of which he was planning to disregard. "As the minister told you, I'm Dylan Hunt, a captain in the old High Guard, and I'm here to offer the Festival system membership in a Restored Systems Commonwealth. I think the Commonwealth is a good idea, and I'll tell you why, and then you'll all have an opportunity to vote, on your individual worlds, on whether or not you'd like to sign up.

"First of all, let me tell you a little about the original Commonwealth, and why we're trying to bring it back. The values the Commonwealth aspires to are these: 'Respect for all life forms, self-determination for sentient beings, and the primacy of basic individual rights. We embrace a simple truth: that galactic civilization can only progress when the many peoples of the stars act as one for the sake of all.' Those words are from the Charter of the Systems Commonwealth, and they hold true today. Those are the goals that drive me. I can only hope that they are also appealing to you.

"The truth is, the Commonwealth did not always live up to its ideals. No one is perfect, least of all me. The best I can say about myself—and by extension, the Commonwealth—is that we keep trying. We don't simply accept our failings, our faults. We recognize that there is room for improvement and we strive for that.

"I can't see a universe in which cooperation is not better than conflict. I can't imagine a system in which every one of us working for the betterment of all of us would not be preferable to one in which we all keep to ourselves, distrust one another, ignore or turn away potential alliances. I can't conceive of any way in which refusing to accept that we all have basic, inalienable rights will improve anyone's lot."

Dylan paused for applause. He was beginning to warm to his topic, and he continued with renewed enthusiasm. "I've seen—I've seen a world that drew away from others be taken into the Commonwealth and turned around, bringing to its inhabitants unprecedented prosperity, peace, and hope. Engaging our neighbors just makes so much more sense than shutting them out, on every level. Identifying and embracing our common ground brings us strength and wealth and wisdom that we can never acquire on our own.

"Joining the Commonwealth is a big step, and it is not without its demands. Membership requires that you stand with other Commonwealth worlds for mutual defense against aggressors. It requires that you accept the basic rights and self-determination of others. It requires that you accept the idea that the universe as a whole has a stake in what its individual worlds do."

A commotion off to one side of the balcony distracted Dylan for a moment. He glanced over and saw soldiers bringing in Tyr, Beka, Harper, and Trance. They all looked unharmed—a little tired, maybe, but none the worse for whatever their experiences had been. Greatly relieved, he tossed them a grin and then launched back into his address.

"The benefits of membership are well worth the costs, though. We live in dangerous times. As members of the Commonwealth you will never face those dangers alone. You will have staunch allies and friends to help see you through your hardest times.

"We are all separated from one another by the vastness of space, but we are united by our common sentience, by our dreams of peace and prosperity, and by our hopes for brighter futures. Together we can lift one another from the dark ages we have experienced. Together we can leave those old fears and hatreds in the past and move into a future free of them.

"Thank you for inviting me to speak to you today, and I look forward to welcoming all of you into the Systems Commonwealth."

He stopped and bowed, accepting the roar of applause that greeted his conclusion. *As a political speech, that stunk up the joint,* he thought. *But whether they like it because they like it, or because they were told to like it, the ovation is nice.* He let their approval wash over him like warm waves from a gentle sea. Then Minister Bet Na stepped back toward the front, and Dylan moved aside to let him have the stage again. As soon as he could he hurried to where Rommie waited with the others.

"That was terrific, Boss!" Harper said as Dylan approached them. "You're a natural!"

"Where the hell have you been?" Dylan demanded. He felt like the father of lost children: relieved that they've been found, but angry that they got lost in the first place, each emotion warring with the other so neither won out.

"It's a long story, Dylan," Beka said. "We'll go into it later. When we have a little more privacy."

Privacy? Dylan wondered. A precious commodity on Festival, he suspected. But the fact that they wanted privacy before they would talk to him was a cause for concern. If they had been out in the city, they had probably learned more about it than he had in his protected confines. "Okay," he replied after a moment's consideration. "We'll talk later."

But not much *later.*

Later came within a couple of hours. After a few more speeches by government officials, the *Andromeda* crew was allowed to gather in Dylan's room. Dylan didn't have a lot of faith that the room wasn't bugged somehow, but short of taking the space elevator back up to the *Maru*, there weren't a lot of available alternatives.

"So what's the story?" Dylan asked. The anger he had felt earlier had faded as time passed. "Where were you guys?"

"We kind of got split up, Dylan," Harper answered. He was still wearing the clothes he had worn to the banquet; they all were, Dylan noted. "Don't even ask where I was, because I don't want to relive any of it."

"The point is that we're all okay," Beka said. "We're here. And we found out some stuff about Festival. None of it good."

"None of it?"

"Dylan, inviting these people to join the Commonwealth might be the biggest mistake you've ever made," Trance said.

"And you've made some doozies," Harper added.

"Thanks," Dylan said with a wry grin. "What do you mean? What kinds of things?"

"They're brutal," Trance said. "And militaristic and oppressive and . . . and mean. They have a curfew, and they kill violators—with no questions asked."

"Those things are not necessarily all bad," Tyr pointed out.

"Maybe not to you," Harper answered. "Because you're the kind of guy who's always going to be on the side of the powerful."

Tyr smiled. "Is there a better side to be on?"

"Most people here live in abject poverty," Beka said, ignoring Tyr. "And in absolute terror of their own government. The rich own everything and the poor have to steal or sell themselves just to get by."

Dylan considered what they were telling him. It didn't make sense—a society like the one they were describing wouldn't fit into the Commonwealth, and didn't seem like the kind that would even show an interest. He'd picked up a weird vibe from Havasu and his ministers, but he had thought they were genuinely shopping for what he was selling, to use Cam Prezennetti's analogy.

"I really think they're freakin' evil, Dylan," Harper added. "Like the Magog, only with better public relations."

"He's not exaggerating," Beka put in. "Not by his standards, anyway. I really was surprised by what I saw last night."

"I can tell," Dylan said. "But there are good and bad everywhere, and I think it's important to maintain some degree of optimism—some faith in my fellow man. Anyway, I've already made the offer. At this point I have to leave it out there and see what they say. In the meantime, we'll try to find out whatever we can about the place."

The others agreed. As they started telling Dylan about their experiences—except Harper, who was oddly taciturn, for him— he began to wonder if he had made a big mistake by coming to Festival.

TWELVE

> "Spreading gossip is like painting a house—you can do a great
> job but you still leave your thumbprints all over it."
>
> —SAMUEL T. BOONE

"Your Regency," Dylan said. "I've come to believe that I need to
visit the other planets in the Festival system. Membership in the
Restored Commonwealth is too important a decision to be made
simply on the basis of a single speech broadcast from here. Especially a speech by me," he added in typically self-deprecating
fashion.

Havasu wagged a long, bony finger at him. "Nonsense, Captain
Hunt," he replied. "I can safely speak for all of our worlds. They
leave the difficult decisions up to us." He chuckled and tried
to arrange his face into something sympathetic—only half-
succeeding, to Dylan's eyes. "Well, they leave the decisions to me,
I should say. Sometimes it's like being the father to a lot of less-
than-brilliant children."

His tone was condescending, which did nothing to improve Dylan's assessment of him. Dylan had already decided His Regency

was self-important, obsessed with power, generally untrustworthy, and not very nice. But he was trying not to let his own impressions of the man affect his mission.

Diplomacy, he had heard somewhere, was the art of overlooking the worst in others while bringing out the best. Not for the first time, Dylan reflected on the twist of fate that had made a diplomat out of a soldier. The roles required such different personal qualities that he felt a schizophrenic disconnect when he tried to embrace both at once.

"That may be so," Dylan allowed. "But I'd like to hear it from them, just the same. The Commonwealth prefers to know that each new signatory to the Charter is aware of all the ramifications and requirements of membership."

"Surely you can accept my personal guarantee," Havasu pressed.

They were in his personal office, high at the top of the Hall of Regency. It was an expansive space about forty meters square, surrounded by windows that looked out over the city. Light from Festival's suns streamed through the window and filled the open, airy space. A dozen chairs were arranged in a loose circle around an elegant table, which Havasu sat behind—setting himself off from the others in that small but undeniable fashion. The ministers, who seemed to function as a chorus of support for Havasu while only occasionally offering up a dissenting opinion, sat in the chairs. Dylan could have sat, but there were no other chairs on this side of the room—the rest were far across the bare stone floor, in differentiated seating areas. The space was awkwardly laid out, Dylan thought—too big and spread out to really function as a conference room, much too huge to be a practical private office. So Dylan stood, arms crossed over his chest. A show of defiance, he thought, was required now. He doubted that Havasu had much experience with that. Dylan couldn't afford to let the man pressure him into rolling over.

"I'm afraid I can't," Dylan said. "Much as I would like to. It would certainly be easier on me. Traveling from world to world, even in such a relatively compact system as this, is going to take me some time. But it has to be done. The Commonwealth is too important for me not to make every effort."

"Your dedication is admirable," Havasu said. The smirk he couldn't quite disguise—or didn't really want to disguise—showed what he really thought of it. "If you are committed to this course, Dylan, then you must do whatever you must do. I'll arrange a military escort to make sure your journeys are safe and your ship and crew remain unmolested. Not all the worlds you'll visit are quite as civilized as ours."

This was something Dylan had failed to anticipate. "That won't be necessary," he assured His Regency. "*Andromeda* is a very capable ship."

"I seem to recall that you needed some assistance when you arrived here," Havasu reminded him.

"We were making a special effort not to be confrontational," Dylan said. "We went closer to Caernaevon Drift than they were comfortable with. I've purchased fuel from them in the past—but more than three hundred years ago, and I guess their attitude toward visitors has changed a little."

"I would be much more comfortable if you accepted my offer of protection," Havasu urged. "Just as you didn't know what to expect at that Drift, you won't know what to look forward to from world to world within the Festival system. Without knowing the local customs, you might just walk into some unpleasant surprises."

"There's always that possibility," Dylan acknowledged. "But it's a chance I'm willing to take. It's kind of what we do."

Havasu looked around at his ministers, as if in expectation of new ideas. None were forthcoming. "I suppose we could allow that," he said. "What do you think?"

There were murmurs of assent, which was just what Dylan expected from them. Havasu nodded sagely and turned back to Dylan with a broad, blatantly phony smile.

"There you have it, Dylan," he said. "If you need anything, you have but to let me know and it will be taken care of. Otherwise, enjoy your trip."

"I'm sure I will," Dylan answered. "Thank you for your hospitality, and I look forward to welcoming Festival—and the rest of the Festival system—into the Commonwealth."

Havasu stood, and the other ministers followed suit. Dylan knew that he was being dismissed, which was fine with him. He didn't especially want to spend any more time on this world than he absolutely had to.

But he really wanted to hear about Harper's night in Gala's red zone.

Rommie really had no special need of human-style emotions. They didn't help her function any better. They didn't even help her understand the ship's crew, although for a while she had thought that they might.

But even though there was no practical function for them, she still felt them from time to time. At least, she thought she did. She had nothing to compare them with, so she didn't know if the sensations she got were the same as the crew would feel. Then again, she supposed the same could be said of anyone else. Nobody ever really knew what was in someone else's head or heart, and everyone had to interpret their feelings for themselves.

But she had been around people—Dylan, in particular—long enough so that she seemed to have just picked up emotions, the way someone might a language or a habit. Like it or not, sometimes she caught herself feeling sad, or joyful, or frightened, or worried. And she was a genuine artificial intelligence, not just a bunch of circuitry. She had the capacity to learn and grow. Just now, she realized that she was glad to be back on the *Andromeda Ascendant*, speeding away from Festival toward the closest planet in the system, called Transitory Primus.

Rommie always felt more comfortable—another emotion,

there—on the ship than away from it. Made sense, she supposed. The ship *was* her, and she it. Separation anxiety could be very strong in sentient organics, and they were almost never separated from themselves.

As much as she hated to admit it, she derived a kind of pleasure from the steady, discreet hum of the ship's engines—thank Harper for that—and the sensation of all her systems online and working at close to optimum performance. Reveling in it, immersed in running the ship and examining the feeling, she almost didn't hear Dylan come in (although "in" was, she knew, an artificial concept). But there he was, in her reality, which was rare since usually she had to go—via her avatar—into his.

"Hello, Dylan."

"Hi, Rommie. I just wanted to thank you for everything you did down on Festival. You know, being patient in all those boring meetings, offering wise advice. . . ."

"Dylan, you know I don't get bored. As for advice, I base that on my data banks. When you've stored tens of thousands of years of history, almost every situation has come up before in some form or other."

"I suppose that's true," Dylan said, smiling at her. He pulled up a chair. She hadn't even realized there was one there, but since there was, in fact, no "there" there, that probably didn't matter much. "But don't dismiss your contribution. You know you're the most valuable member of my team."

"Well, thank you, Dylan." Rommie returned his smile. She suspected from time to time that he took her for granted—she was essentially, after all, an assortment of parts doing what they had been engineered to do. So getting thanked, being shown appreciation, was always gratifying. "I'm glad I could help."

He rose from the chair again—it vanished immediately—and came closer to her. "I just wanted to say that," he said again. He looked a little flushed, and seemed tongue-tied. Maybe there was something else he had wanted to say, but couldn't manage to find the words for. "And any data you can turn up on Transitory Primus would be great," he added, as if to fill the awkward gap.

Then he was gone, vanishing as suddenly as the chair had, leaving Rommie alone again.

That was strange, she thought. Strange, but kind of nice. She—back to emotions, she knew, but there it was—couldn't help liking Dylan. She had known him for a very long time, and they had been through a lot together. Quite literally, war and peace, life and death, all those big, important concepts. It would have been completely natural for a man and a woman to be drawn together by such events. Somewhat less natural for a man and a Glorious Heritage class heavy cruiser. But then, Rommie was more than a ship. She was, like it or not, sentient, or she couldn't have been thinking about these issues. She had a personality, of sorts.

She knew that because if she didn't, she wouldn't have felt the pain of knowing what she could never have.

There were a lot of good pilots around, and a few great ones. Beka Valentine was pleased to know—*screw false modesty*—that she was one of the latter, and further, that she had never met one better than herself. She couldn't have been happier to leave that stupid planet behind, and now that she was back at the pilot's console of the *Andromeda Ascendant*, she was able to relax again. A lot of people would have felt just the opposite, she knew. Control of an enormous spacecraft brought with it a lot of responsibility, while her time on Festival's surface could have been considered vacation, more or less. But standing on solid ground put her on edge, while piloting the ship soothed her.

"Was it everything you expected?" Rev Bem asked as he walked onto Command. It was the first Beka had seen of him since they'd returned to the ship. "I prayed for you the entire time you were down there."

"Maybe that helped," Beka said. "It was a little hairy for a while."

"Those people have lost the Way," Rev Bem confirmed. "If they ever knew it in the first place. Living only for the pleasure of the moment, without a thought to their spiritual path . . ." He shuddered. "Horrific."

"It's not quite that way," Beka told him. "Yes, there was what seemed like a pretty desperate effort to have a good time, but I think that's mostly to blunt the pain of living in that society."

"The Way can do that as well," the Magog reminded her. "Better, in fact."

"Beka exaggerates," Tyr put in. He had been hanging out on Command Deck with Beka when Rev Bem showed up in all his frightening, formerly-flesh-eating glory. The Magog still sounded like something that could crush gravel, and looked like an apparition that parents might use to scare their children into acceptable behavior, but she knew he was harmless. His spiritual epiphany had made him into a seeker of peace and knowledge, a gentle monster who would never intentionally hurt anyone.

The same could not be said of Tyr, who continued his thought. "The entire population of the city of Gala—much less the whole of Festival—does not engage in the frivolous pursuits she describes. Many of the inhabitants are serious, practical, disciplined individuals."

"I guess I missed those," she said.

"You had only to open your eyes and look around."

"Maybe my eyes were blinded by the bright lights and lack of sleep."

"We make our choices. . . ." Tyr let his voice trail off.

"Be glad you didn't stay down there any longer than absolutely necessary," Rev Bem put in. "A place like that can become like a spiritual vampire, sucking the innate decency and goodness right out of you."

"Did you observe any of that?" Tyr asked with an arched eyebrow. "You met a man, right?"

"Yes, but there was no—never mind. I never really got a chance to know him, what with looking for Trance and Harper all night."

"You and Mr. Harper looked a bit the worse for wear when our patrol found you," Tyr pointed out. "Too bad you didn't just stick with Trance, who at least was able to find her way back to the Hall of Regency."

"Yeah, because spending the night with criminals would have been so much better than—" Beka stopped, mid-sentence. Tennyson had been a lot of things, but strictly law-abiding probably wasn't one of them. She'd have liked a chance to really get to know him, in every sense of the word. "Okay, I probably did that anyway. But not with criminals actively involved in the commission of crimes."

Rev Bem let out a low moan. "This sounds worse and worse."

"Just don't ask Harper about Abundant Mercy," Beka said with a laugh, remembering the pained look on Harper's face when she'd teased the story out of him. "The one who got away."

"I like the name," Rev Bem admitted. "But I suspect that is all I'd like."

"I can virtually guarantee it," Tyr said.

"If any of you need one-on-one spiritual counseling after your ordeal, I'm available," Rev Bem offered.

"Thanks, Rev," Beka replied. "I think I'll be fine. The only lingering problem I have is that this whole Commonwealth deal makes it kind of tough to make friends, you know? Always flying off to someplace new. Which, admittedly, is what I've always done. But usually I could stick around for a few days, if there was someone interesting who I wanted to know better. Now a brief encounter has to be really, really brief, and sometimes a girl likes to take her time."

"I'll be in my quarters," Rev Bem announced. He practically ran from the deck.

"Guess he doesn't like to hear about stuff like that," Beka opined.

"I imagine not," Tyr agreed. "Unless your point was that you rarely find the time for a prolonged spiritual dialogue with these new friends you speak of."

Beka smiled. "A time or two, I might have put it that way," she admitted. She allowed her thoughts to drift for a moment, remembering certain occasions, but then snapped her attention back to the here and now. "What about you, Tyr? Are you okay with the constant travel?"

"Nietzscheans are nothing if not adaptable," Tyr answered. "But as you know, we are pride-oriented. We prefer to travel with our clans, if at all. Moving from place to place, never having roots . . . that would not be my first choice. It is acceptable for a short while. Certainly not for a lifetime."

Beka glanced at him. The powerful Nietzschean seemed lost in thought, maybe trying to imagine what his life would have been like had he not been the last surviving member of Kodiak Pride. There were times she thought she could relate—she had a brother, Rafe Valentine, out there somewhere, but he was bad news and only showed up when he wanted something. Her mother had been missing for years, and her father was dead. She was not the last of her family, but sometimes she might as well have been. She had known loss, too.

Somehow, she suspected it wasn't quite the same.

Beka couldn't have known it, Tyr Anasazi realized, but she had come very close to pinpointing his immediate concern.

Most Nietzscheans thought nothing of extended periods of space travel—but then, most Nietzscheans had a clan with them when they went. Not Tyr. He was alone in the universe. Those he served with on the *Andromeda* were temporary colleagues, nothing more. He had always thought—well, once he had given up thinking that he would just kill them all and take the ship—that he would stay with them until something better came along.

Now, maybe it had.

He hadn't told anyone about the offer that Tartagus had made him, but it had not left his mind, either. The idea of being part of a regimented military unit held great appeal to him. The soldiers of Festival were trained and disciplined, well equipped, and respected by the populace.

Respected, or feared.

Either was fine with Tyr.

Other Nietzscheans considered Tyr something inferior to them, because his pride was gone. Tyr knew he was not a lesser being. But had he put his own Nietzschean nature in jeopardy by tying himself to a ship, to these mere humans? With the exception of Dylan—who wasn't just human, but a mixed breed, son of a human and a heavy-worlder, and therefore tougher than the rest—his shipmates were all civilians. Tyr worked out, trained, exercised, and saw enough combat to keep his skills and senses sharp. But in this company, would he even know if he started to grow soft?

So an established military had a lot to offer him. He didn't know if Festival was the place he would want to do it. But the things that bothered Beka, Harper, and Trance about it didn't concern him in the least. A big, crowded planet needed a strong military. Without that guiding hand, the place would be sheer chaos.

They would be in the Festival system for a while, he knew. He had time to mull things over. No need to jump into a decision; there were many things to consider. He did feel a certain loyalty to Dylan, and didn't want his own absence to put the captain's life in danger. He had grown to care for the others, as well, although not to such a degree that he couldn't walk away from them, if it seemed like the best course. And there were other military forces around.

But only one that had offered him a place.

He touched his chin. It would certainly bear further consideration.

———

Cam Prezennetti felt an unfamiliar sense of unease as he approached the Hall of Regency. He had been here plenty of times, of course, and now he had hitched his future to the place, and to its most prominent resident. What fueled his anxiety was that he had come, on this occasion, to visit a somewhat less prominent personage, but one who could, if she chose, have an equally powerful impact on his future.

He hadn't been able to get Ashala off his mind since meeting her in the waiting room the night before. He had done a little research—sales and marketing was all about research, after all—and had learned her name and bits and pieces of her background. Poor, as he had suspected. From the distant city of Vidona Narrows, a small burg of only twelve million. Havasu had happened across her on one of his rare excursions outside Gala and brought her back with him. Some wags whispered that all the fine clothes, excellent meals, and privileges of the court couldn't make a lady out of her, and that Havasu was getting tired of trying.

All of which meshed with what Cam had believed from the outset. He knew that he, like Havasu, could be easily bored, but he believed that she was worth making some effort for, in any case. He couldn't take her away from Havasu—not without forfeiting his life—but he could be there when His Regency finally discarded her. Maybe he could even speed up the process.

To be in place, though, he had to be right in her sights. Which meant this visit, nerve-wracking though it might be.

He made his way to the upper floor residences with no problem, since he was a regular visitor. But once there, he needed an excuse to see Ashala. At the door, he presented himself to Nesdran, His Regency's personal aide, and took the man aside. "I'd like to purchase a gift for His Regency," he whispered. "Something to express my deep appreciation for a business opportunity he's afforded me. I was asking Ashala about it last night, when we were waiting together for him, and she had some good ideas, but I was pulled away before she could finish telling me. I wonder if I could get a couple of minutes with her."

Nesdran nodded. "I'm certain that can be arranged, Mr. Prezennetti," he said. "Please wait here and I'll fetch her."

Cam waited, hoping that His Regency wouldn't choose this time to pass through the entryway. He was pretty sure Havasu was already ensconced in his office, however, and had timed his visit accordingly.

A few minutes later, Ashala came in, unaccompanied by Nesdran. "You wished to see me?" she asked. "So badly that you made up a ridiculous story?"

"Not so ridiculous," Cam corrected her. "If you do have gift ideas I'd be delighted to hear them. But you're right, in fact. I did want to see you, and that's really why I'm here. I have a feeling you wanted to see me, too, and that's why you're here. You could just as easily have told Nesdran to throw me out, or worse."

"Maybe I should have."

"Maybe so. But you didn't. And you still haven't. I've got to think that means something."

"It means I'm curious by nature," she said. "Even when it gets me in trouble."

"No trouble here," Cam assured her. "I'm nothing if not discreet."

"Nothing?"

"Okay, nothing may be too strong a word for it. But I am discreet. That's a guarantee."

"Of course you are. It would mean your life if you weren't."

"It could. If you're talking about doing anything beyond having a simple conversation about gifts." He paused, regarded her carefully. She stood with her arms at her sides, weight on her left foot, hip cocked. Open, not hiding anything. She looked directly at him. "Are you?"

"You wouldn't be here if you didn't think so."

"You're a smart lady," Cam said. "Are you also adventurous?"

"Like I said, I'm curious," she told him. "Sometimes it's the same thing."

"Sometimes it is," Cam agreed. "Can you meet me someplace?"

"Name it."

This was even easier than he'd expected, and he had been sure during their brief encounter the night before that she wouldn't put up much of a struggle. He named a place and a time, and she nodded her assent.

"I'll take my leave, then," he said once the assignation was set.

"If I were you, I'd go shopping for a really good gift," she said. "Just in case."

Cam nodded. "Just in case." He made his departure then, anxious to go up to His Regency's office to share an idea he'd had during the night—one that might help to ensure the results His Regency desired, vis-à-vis the whole Commonwealth situation. Stopping off to see Ashala had taken precedence, though; one had to have one's priorities straight, after all.

THIRTEEN

> "When traveling, it's always a good idea to learn the local
> customs. For example, on the eastern border of New Anglia,
> one must be careful not to touch one's own head in public.
> Touching the head is considered unclean, and is an invitation to
> the locals to remove it by any means necessary."
>
> —*DESPERATION DRIFT: A GUIDEBOOK*

Transitory Primus was a very different sort of place from Festival.

Festival, the dominant world—at least according to Angar an Astalat, Transitory Primus's world chief—was vastly overpopulated. All of those people had to eat, and Transitory Primus was predominantly agricultural, with almost all of its produce being consumed by a single customer: Festival.

Angar an Astalat seemed to Dylan to be a pretty representative specimen of this planet's main populace. Where Festival's inhabitants were almost all humans, Transitory Primus's humans were in a distinct minority. The majority were beings more like the world chief—a large, bulbous female with a big round head on a bigger and rounder body. Evolution had given her two arms, but they ended in elaborate multijointed pincers instead of hands. Likewise, she had two eyes, but they were so small and beady as to be hardly noticeable on such a huge head. Transitory Primus was the closest of Festival's planets to the system's larger sun, and its periods of darkness were brief, its light almost blindingly intense. Dylan could have used smaller eyes himself. He was glad they were sitting in the shade.

"I enjoyed your address," the chief said to Dylan with her mouth pulled back into a wide, toothy grin. Her voice was high-pitched, almost squeaky—surprising in someone so large and rotund. They sat inside the open-air Great Hall of the rough wooden compound that served as an Astalat's headquarters, personal dwelling, and center of government. *Andromeda*'s crew was scattered about the room—even Rev Bem had come along this time—but Dylan and an Astalat sat together on a central pillowed banquette. The world chief had an earthy, slightly sweet odor that reminded Dylan of some of the flowering plants on *Andromeda*'s hydroponics deck. "You raised many important points."

"Thank you," Dylan said. "I didn't have a lot of time to prepare, but the Commonwealth is very important to me."

"That much was clear," an Astalat observed. "And you are a fine spokesperson for its ideals. Ideals which we here on Transitory Primus share."

"I'm glad to hear that," Dylan said. "I've done some research, but if you could tell me a little more about how your political system is organized I'd appreciate it. I take it from your title that you are the equivalent to His Regency on Festival?"

The world chief smiled again. "With considerably fewer subjects, but yes, essentially. We have been traditionally split among tribal lines, for the most part. Tribes that occupy vast areas, but areas that are sparsely populated. There were at one time enormous tracts of untouched, undeveloped land all over our world, but with the constant demand from Festival we have been turning more and more of it to agricultural use. As a result of this activity, economic realities have tied us together, with the result that the tribes have become allied. There are still many tribes, but two generations ago it was decided that there needed to be someone at the top, coordinating and overseeing the relationship with Festival, so that the tribes could continue to live and work in harmony with one another while maintaining their own tribal integrity. That position became the world chief, which is an inherited title passed down along matriarchal lines."

She stopped, and Dylan realized the lecture was over. "Thank you," he said. "That helps a great deal."

"I don't make decisions in a vacuum," an Astalat said. "I consult with the heads of the various tribes, and have done so since your speech. We are all in agreement about membership in your Restored Commonwealth. If the offer remains open, we should very much like to join."

"I'm delighted to hear it," Dylan said. "I admit, I was a little concerned that Festival's leadership might try to influence the other planets in the system, and I wanted to get honest answers, in person, from each of the individual worlds."

An Astalat made a motion with her head that might have been a negative indicator. "Festival is our primary client. We are economically bound to it in an inextricable way. But we have our own minds, our own agenda. His Regency can dictate certain financial terms to us but he does not rule over us."

"Very well. Does the same go for the other planets in the Festival system, Chief an Astalat?"

"I cannot presume to speak for them all," she answered. "Only for our own."

"Of course," Dylan acknowledged. "That makes perfect sense. I was only asking for your general impression, not for any kind of certitude."

The world chief considered for a long moment before answering. "I'm sorry," she squeaked. "I cannot say. Our trade and dealings are mostly with Festival, not with the other worlds."

The other members of *Andromeda*'s crew were sitting around in various states of interest or lack thereof. Harper was downright fidgety, running his hands through his hair, tapping his feet, adjusting the way his clothing hung, then back to the hair. Tyr was his typical stoic self; he might have been mentally reciting an old Nietzschean epic poem, if such things existed. Beka looked like she was barely awake. Rev Bem seemed interested in the conversation, and while his appearance had discomfited the world chief at first, she had quickly come to accept that the Magog was not here to eat her or to implant his eggs in her body. Trance, like Tyr, seemed lost in thoughts of her own, maybe charting the paths of probability that this whole effort would pay off. And Rommie—who insisted she didn't get bored—was gazing at Dylan with a strange, almost beatific smile on her face. Dylan returned it with one of his own, and he could have sworn that she sparkled when he did.

"Well," Dylan said. "This was easier than I expected, then. We're still hoping to get all the planets of the Festival system involved, but I'm sure you'll be accepted into the new Systems Commonwealth."

"Festival itself has already been accepted?" an Astalat asked. Dylan didn't know her, or her species, well enough to be certain, but it sounded to him like there was an edge of worry in her tone.

"Not yet," Dylan replied. "No definitive answers will be made until we've visited everyone."

"I see. Our application to the Commonwealth, is, of course, predicated on Festival's entry. If our primary client is not part of it, then we won't be either."

Dylan wished he could read her body language better. He had thought that she was anxious to join, that she agreed with the Commonwealth's goals and precepts. He was a bit taken aback that she would make her world's membership dependent on another's. But she seemed pretty adamant about it. He'd try to raise the issue again, subtly, on some other occasion.

"Since you are here, we would love to show you around a little," an Astalat said. "And show you off too. Our tribe would love to get a glimpse of the famous Dylan Hunt."

Harper audibly snickered at that. "Sometimes just a glimpse is best," he teased. "Because then he can't make you rebuild something you've already spent eighteen hours on."

"Mr. Harper refers to the Phased Array," Dylan explained. "Which is supposed to be a System Search Sensor, but after eighteen hours wasn't searching or sensing anything."

"But it looked great," Harper added.

"That's true," Dylan admitted. "And yes, Chief an Astalat, we'd be very interested in seeing some of the local sights."

An Astalat rose from the banquette they shared. "Very well," she said. "Follow me, please."

Harper kept having to go back for Trance.

The world chief gathered a few more of her local counterparts and took the *Andromeda* crew on a walking tour of Port Angar, named after her great grandmother. But it wasn't really much of a port—the real commercial activity, she explained, took place several kilometers from the town's center. Wasn't much of a town either, for that matter. A few scattered clutches of commercial buildings were joined by unpaved paths. Most residents, an Astalat said, lived out among their fields.

But there were plants everywhere, flowers and towering green reeds and tall trees. They all were infested with animals, birds, and bugs of various sorts, iridescent sharp-winged flitters and six-legged, furry loping creatures as tall as Harper's chest, and many more. Trance kept being enchanted by the sheer volume of living things. Harper tried to keep an eye on her, but every now and then he would realize he hadn't seen her for a while, and would have to backtrack and find her.

He wasn't that interested in an Astalat's running monologue about the place, however, so he didn't mind being the designated Trance-fetcher. Port Angar was almost the polar opposite of Gala. Certainly of Gala's red zone. The pace of town life here was so slow as to be nearly comatose. Maybe it was because the real work was done out in the fields surrounding the town and at the actual port, but it seemed like most of the locals they saw were sitting around doing nothing, except for the really ambitious ones who were eating or drinking.

The main exception, he noticed, were the military patrols moving from place to place: human, and clad in the uniforms of Festival. They were as brisk and efficient in their motion as they were back on their home planet. "The Festival goons run this place?" he asked Tyr.

"I would not necessarily agree with your characterization of them as goons," Tyr said. "But yes, so it would appear."

Harper looked around, hoping to see an equivalent local show of force, but there was none. Only the Festival soldiers. They weren't as numerous as they were in Gala, but then, they didn't have anywhere near the population to keep in check. "That's kinda freaky," he said.

"It is surprising," Tyr admitted. "Perhaps they don't have a military force of their own."

"Perhaps they don't need one," Harper argued. "They're just a bunch of farmers."

"That does not mean that there is no need for defense or law enforcement," Tyr said.

"If they did, it'd seem like maybe a good idea to provide their own," Harper suggested. "This way it looks like they're living under Festival occupation."

"Perhaps they are." Tyr didn't sound as if he saw a problem with that, and probably he didn't.

Harper glanced around and noticed that Trance was missing again. "Be right back," he said. He turned around and hurried back the way they had come. Before they had entered the town itself—though the transition was hard to distinguish, because the town was so thickly planted—an Astalat had led them down an unpaved path lined with tall trees, and beyond the tree line was thicker jungle. He hoped she hadn't wandered out into that. If she had, she could wind up lost for days. The other times she had fallen behind, though, she had stayed close to the path.

And she had again. He found her after backtracking for about five minutes. She had, in fact, stepped beyond the tree line, but had not gone very far into the dense growth. She was sitting cross-legged on the ground in front of a sapling, a pale blue tree with branches that drooped toward the ground as if weighed down by their broad yellow leaves. The double shadow from the system's two suns threw a shifting, splotched pattern on her light purple skin.

"Trance," he said. "You gotta stop disappearing."

"It's so beautiful," she said. "But it's sad. It wants a lot more light than it's getting here."

"Well, unless you're gonna go up and cut a window in the bigger trees, it'll have to make do," Harper pointed out. "Come on, I don't want to lose the others."

Trance wished the sapling a long, happy life and joined Harper. Together, they hurried back up the path, breaking out of the jungle when they entered the town. Once again, Harper saw patrols of soldiers, and Trance stiffened beside him, noticing them too. "Harper!" she whispered. "Look!"

"Seen 'em," he said. "Looks familiar, huh?"

As they watched, unnoticed at the edge of the thick forest, a couple of the soldiers peeled off from their unit and approached one of the native inhabitants of Transitory Primus. Harper had not yet learned how to distinguish the males from the females, although he assumed there was a distinction, so he didn't know which this was. He also wasn't sure what he or she had done. But whatever it was, it had ticked off the soldiers.

One of them poked the big non-humanoid in its round belly with the butt of an energy rifle, and then both soldiers laughed. The first soldier, the one who had been doing the poking, said something—Harper couldn't hear it, but the tone sounded angry—and then slammed the butt home again, harder this time.

The local collapsed against the wooden wall of a nearby building. Harper saw that the rest of the patrol was now standing around watching the altercation with various degrees of amusement showing on their faces. "Come on, Trance. We don't want them to spot us."

"But we should stop them," she said. "Did you see what they did?"

"I saw," Harper confirmed. "But we don't know why, or what it's all about. We can tell Dylan, and he can say something to the world chief, but we shouldn't just put ourselves in the middle of a situation we don't understand."

"I guess," Trance agreed reluctantly. "Let's hurry, though."

Sounds good to me, Harper thought. Like Trance, he would have liked to jump into it and straighten out those soldiers, who looked as if they were being unnecessarily brutal. But he really was concerned about misinterpreting things: what if those soldiers had just caught a wanted killer, and by interfering they would let the killer go free? They were so ignorant of local affairs that they might only make things worse by getting involved.

They moved on, trying to catch up to the rest of their party and hoping they hadn't struck out across the town on one of the other roads. After a few minutes, though, they saw the group. The world chief had taken them out into a grassy square, banked on all sides by two-story wooden buildings with elaborately painted façades and carpeted with deep blue grass, ankle high and decorated with flowerbeds. Every time someone moved in the tall grass, tiny insects burst into the air like motes of dust or sparks from a fire. An Astalat was spreading her hands as if pointing out the glorious sights surrounding the square, and the *Andromeda*'s crew was gathered around her.

They were standing near the center of the square, making ready to move on, when the first explosive rounds tore up the ground around them. Trance let out a little scream, and she and Harper started to run toward their friends.

FOURTEEN

"Learn 'duck' in as many languages as you can—and I don't
mean the name of a water fowl."

—NIETZSCHEAN FOLK WISDOM

Dylan and Tyr were the quickest to respond.

Dylan shoved the world chief to the grass and shielded her with
his own body, unholstering his force lance at the same time. Tyr
drew his huge Gauss pistol.

"Where?" he demanded.

Dylan pointed his force lance toward a row of buildings north-
west of their position. He hadn't seen anyone, but there were dark
windows, where someone might have been hiding. "I think," he
said, "but I'm not sure."

"Good enough for me," Tyr said. He pushed himself to his feet
and started toward the distant building, running in a zigzag pattern
so as to make himself a less predictable target.

Dylan noted that Harper and Trance had caught up to the rest
of them. Beka was flat on the ground, her own force lance aimed
and ready. Rev Bem was hunkered down toward the grass, mutter-

ing prayers that Dylan couldn't make out. Rommie had dropped along with the rest of them, but was getting up on her knees. The world chief and her colleagues were in no hurry to make themselves better targets, and remained flattened in the high grass.

"Stay down, everyone. Tyr will try to draw their fire so we can confirm their location. Chief, do you have any idea what this is about?"

"I don't, Captain Hunt," she said. He wasn't inclined to doubt her word. The attack seemed entirely unexpected on her part.

"No political enemies who might pull something like this, trying to make a statement?"

"Not that I'm aware of," she replied. "There are always some who despise those in power, of course. But there's no way of knowing who this is until we get quite a bit more information."

Phosphorescent tracers streaked the air and more charges blew around Tyr, who threw himself to the ground and rolled, firing his force lance at the same time. This time, everyone could see which building they came from: one of the ones Dylan had identified in the first place.

"Return fire!" Dylan commanded. Everyone with a weapon obeyed. A blistering barrage tore at the building's rough wooden walls, splintering them.

In spite of that, whoever was inside kept shooting. Some aimed at Tyr, who had rolled to his feet and continued his advance. Others fired at the rest of the *Andromeda* crew. Dylan ordered Trance and Rev Bem to escort the world chief and her retinue to safety while the ship's crew held off the attackers, and he noted that when the locals and the offworlders parted ways, the attack continued to center on the crew of his ship.

The realization hit him like a knife in the gut. *They aren't after the world chief. They're shooting at us!*

It made no sense. They hadn't been on the planet long enough to make any enemies. But as Trance and Rev Bem got farther away with an Astalat and the others, and they were no longer targets, he knew that it had to be.

For some reason, whoever was in that building had targeted *Andromeda*'s crew.

And that made him just furious.

"Come on!" he shouted. He took off after Tyr, assuming the others would follow his lead. Which they did. As they ran, they kept up the assault on the building. Tyr had made his way close enough to lob a couple of EMP grenades in through the open windows, which would not only stun anyone inside but would knock out the electrical systems that powered their weapons. Dylan saw the sun-bright bursts of light when they went off, and no more fire came toward them.

"I think they're down!" he called to the others. "But stay sharp. We don't want any nasty surprises."

They closed on the building, weapons at the ready. Their earlier onslaught had shredded the wooden walls. Some of the wood smoldered, and tongues of flame licked in a few spots, ribbons of smoke coiling toward the sky.

"It's quiet," Tyr said when Dylan approached. He had pressed himself up against one of the outer walls; for anyone to shoot him from inside they'd have to fire through the wall or lean out the window, at which time he'd have been able to pick them off easily.

"Let's go in," Dylan suggested. "But carefully."

"My watchword," Tyr agreed.

"You guys wait out here," Dylan said to Beka, Rommie, and Harper. He and Tyr went to the main door, and Tyr leapt across the doorway, so they would enter from different sides.

Weapons raised, they swung around the jamb and into the shadowed interior. They found themselves in a large lobby-type area, open and unoccupied. Various doors opened off the lobby, but only one seemed to lead in the direction from which the weapons fire had come. Tyr cocked his head toward it, and Dylan nodded in agreement.

Once again, they went in from both sides at once, weapons preceding them. Again, no warning or gunfire met their advance.

But this room was not empty. It was some kind of office complex, Dylan realized, full of tables, paperwork, and primitive calculating machines.

Over by the windows, tables had been upended and shoved against the walls. Papers were strewn and scattered everywhere.

Behind those tables, nine people lay dead on the floor.

The acrid stink of the smoke that hung on the air mixed with the bitter tang of spilled blood. The nine wore dark, nondescript clothes, ideal for an attack from ambush. Dylan and Tyr made a quick circuit of the complex and then holstered their weapons, returning to the mass of corpses behind the cover of the tables. Both men realized that something was wrong at the same moment, but Tyr gave voice to it first.

"EMP grenades would not have killed them," he said.

"But they would stun them," Dylan added. "And we didn't fire after they went off. So either they were dead before you threw the grenades, or . . ."

Tyr turned over one of the bodies, which had been lying on its stomach. It was human, as they all were, and female.

The woman's throat had been slit wide open. A sharp knife clattered to the floor as Tyr rolled her. Old-fashioned steel, with a wooden handle. Sticky dark blood pooled on the floor beneath her corpse.

"Or some of them killed themselves," Tyr finished. "With weapons that the electromagnetic pulse would not have affected."

Dylan nodded, speechless. He and Tyr examined the rest of the bodies. Most had obviously been killed by weapons fire from outside, but three of them had died at their own hands.

"They were the last three to go," he speculated. "They would rather die than be captured."

"The hallmark of a fanatic," Tyr said.

"They definitely didn't want to be interrogated," Dylan said. "Is that because they were afraid of the authorities on Transitory Primus? Or were they afraid of us?"

"They were shooting at us," Tyr reminded him.

"Good point."

"Thank you."

Dylan glanced out the window toward the square, where he could see Trance and Harper leading the world chief and her colleagues back toward Beka and the others.

"I would keep well away from that window," Tyr suggested. "Unless you have informed the others that we have neutralized the threat."

Dylan took Tyr's advice and moved away from the open window, just in case. "You suppose anyone's called a cop?"

Captain Zanitz, the officer in charge of the investigation, was exactly the kind of person who most annoyed Dylan: officious, self-aggrandizing, critical of others, and with a spoonful of smarminess thrown in for good measure. His swagger seemed forced, as if it had come with his uniform instead of being an organic part of his personality. While his underlings scanned the bodies, making instant identifications based on the DNA readings they took, he stood with his legs thrown wide and his arms across his chest, head tilted back so he could look down his nose at Dylan and Tyr, despite the fact that both were taller than he was.

The captain and his people were all human, wearing the uniform of Festival's military. There was one local accompanying them, Pestin ab Petingule, of the Transitory Primus Tribal Defense and Compassionate Justice Administration. The "ab" of his name was the only way Dylan knew his gender, and his job seemed to consist of staying out of the way while Zanitz's team worked.

"We'll know who they all are in a matter of minutes," Zanitz promised. "An hour after that we'll have rounded up any known associates, determined if there was a political motivation to their attack, and—"

"What other motive might there be?" Tyr interrupted. "Do you believe they were simply trying to shoot us from a distance of fifty meters so that they could pick our pockets?"

"Well," Zanitz said, momentarily flummoxed. "We . . . we don't know, do we, until we investigate? We don't know if there is any connection between you and them, and we don't—"

"Here's a freakin' clue, Captain," Harper said. "We've never been here before, and since we landed we've been hanging with the world chief, who, unless I'm missing something, is the chief of the whole world. If you can identify these bozos as fast as you say, it's because you already have them in your DNA database, which must mean they're from around here. Put two and two together and you usually come up with a number, not a rectangle or a member of the cheese family."

Dylan smiled at Harper's outburst. "Mr. Harper's language is . . . colorful, but he makes a good point. I can tell you right now I've never seen these people before, and I'm sure my crew hasn't either. With the exception of Festival's military presence, what is the size of the human population on Transitory Primus? Something like one hundredth of one percent? It doesn't seem like it'll be that difficult to find out what they were after."

"Trust me, Captain Hunt," Zanitz said. "We will get to the bottom of this."

"We'd like to offer our assistance," Dylan said. "We can—"

Zanitz cut him off. "That won't be necessary. Our investigatory methods are unsurpassed, and—"

"I'm sure they are," Dylan pressed, struggling against an overpowering impulse to simply deck the guy. "But they were shooting at us, which makes it kind of personal, you know? I'd hate to think there might be others out there waiting to ambush us."

"The only way I can guarantee your safety is to offer a military escort," Zanitz said. "I hope you know the offer is extended indefinitely, as long as you are within the Festival system. But I'm afraid I will have to insist that you and your crew refrain from interfering with our criminal investigation."

Dylan turned to ab Petingule, who made a motion that Dylan took to be the equivalent of a shrug. "I can't overrule Captain Zanitz during an ongoing investigation."

"It's hardly ongoing," Beka pointed out. "So far all he's done is nudge some corpses around with his shiny boots."

Realizing the futility of trying to argue with a low-level functionary, Dylan stalked over to where an Astalat was waiting nearby. "Chief," he said. "Those shots were meant for us, not for you. But this . . . this Festival martinet doesn't want to let us be involved in the investigation, except possibly as suspects."

"Captain Hunt, you must understand our position," an Astalat implored.

"What position is that?" *Supine?* he thought but didn't add.

"Transitory Primus has several hundred million hectares dedicated to the cultivation of food crops," an Astalat said. "All of it grown for a single client, a single destination."

"Festival."

"That is correct. If we lost Festival's business, we would be well fed. But that is all we would have. Our economy would collapse. We'd revert to our old tribal ways."

"You say that like it's a bad thing. As long as you can feed yourselves, you're a lot better off than some."

"But how long until the starving masses on Festival came to take by force what they had been paying us for? How would we stand up against that?"

Dylan had no ready answer. Membership in the Systems Commonwealth would help, he knew, because Commonwealth member worlds were sworn to help defend one another, and they'd provide new, competitive markets for the planet's crops. But for Transitory Primus to join the New Commonwealth, the world's leadership would have to be in agreement, and from what an Astalat had indicated, her position as world chief might be a tenuous one without Festival's assistance.

And if the world government did collapse because of Dylan's interference, the tribal leaders on the planet might not look too kindly on the Commonwealth.

He knew that all this speculation was far-fetched. In spite of what an Astalat claimed, it was unlikely that Festival would consign itself to starvation—or turn to a new, more distant food supplier— just because one of its military officers had been overruled. Taking the food by force seemed by far the likeliest option. Anyway, what an Astalat believed was what counted, and she didn't seem willing to risk Festival's displeasure.

"Fine," he said after contemplating the situation. "We'll continue our tour of the Festival system. If we can answer any questions with regard to the investigation, you'll know where to find us."

"I hope you don't think . . ." An Astalat let her statement trail off. Dylan wasn't sure what she didn't want him to think. But he was pretty sure that he thought it anyway.

FIFTEEN

> " 'Great' is a word that is appropriately applied to very few
> individuals. Otherwise it would have a different meaning, a
> synonym for 'average' or 'common,' perhaps. Sani Nax Rifati is
> one of the few people I can think of to whom I would apply it
> without hesitation."
>
> —CADET DYLAN HUNT, HIGH GUARD ACADEMY,
> TARN-VEDRA BRANCH

When Dylan came to Rommie en route to Cenatex, the third
planet in the Festival system, she didn't even question it. This time,
he wasn't quite as tongue-tied as he had been before, nor did he cut
his visit short after only a few minutes. Instead, he stayed for more
than an hour, and their conversation was deep and wide-ranging.

And when it was over, instead of awkwardly squeezing her
shoulder, Dylan gave her a long, crushing hug. It all happened on
the purely virtual level, but the sensations were thrillingly physical.
She knew that it couldn't develop to anything further—he was
flesh and blood and she was not, and there was no way to bridge
that gulf—but that didn't mean that she couldn't enjoy every moment of whatever this was.

And she intended to.

———————

"Andromeda," Beka said. "I need a status report on—"

The sentence wasn't even out of her mouth when Rommie's face appeared on a viewscreen. The look she wore wiped the thought right out of Beka's mind. Rommie wore a dreamy smile that reminded Beka of girls she had known in her much younger days—maybe even herself, from time to time.

"Yes, Beka," the on-screen image prompted.

"Rommie," Beka said, unable to contain herself. "You have a crush on someone!"

"No, I don't," Andromeda's holographic avatar answered from behind Beka. The pilot turned around to see this version, who was trying to organize her face into its implacably businesslike expression. But she couldn't do it. There was a twinkle in her eyes, and her lips kept curling up, dimpling her cheeks.

"You do," Beka insisted. "You're crushing like crazy. Who is it, someone on Transitory Primus? God, I hope not, that would mean you had worse taste than I thought. Maybe some nice big muscular battleship from the Festival fleet?"

"Beka, it's not . . ."

"I know that look, Rommie. I *know* that. It's okay, you can tell me. You know I can keep secrets."

"Like you kept the one Harper told you? About that incident on Hella Drift?"

"Oh, that?" Beka asked, a little embarrassed that Rommie remembered. But Rommie remembered everything. No memory holes there. "He was just a kid. And the woman was—she was very understanding. Anyway, he really wanted everyone to know about it or he never would have told me."

"I seem to recall him being quite upset about it," the Andromeda on the viewscreen said. Her face vanished and was replaced by an image of Harper, red-faced and screaming.

"I can't believe you told Trance!" he shouted. Beka remembered all too well the dressing-down he had given her at the time. "And of course she told Tyr, and somehow it got to Dylan, and . . . I guess that's the last time I can trust you!"

"That doesn't support your theory very well," the holographic Rommie said as Harper disappeared and the screen went blank.

"Okay," Beka admitted. "Maybe I did blow it that time. But it was just such a good story, that . . . okay, you win, I should have kept my big mouth shut. Is that what you're looking for?"

Beka's momentary discomfiture had given Rommie the time she needed to compose herself. When Beka took another look at her, the holograph was back to her normal poker-faced self. Beka wondered briefly if she had misread Rommie's expression in the first place. But no, she couldn't have. On anyone else, maybe. But on Rommie it had been so out of place, so unexpected, that it just had to be real. Beka would never have imagined it because she never would have expected such a look on Rommie.

"Perhaps you should have," Rommie suggested. "Was there something you wanted?"

"There was," Beka said. "But I'll be damned if I can remember what it was. Give me a minute, it'll come to—"

"Beka, I'm receiving an emergency summons," Rommie interrupted. Now her face was on the screen again, speaking in concert with her holographic self.

"Put it through," Beka ordered.

After a moment's hesitation, Rommie said, "They're asking for Dylan specifically."

"Then put it through to Dylan. Where is he?"

"I'm right here," Dylan answered, striding onto Command Deck. "Put what through to me?"

As Rommie turned to answer him, Beka thought she saw a slight pinkening of her cheeks. That was impossible, though. A blush was an involuntary physiological response, the result of capillaries close to the skin dilating, allowing more blood to rush in. Rommie was very realistic on the outside, but she didn't have capillaries or blood:

"A distress call," Rommie answered. "From Breckenridg
Drift."

"Put it on screen," Dylan ordered.

Rommie's image disappeared from the screens and a statick
broken transmission replaced it. Beka could barely make out th
image of a human-looking female. She seemed to be transmittin
from a dark room inside a tunnel, with occasional flashes of lig
illuminating her face but not much else.

"This is Captain Hunt of the Systems Commonwealth," Dyla
said. "What is your location and situation?"

"Captain Hunt," the woman said. "I am hailing you from th
diplomatic courier vessel *Argent*, near Breckenridge Drift."

Dylan glanced at Rommie and mouthed, "Get me data. Now.
Then he turned back to the woman, who hadn't even noticed.

"We are under attack," she went on. "I believe that the attacke
are pirates, based on the Drift."

"Are there injuries?" he asked.

"Many. And many fatalities. Our defensive capabilities hav
been almost totally expended, and they have succeeded in crip
pling our ship, so we cannot run or hide."

"It sounds like you're in need of immediate assistance," Dyla
speculated. "And Breckenridge Drift is . . ." Rommie put a cha
on screen, and Beka glanced at it at the same time Dylan did. "Ba
sically at the far end of the Festival system from where we are
There must be someone closer who could lend you a hand."

The transmission shook violently, and the picture went blac
for a moment. When it came back online there seemed to b
clouds of smoke around the caller, and her face—worried to begi
with—looked close to genuine panic.

"Looks like three Slip jumps," Beka whispered. "At full spee
we could be there in a couple of hours, best case. Probably a litt
more."

"Captain Hunt, there really are other things with which
should be occupying myself," the woman said. "Please do not re

veal our location to anyone else. It is imperative that you comply with this request. But if you can assist us, it would be greatly appreciated. My name is Limm'ta Nax Terani. I believe you know of my great great grandfather, Sani Nax Rifati. If using his name will help persuade you to aid us, I am not above—"

The screen went black again, and this time the image did not restore itself. "Transmission is ended," Andromeda reported.

"We should call an alert for other ships in that vicinity," Beka said. "Asking us not to is just crazy—or some kind of a trap."

"Set a course," Dylan instructed, overriding her.

"But, Dylan—"

"Set a course for Breckenridge Drift. Rommie, find out anything you can about the *Argent* and Limm'ta Nax Terani. I want the data in my office on the double."

He left Command Deck as abruptly as he had come in. Rommie watched him go, then phased out herself. Beka shook her head, wondering just what exactly had transpired here.

She didn't have time to worry about it, though. She had a new course to calculate.

Sani Nax Rifati. Former High Guard Supreme Commander, and the man Dylan looked up to as a personal hero and role model, above anyone he had ever met. Without him there never would have been a Systems Commonwealth in the first place. Sani Nax Rifati was the champion of Tarn-Vedra, so most kids growing up there knew the stories about him and admired him. Dylan had taken that admiration to an extreme, studying his exploits, visiting places he had walked, finally joining the High Guard himself once he came of age.

Before Rifati, the Vedran Empire had reached far and ruled hundreds of worlds. But civil wars shook its foundations, and rage directed at the Empire from subject races threatened the intergalactic stability that had resulted. Sani Nax Rifati, a remarkably forward-looking soldier, led a coup that resulted in a reform of the government. The Vedran Empire became the Systems Commonwealth, with the empress as its titular head of state. Under Rifati's plan, the Commonwealth expanded faster, and with far less blood spilled, than under the old empire. Finally, more than a million worlds had joined, and they coexisted in relative peace and prosperity.

All it had taken was one man with a good idea and the fortitude to fight for it despite long odds.

Joining the High Guard had only been Dylan's first attempt at following in his hero's footsteps. In his moments of quiet introspection—which terrified him as often as they brought him pleasure or satisfaction—he knew that he was now embarked on his second attempt. Only this one was a much bigger challenge. If it paid off, it would be well worth it. But it would take everything Dylan had to offer, and then some, to rebuild the dream that Rifati and Dylan shared.

Was it possible that a descendant of Rifati's was still alive? He hadn't heard of any. But then, Tarn-Vedra itself had been lost since the Fall. That didn't mean it no longer existed, or that there weren't other Tarn-Vedrans out there.

He didn't know if this Limm'ta Nax Terani was for real or not. But even if he had been inclined to pass her distress call off to a different ship—which he was not—he had to check this out. Beka was right, of course. The request not to alert any closer ships seemed rather suspect, so they had every reason to believe they were sailing right into a trap of some kind. And the fact that they had so recently left the scene of an attack on themselves didn't diminish his concerns. Someone had it in for *Andromeda*'s crew, for an unexplained reason.

Since that was the case, though, and since they had been invited into what might turn out to be the maws of the beast, Dylan figured they might as well go in with eyes wide open. He tried to keep a grip on his innate desire to trust others, to assume that the woman was telling the truth, but also to keep one hand on his weapon at all times. They might be headed for trouble, but what better way to find out what was really going on around here?

Almost as if Dylan's thoughts had been read, Rommie's face appeared on a viewscreen. "Dylan," she said. There was an odd smile on her face. He smiled back.

"Yes, Rommie?"

"There's an incoming transmission from His Regency."

"Put it through."

"Okay. Good-bye, Dylan."

That was just as unusual as her smile, but he didn't give it any further thought. Havasu's visage appeared on the screen, looking solemn and pale.

"Dylan, I've been told that there was an attempt on your life today, on Transitory Primus."

"It looks that way," Dylan acknowledged.

"That's absolutely unacceptable. Absolutely. You are an honored guest of mine, and of Festival. No effort will be spared to get to the bottom of this at once."

"We offered to help, at the scene, but we were turned down flat."

"Of course," Havasu said. "You've been the victim of a horrible crime. You should not have worried yourself about trying to deal with it. Our security forces are unparalleled."

"Thank you, Your Regency. Nonetheless, I don't mind getting my hands a little dirty when someone's taking shots at my crew."

"Yet one more reason why you are such an esteemed individual, my dear Captain Hunt. I'm afraid I must insist, in light of this turn of events, that you accept my offer of a military escort for the duration of your stay in our system."

Dylan had to think about that for almost an entire millisecond. The *Argent* asking that no other ships be alerted to their peril, and then Havasu demanding that *Andromeda* be accompanied on its rescue mission. It all added up to something. To borrow Harper's bizarre metaphor, it may not have added up to four, but maybe to a rectangle. Or possibly something in the cheese family.

"I appreciate the offer, but once again I have to decline," Dylan said forcefully. "I need to talk to representatives of these other planetary governments without any Festival presence whatsoever. *Andromeda* is absolutely capable of defending itself against any threat that might arise."

"Although," Havasu pointed out, "today's attack came when you were away from your ship. If you persist in visiting each planet individually, you will be away from the ship quite frequently."

And if you persist in offering me protection I don't want and won't accept, I'll have to smack you one, Regent or no, Dylan thought. As usual these days, he chose to word his objection in a more diplomatic fashion.

"If I genuinely believe that we're in any danger, I'll let you know, Your Regency. Until then, I would very much appreciate your cooperation in keeping your forces away from us."

Havasu blew out a heavy sigh. "As you wish, Dylan," he said grudgingly. "Your safety cannot be assured if you will not accept my protection, and I would dearly hate for anything unfortunate to happen to you or your crew. But I humbly accede to your request."

"Thank you, Your Regency," Dylan said. He had been worried that Havasu would do more than insist; that he might send a fleet, or at least a couple of escort ships, along in spite of Dylan's desires. His willingness to accommodate didn't do much to put Dylan's mind at rest about this whole Breckenridge Drift side trip, but then he wouldn't have a whole lot of time to think about it. As soon as he signed off, Beka took them into Slipstream for the second of the three jumps. They'd be at the *Argent* before long, and then maybe they'd get some answers.

SIXTEEN

> "An open-minded Perseid can even learn to trust a Nightsider.
> But only one Nightsider. And only one time."
>
> —PTHAF TTWAN, CY 7995

The *Argent* held no answers for them.

By the time they arrived, it was a holed wreck of a ship, floating in space, as dead as the goldfish Dylan had tried to keep in his quarters as a young High Guard officer. After the fish's first Slipstream experience, Dylan had found it belly up in its bowl. The *Argent* drifted upright, but otherwise the visual impression was very similar.

She was a small ship, light and agile, and not suited to a sustained battle by herself. Dylan didn't recognize the design and asked Rommie to identify it.

"I believe it's Vedran, Dylan," Rommie answered.

"It can't be. If it was High Guard, I'd know it."

"I didn't say High Guard, Dylan." Rommie's avatar appeared on Command Deck next to him. "I said Vedran. There is a difference."

"Old Vedran? From before the Systems Commonwealth? That's impossible."

"No," Rommie said. "New Vedran. From after the fall of the Commonwealth. Look." She displayed an image of the *Argent* on one of her screens, and then superimposed a High Guard diplomatic courier over it. Dylan saw what she meant: its lines were similar, but the *Argent* was an improved, modernized version.

"That's . . . that's amazing," Dylan said, almost speechless. If this ship, and Limm'ta Nax Terani, were clues to the location of Tarn-Vedra, he would . . .

. . . Well, he didn't know what. But he would.

"I'm going to board her," he announced.

"I recommend against it," Tyr said. "Amend that. I strongly recommend against it."

"I've been scanning her, Boss," Harper added. "There's no one alive on that ship."

"From the looks of her, I didn't think so," Dylan acknowledged. "But I'm going to take a look anyway."

"You have never been willing to accept good advice," Tyr said. "Why should you start now?"

"Excellent question," Dylan replied. "I guess there is no reason. Why break a habit that hasn't killed me yet?"

Tyr shrugged. "A brilliant philosophy."

The cruiser was too big to bring onto *Andromeda*, so he decided he would take the *Eureka Maru* down to her. "Anyone want to come along?" he asked.

"Want to?" Tyr echoed. "You might as well ask if anyone would like to commit suicide today."

Dylan waved a hand toward the wrecked ship, floating alone in space. "Do you *see* any pirates?"

"Do you really believe there were pirates?" Tyr shot back.

"Something put those holes in her," Dylan pointed out. "She didn't shoot herself up like that."

"Point taken," Tyr relented. "Very well. I will accompany you."

"Me too," Beka volunteered.

"You should stay here," Dylan replied. "If those pirates come back, we'll need you piloting *Andromeda*."

Her face fell, but she nodded. "Okay," she said. "But you two be careful."

"I really don't think there's anything left on the *Argent* that can hurt us," Dylan speculated.

"Who's talking about the *Argent*? You're going to be flying the *Maru*. I don't want anything to happen to my ship!"

The *Argent* was such a mess that the environmental and AG systems were offline. Tyr and Dylan wore EVA suits and gravity boots. They clomped and lurched around on the ship's decks like drunken dinosaurs, and Tyr was deeply appreciative that there were, in fact, no pirates lurking around on board.

There were also, as Harper had claimed, no other living beings. There were bodies and charred decks and bulkheads, twisted steel, and melted plastics. And there was evidence of looting: storage containers on the cargo bay had been broken into, as had supply lockers in the medical wing. It looked to Tyr like a quick job: pummel the ship with heavy weapons fire for a while, then board her, eliminate any remaining defenders with small arms fire, and grab any valuables around. The pirates—he had to admit that he was now convinced of the reality of the pirates—had probably not spent more than a half hour on the ship.

After a quick look around, he and Dylan retreated to the *Maru*, and returned to *Andromeda*.

"The pirates think they're sneaky," Dylan said, back on Command Deck. "But we already know they came from Breckenridge Drift."

"Which is just what they deserve," Harper suggested. "I've heard stories about that place, none of 'em good. They can have it, if you ask me."

"Which no one did," Dylan pointed out. "Anyway, we're going."

Tyr knew he had heard correctly. He nearly always did. He jus
didn't like what he had heard, and he had no compunction abou
letting Dylan know it. "You are joking, correct?"

"I am joking, incorrect," Dylan said. "Limm'ta Nax Terani wa
not among the bodies we found on the *Argent*. Therefore, the pi
rates have her. Therefore, we're going to get her back."

"'Back' implies that we had her once," Tyr countered. "An
have you considered the possibility that she was vaporized?"

"I haven't," Dylan answered. "And I'm not going to. She's or
that Drift, I'm convinced. We can ask nicely, and see if they giv
her up. But if they don't, then we'll make them wish they had."

"I love it when you talk all tough and everything," Beka put i
from the pilot's console. "But what if they just decide it's easier t
kill her?"

"Then they'll wish they hadn't," Dylan replied. "Works eithe
way."

"Except one way she ends up dead," Harper observed. "Mayb
both ways. Someone check my math."

"They won't kill her," Trance said. She sat on the upper sectio
of Command, her tail wrapped around herself, and she was caress
ing its tip with a gentle touch.

"Are you sure of that?" Tyr asked her.

"Sure enough," she said. "They wouldn't have taken her if sh
didn't have something they want—information, most likely, sinc
if it was something physical they could have just taken it when the
took the ship. Unless she has given it up, they'll keep her alive."

Logical, Tyr had to accept. But it was Trance Gemini talking
Logic was only one consideration for her. Probabilities were th
primary consideration. He didn't understand her, didn't know how
her processes worked, but he had learned to trust her hunches. I
she thought the woman was alive, then she probably was.

"All right, then," he said. "Shall we pay a visit to the pirates?"

———

The spokesperson for the pirates called himself Antonio Salazar Fitzpatrick Spaulding IV. "Fitz for short," he said with an unfriendly snarl. "And short is good, because I don't think you'll be wantin' to talk to me for long."

Fitz was human, or at least appeared so. His hair was long and snarled, dark brown with streaks of black and blue in it. His eyes were an almost flat black. *Shark's eyes*, Dylan thought. *Dead eyes.* On his forehead, cutting down like scimitar blades toward the outer edges of his eyes and almost meeting in the middle, was a series of elaborate red tattoos. He was bundled in heavy, layered clothing, wrapped high around his neck.

"Believe me, I have no interest in chatting," Dylan replied. "But you have someone I want."

"Let's leave your personal life out of this," the pirate said with an unpleasant grin.

"Yeah, let's," Dylan agreed. "And just to make things explicitly clear, let me put this in formal terms. I hereby demand, on behalf of the Systems Commonwealth, that you immediately surrender your captive Limm'ta Nax Terani to me."

Fitz elevated his eyebrows and gave Dylan a pained expression. "You demand? You demand? And just what do you back that demand up with, soldier?"

"Have you seen my ship?"

"I've seen it. Very impressive. So let me get this straight. You're willing to pound the entire drift just to get one puny captive you think I have? Lots of innocent people here. But then maybe taking the moral high ground doesn't enter into your calculations."

Dylan allowed himself a small smile. "Funny, getting a lesson on moral high ground from an admitted pirate."

"Did I admit to being a pirate? When was that?"

"Must have been about the same time I assured you that I couldn't locate your precise ship and would have to blow up the whole Drift. Just how backward is your technology, if you think that's the case?"

"Let's not talk about my technology," Fitz responded. "Let's tal about a price."

"Ransom?" Dylan asked. "That's your idea of morality?"

"It's tradition," Fitz said. "Not exactly the same thing, I admi but take what you can get. Anyway, it's where this conversation going, or else it's over."

"Then it's over," Dylan said. "The only payment you get is i the form of missiles. And not the kind you can reuse."

"Are you sure you want to risk her life?"

"So you admit you have her?"

"I said no such thing. I was simply asking if you've considere that aspect."

"I've considered," Dylan promised him. "That's all the tal we're having, unless you're ready to hand her over."

"Bite me," Fitz said.

Dylan broke the connection. "Tyr," he said. "Make him regre having said that."

"Happily," Tyr said from his post at the weapons console. "B the woman . . ."

"Don't destroy his ship," Dylan answered. "Just soften it u some."

Tyr was never one for big displays of emotion, so the grin o his face as he complied was a surprising sight. His dark eyes flashe with something that looked like glee. "Softening," he said.

Rommie's face sparked into life on a viewscreen. "Dylan," sh said. "We're being fired upon."

"They're shooting at us?"

"So it would seem."

"Deploy defensive measures," Dylan commanded. "PDLs, drone Tyr, are we shooting at them yet?"

When he answered, there was an unusual tightness to Tyr's voic "I am trying to," he said. "But the ship is not being very responsive.

"Rommie?"

Her avatar walked up to Dylan. "I don't know what's wrong, Dylan."

"Run diagnostics," he said sharply.

"I have been. All my systems seem fine."

"Missiles away," Tyr reported. Dylan noted the hard look he reserved for Rommie.

"Brace for impact," she warned. "We've blocked most of theirs but a couple are getting through."

"That's what I love to hear," Dylan said sarcastically. "Because we haven't been knocked around enough the last few days."

Before Rommie could even answer, the impacts came, subtle vibrations shaking the deck.

"That isn't so bad," Beka said.

"But let's keep it from getting worse," Dylan suggested. "Tyr, continue hammering them."

"As long as the ship cooperates."

"I'm not finding anything wrong, Dylan," Rommie insisted. She wrinkled her brow in a very human fashion, and kept her eyes locked on Dylan's. He was reminded of a child who's been caught in the act of something naughty but doesn't want to admit it.

"Keep checking."

"Another volley off," Tyr announced.

Dylan watched on his tactical screen. The pirate ship had hunkered down close to the Drift, in an area where various junk—wrecked ships, satellites of various sorts, and a couple of wedges of planetary matter—floated about in a kind of orbital dumping ground. The debris made it a little hard to get a bead on the ship, but conversely, Dylan wasn't too worried about hitting any of it. He hadn't wanted to admit it to Fitz, but he was concerned about the possibility of Limm'ta being hurt in an extended battle. And he knew the possibility remained that the pirates might just decide to kill her out of spite if the fight didn't go their way.

A quick resolution to the situation would help in either scenario.

And, of course, a fully functioning ship would help bring abou
that quick resolution. Tyr was working the offensive weapons–
Dylan could see the look of intense concentration on his hand
some face. And the ship's multiple defensive systems were blockin
most of what the pirates fired their way. Occasional shudder
rocked the deck as missiles and plasma charges slipped through.

"Hold her steady, Beka," he said. Redundant, he knew. On
glance at her and it was obvious she was doing just that, hair in he
eyes, worrying at her lower lip. Harper was in Engineering an
Trance in Hydroponics, and who knew where Rev Bem was
Somewhere praying for everybody's eternal spirits, most likely, o
else back on his memoirs. But those who were on the bridge wer
doing their jobs, slugging away at the pirates.

After another few minutes of the same, Tyr glanced over at Dy
lan with a grin on his face. "That should do some damage," he an
nounced. Dylan checked the viewscreen and saw missiles streakin
toward the pirate ship, then the flash of their impact.

"Hail the ship," he instructed Andromeda. "Let's see if they'r
ready to talk about surrender."

"Hailing," Rommie said.

Dylan waited a moment, and then she gave him a frow
"They're not answering."

"Let's move in," he said. "Fast. Let's catch them off guard.
want Limm'ta alive if at all possible."

"She's alive, Dylan." It was Trance, bounding onto Comman
Deck.

"You're sure?" Stupid question. Trance didn't make definitiv
statements unless she was sure of things.

"Positive," she confirmed.

"Okay, then," Dylan said. "Mr. Anasazi, Ms. Valentine, we'r
boarding a pirate ship. Look out for parrots and planks."

SEVENTEEN

"Don't forget your mittens!"
—NOTE TACKED TO THE INSIDE OF A DOOR OF A
    DORMITORY AT THE KELSO SHIPWORKS,
    BRECKENRIDGE DRIFT

During the time it took *Andromeda* to reach the pirate ship, Dylan summoned Harper from Engineering. He would join them on the other ship, while Trance and Rev Bem stayed behind.

But the ship wasn't as crippled as the wreck of the *Argent* it had left behind. Instead of sitting around waiting for them, it headed for Breckenridge Drift and put down on the surface. Worried that the remaining pirates would take Limm'ta and disperse themselves among the drift's populace, Dylan, Beka, Tyr, and Harper took the *Maru*, and landed just a few minutes behind the damaged pirate vessel.

Breckenridge Drift was bitingly cold, and so distant from either of the Festival system's twin suns that the sky remained dark all the time. Thin air made breathing difficult, and shallow exhalations came with visible puffs of steam. Artificial lighting, atmosphere, and gravity made the Drift livable, but just barely. The pirate ship, Dylan noted with some satisfaction, had come down hard, crash-landing in the middle of one of the half dozen shipyards that were the main source of income and employment for the Drift's residents. *Piracy*, Dylan supposed, *being only the second-largest employer.*

The shipyard was vast, crowded with construction stations, huge pieces of equipment, and the skeletons of several in-progress spacecraft. It looked, at a glance, like the pirate ship had not caused any casualties, but it had taken out a couple of smaller buildings. Beka expertly and appropriately brought the *Maru* down on a wide, empty stretch presumably used as a landing pad. As soon as they had settled, she opened the hatch and the four of them ran out into the shipyard.

"Let's check their ship first," Dylan shouted, running toward it with his force lance at the ready. The others kept pace with him, their feet crunching on the frozen ground. He couldn't see anyone, or any activity, around the pirate's vessel, and his guess was that any survivors had already cleared out. But with any luck, they might have been in too much of a hurry to take Limm'ta Nax Terani with them.

The pirate ship had plowed into the ground nose-first, and a hatchway gaped open near the rear, a couple of meters above the ground. Jumping down from it wouldn't have been too difficult, but getting into it from here—without getting one's head blown off, in case there was someone waiting inside for precisely that purpose—might be a challenge.

"What do you think?" Tyr asked.

"I think anyone who sticks his face up there has a good chance of losing it," Harper offered. "Of course, mine's about to freeze off anyway, so what's the difference?"

"So you're volunteering?" Beka asked.

"Hey!"

"Someone's got to."

"Boost me up," Dylan said impatiently. He didn't like standing out here in front of the ship, where they were easy targets for any pirates who had hidden themselves around the crash zone. "I'll do it."

"No, Boss," Harper countered. "Beka's right. I'll go first."

Tyr made a stirrup of his hands and Harper stepped into it. Tyr hoisted him much faster than he was ready for, and a second later he was rolling into the ship. "It looks clear," he said.

Dylan went up next, then Beka. Tyr, left behind, pulled himself effortlessly up into the hatch. Inside, the ship's corridors were dark, the walls and floors black with age or corrosion or maybe smoke. There were light fixtures, but it looked as if all the power was shut down. Artificial light from outside leaked in through the open hatch, but overall, standing on the sloping deck was like looking down a long, black tunnel.

With a shrug, Dylan said, "It's not like they don't know we're here, if there's anybody left on board."

"Probably true," Tyr agreed.

"Limm'ta!" Dylan shouted, his voice echoing through the quiet ship. "Are you here?"

No answer came back to them.

"I guess she's not," Beka said.

"I hope they didn't have ground transport, then," Dylan said. "We've got to find them fast, before they get far away."

"We should check the rest of the ship, first," Harper suggested. "In case . . ."

"In case they killed her," Tyr finished, less worried than Harper about sparing anyone's feelings.

"Let's make it fast," Dylan said. This would be the second ship he had searched looking for Limm'ta Nax Terani, and—as he had been the first time—he was reasonably certain she was no longer on it.

But he couldn't dispute the logic, and their little contingent was too small to split up. When they did catch up to the pirates they'd need all hands. They moved rapidly down the corridor, checking each hatchway they came to. From time to time they found dead pirates, but no sign of their captive.

When they had covered most of the ship, Dylan brought the search to a halt. "We're wasting time," he said. "Let's get out here and find them."

They left the ship the same way they had come in. When they hit the ground, Dylan used his subdermal comm unit to call *Andromeda*. "Rommie, can you get a read on the pirates?" he said. "I can't get a visual here—too much stuff around. They could be anywhere."

"There are some random groupings not far from you," Rommie reported. "I can't tell who they are, though."

"They could as easily be shipyard workers," Dylan said. But he got their locations from her just the same. The nearest grouping was inside one of the larger buildings, just a couple hundred meters from the open space where they'd landed the *Maru*. He told the others where it was, and they all struck out for it.

The buildings were primitive, thrown together for function, not beauty. The one they ran toward was washed with stark white light, but its walls were flat and gray, without texture or decoration. It was, Dylan thought, nothing but a big, rectangular box. There were a couple of huge doorways visible from here, big enough to move ships in and out of, and probably more on the other sides.

They were almost to the closest door when someone came running out of it. She was a blond woman wearing worker's clothes, plain and unadorned except for the shocking streak of blood that ran down her front. With a look of horror on her face, she ran toward them, gesticulating wildly behind her as she did.

She was almost close enough for them to hear what she was shouting when a shot from behind threw her to the ground. The big, smoking hole in her back was visible even from where they were.

Instantly, Dylan dropped to one knee and opened up with his

force lance, blasting toward the slightly open doorway from which the shot had come. Beka and Harper fired Gauss pistols and Tyr joined in with his big multibarreled gun.

After the doorway was more or less incinerated, however, they stopped firing. There had been no return fire, no guarantee that there was actually anyone still on the other side.

"I guess we're going in," Dylan said.

"This is a lot of effort on behalf of someone you have never met," Tyr suggested.

"Are you saying we shouldn't do it?"

Tyr smiled. Survival was of paramount importance to him, but without combat, Dylan suspected, he would find life almost too boring to make survival worthwhile. "Not at all, Captain."

They covered the rest of the ground to the doorway without being fired upon, passing the dead woman on the way. Dylan wished she had lived long enough to let them know what was going on inside. Had the pirates taken hostages? Or had they just moved through the building, brutalizing those they came across—hence the blood on her front—and then moved on? And how many of the pirates were still alive?

At the doorway, they paused again, checking the inside before entering. There might have been a single pirate left behind to guard this door, or the whole crew might have been chasing the one runaway woman. No way to tell now. There were so many uncertainties, Dylan wished for a moment that he'd brought Trance along to help untangle them.

Inside, the building was a vast manufacturing plant, one giant room with a stratospheric ceiling. *Andromeda* couldn't have fit through its doors, but a handful of *Eureka Maru*s could have. Heavy machinery was everywhere: giant cranes and hoists, steel-working stations, and the like. The more complex circuitry was no doubt done in one of the shipyard's other facilities; this building was geared more toward the big work of crafting the skeletons and exteriors of the ships. Big pieces of works-in-progress were everywhere. The lights were on. As dark as it was outside, it was bright in here, and machines were running, warming the air a bit. A shift must have been hard at work when the pirates crash-landed. Some of the machinery was so loud, Dylan guessed the workers in here might not have heard anything, were probably taken by surprise when the pirates came in.

The stink of blood in the air and the bodies he saw once he'd blinked in the bright light a few times confirmed his guess. People in outfits like the murdered woman's were collapsed on the floor near what he assumed were their workstations. Trails of blood on the floor led away from the bodies. No telling at a glance if the blood had belonged to the dead workers, or—as Dylan fervently hoped—to wounded pirates.

"Better than Hansel and Gretel," Harper said, pointing to one of the blood trails. "Unless some vampire comes along and licks it up, we have something to follow."

"The way this trip is going so far, I wouldn't count out the vampire theory yet," Beka returned.

Dylan shushed them and they followed the trail into the interior of the cavernous space. The pattern of spatters on the bare, utilitarian floor wound between huge machines, gradually lessening as it went. Machinery growled and shrieked around them as they went, all of it abandoned. It was like walking through a jungle full of wild beasts, not knowing which one might attack, or when. An entire army could have been massing around any of the blind corners, and Dylan wouldn't have been able to hear them, although Tyr might have.

But then he saw them—not an army at all, but a ragtag band of pirates. They had run into a dead end. The mazelike interior had channeled them to a blank wall. There were mounds of parts on racks and piled on the ground in front of and around them, and the dozen or so pirates had several workers with them. The workers, humanoid males and females alike, were frightened, some bloodied and battered at the hands of their captors.

Dylan recognized one of the pirates as Fitz, their captain. Blood streaked his face and a rag had been tied over what looked like a bad gash on his right temple, but his tattoos could be seen spiking down from under the rag. One hand held a gun, and the other was wrapped around the upper arm of Limm'ta Nax Terani. The gun was pointed more or less at her head.

"That's close enough, Captain Hunt!" Fitz shouted when Dylan and his crew came around the corner and saw them. "You wouldn't want anything to happen to these hostages, would you?"

"Are you sure that's the right question?" Dylan shot back. "If you hurt them, you don't come out of there alive. If you let them go, you might. Up to you."

"That isn't how it works," Fitz growled.

"It is now," Dylan corrected. "You can't get out of there without going through us. And that's just not happening."

He really hoped the pirates fell for it. They were all looking a bit haggard, as if the crash-landing, and the battering they'd had before that, had taken most of the fight out of them. But if they chose to fight, they could easily kill the hostages, including Limm'ta—which would render this whole expedition just a pointless side trip.

There was some hushed conversation on the pirates' side. After a moment, Fitz called out, "We have the hostage you want, Captain Hunt. You didn't come all this way just to collect her corpse. That means we make the rules."

Damn, Dylan thought. He had been hoping that wouldn't occur to them. "Let's just say—hypothetically speaking—that we agreed with you," Dylan offered. "What would those rules be?"

"Safe passage out of here," Fitz said. "We have friends on the Drift, we just want to get to them."

"In other words, you get to raid the *Argent* and then get off scot-free," Dylan translated.

"Scot-free? You wrecked our ship, killed most of our crew. What more do you want?"

"Just those last few hostages released unharmed," Dylan said. "And then we turn you over to whatever passes for law enforcement here." That last part was just for purposes of negotiation. Once the hostages were freed, he didn't especially care what happened to most of the pirates—Fitz excluded. Knowing that he'd cost them their ship and most of their crew was good enough for him.

"Dylan," Tyr whispered. "This is foolish. We should just kill them and go."

"We're almost there," Dylan replied. "Another minute or two, and—"

But before he finished his thought, one of the pirates fired at them. Her shot went wide and a plasma burst struck one of the big pieces of machinery behind them. The shot disrupted the negotiation, and everyone went into action at once. Dylan lunged forward, ducking down behind one of the piles of polished steel parts, and let off a blast from his force lance. His shot hit Fitz in the shoulder, spinning him around and away from Limm'ta. Smart bullets from Tyr's multigun slammed into more of the pirates. Pirates fired back toward them, but their shots slammed harmlessly into the steel behind which the *Andromeda* warriors had taken cover.

The air was filled with flashing light and smoke and the whirr and bang of explosive charges. It only lasted for a few seconds, though, and when it had died down Dylan made a quick head count. He saw Tyr, Harper, and Beka, all apparently unscathed.

Then he looked back toward the pirates, and saw Fitz dragging himself to his feet and lifting a gun toward Limm'ta, who had been knocked to the ground. Her face and chest were bloody, but there had been so much spray among the pirates it was impossible to tell from here if she had been hit or not.

He had dared to hope that Fitz would survive this whole thing, so he could be brought to justice, or at least be made to explain why he had targeted the *Argent*. Dylan hadn't been able to shake the nagging belief that there was more to the story than what Limm'ta had told him. He didn't know if Fitz could fill in any of the pieces or not, but he'd at least like to interrogate the guy. So while he knew he had to shoot Fitz before the pirate could shoot Limm'ta, he aimed for Fitz's legs.

Limm'ta, however, didn't.

She had apparently fallen on or near a pirate's gun, which she brought out from behind her back. Holding the big weapon in two hands, she pointed it squarely toward the surprised pirate's head and squeezed the trigger. Fitz's skull exploded in a fine, red mist.

Dylan felt Harper's presence close to his back. "Hey, Boss," Harper said. "Isn't she the one you thought needed to be rescued?"

EIGHTEEN

"The best scams end with the mark thanking you for taking his money."

—IGNATIUS B. VALENTINE

Walking into what had most probably been a trap struck Tyr as not being the most sensible move Dylan Hunt had ever made. Then again, Dylan had a long habit of doing things that Tyr would not have considered wise. The High Guard captain was a good combatant, but maybe not such a great soldier: too willing to let his emotions, instead of tactical or survival-oriented considerations, dictate his next move.

Now they were back on *Andromeda*'s Command Deck with Limm'ta Nax Terani, whom Dylan had absolutely no reason to believe was who she said she was. The "fact" that she was descended from Dylan's lifelong hero only made her story *less* believable, Tyr thought. It had always been the way of con artists to tell their marks just what they wanted to hear, letting them hook themselves. Tyr was afraid that Dylan might be falling for just such a line.

For the moment, though, the captain was all business. "Mr. Harper," Dylan said. "I want you to run a full diagnostic on *Andromeda*. Pay special attention to weapons systems, but check out everything. I don't want to be taken by surprise again by missiles that won't fire."

"Gotcha, Dylan," Harper said. "Anyone needs me, I'll be somewhere in Rommie's innards."

"Yuck," the ship's android avatar said.

"Figuratively speaking," Harper amended. "Or, I guess literally speaking. You're the part that's figurative."

"Still . . ."

"Today would be good, Harper," Dylan suggested.

"On my way." Harper exited Command.

"Beka, take us back toward where we were, on the way to Cenatex. We've got to finish our mission here. I want to keep hitting each planet in order."

"Right, Dylan," Beka agreed. "I'll set a course."

"But go easy on the engines," Dylan said. "Until Harper's checked them out thoroughly."

"It'll take us a while, then."

"Slow and steady," Dylan told her. He turned to Trance. "Trance, please take our guest to Medical and see to her wounds."

"Okay, Dylan," Trance said brightly. She took Limm'ta's hand and helped her toward the door. "My name's Trance Gemini," she said as they went. "You'll like me."

Tyr took his place at the weapons console. He liked the brisk, efficient way Dylan had taken care of that. But it didn't negate the fact that the whole reason they had come so far off course, slowing down their mission and putting all their lives at risk, was because Dylan had let his emotions take over.

The truth was, Tyr enjoyed fighting, and like most Nietzscheans he was good at it. Going up against the pirates had been fun. With only four of them, however, they were lucky that the pirates had been weakened first by *Andromeda*'s pounding and by their crash onto the Drift. A larger, more organized force could easily have overwhelmed *Andromeda*'s tiny crew. Once again, he realized, the idea of joining a bigger, more potent military unit was starting to appeal to him.

He had no illusions about his place on *Andromeda*. The people on the ship had every reason to hate Nietzscheans, and though Tyr Anasazi was without a pride, and therefore not welcome among his own kind, he doubted that he was fully accepted here either. Of course, they tried to appreciate him, and they liked what he did for them—most of which revolved around firing weapons at various enemies.

But would they ever truly welcome a Nietzschean in their midst? Given what the Nietzscheans had done—destroying the original Systems Commonwealth, among other things—Tyr had his doubts.

He hadn't made up his mind yet, and he was determined to stay with *Andromeda* at least for the duration of this particular mission, visiting the planets of the Festival system. By the time the mission came to a close, however, he would make his decision, once and for all, before *Andromeda* left the system. If he chose to leave the ship, he didn't think Dylan would object too strenuously.

And if he did—well, the question of who would prevail in a fight between them had never really been settled. Tyr was pretty sure he knew what the outcome would be. As much as he'd hate to be forced to kill Dylan Hunt, he would if he had to.

Independently of Tyr, Beka had also come up with the theory that Dylan was being conned. She came, after all, from a long line of con artists and crooks. Her dad, Ignatius, had built the *Maru* with his brother Sid, and before Dad's untimely death, the two of them had used it to smuggle just about anything that could be smuggled. Magdalena Valentine, her mom, had disappeared long ago, and while presumed dead, there was every possibility that she was just running cons someplace Beka hadn't been yet. And her brother

Rafe was still engaged in the family trade, showing up from time to time to bedevil Beka in his attempts to draw her back in with him.

So she was a girl who knew a snow job when she saw one. And she was pretty sure she saw one in Limm'ta. Whether or not she could persuade Dylan was, of course, a different story altogether.

The pieces added up—to what, she wasn't yet sure. They had been pulled away from the task at hand, visiting each of the planets in the Festival system to talk one-on-one about Commonwealth membership, and lured to the farthest reaches of the system. If they ran into trouble here, there would be no one around to bail them out, as the Festival ships had done upon their arrival. It seemed that there might be something wrong with the ship. At any rate, while they found out if there was or not, they were limping, not speeding, back to where they had left off. And now Limm'ta was on board. If she was the grifter Beka assumed she was, it wouldn't be long before she started sweet-talking Dylan again, and who knew where they might end up then?

She guessed that in the long run, it didn't much matter to her. She was at the helm of a ship, cutting through space, not tied down to some mudball or other. She had chosen this life long ago, and she wouldn't have it any other way.

Or would she? Guiding *Andromeda* slowly toward the first Slippoint, it suddenly occurred to her that she hadn't really chosen this life at all. If anything, it had chosen her. She'd been born on the *Eureka Maru*. The transient life—home being a vessel, instead of a place—was all she had ever known. Maybe her decision had simply been abdicating the responsibility of making a decision. She had chosen by ignoring the possibility that there was a choice, not by actively considering the alternatives and picking one. It was perfectly likely that she was in a rut just as deep as if she'd moved to a planet and stayed there.

Beka felt a weight press down on her shoulders, as if the roof had suddenly collapsed on her. She had felt free, but she had not carefully examined that freedom. Self-reflection wasn't her strong point, she figured. Now, however, she wondered if her freedom was that of a bird in a big cage; just because she couldn't see the bars on either side didn't mean they weren't there. A person, she supposed, could be chained as easily to a moving object as to a stationary one.

She had hardly met Limm'ta, but now she had a good reason not to like her. Anyone who could get Beka Valentine depressed about piloting a ship was someone she didn't need in her life.

Rev Bem had long since given up trying to understand why Dylan made some of the decisions that he did. In his company, they flitted about the known universe like a confused moth at a candlelight vigil. But where he was made little difference to the Magog; his spiritual journey, not his physical one, was what he cared about.

Except that it was hard to focus on his memoirs with the ship bouncing and jolting, lights flickering, the dull pounding of explosive charges hitting her hull. He had been coming to an important part of his tale—the story of his first experience implanting his eggs in another being and the pride with which he had imagined his young eating their way out—when the barrage had started. He had interrupted his dictation long enough to ask Andromeda what was going on, and she'd told him that they had gone several million light-years out of their way to engage in combat with a pirate ship. Rev Bem had shrugged and tried to remember his place. He had been closing in on a point—the story about his eggs had been a parable for something else—but with the noise and the flashing lights and the knowledge that any breath might be his last, he couldn't remember what it had been. Instead, he started praying for the eternal lives of everyone involved in the battle, himself included.

Rommie knew it didn't make any sense to resent Harper's poking around in her guts. She was, after all, a warship, made of engineered parts, and he was her engineer. But she had run self-diagnostics at Dylan's request, and had come up blank. So it bothered her a little that Dylan had ordered Harper to explore further. Maybe her responsiveness was off a little bit. That happened to the best of ships, didn't it? Everyone had a moment or two of hesitation from time to time. It didn't necessarily mean anything.

She was still stewing about it when Dylan showed up in the virtual reality matrix. Rommie had thought he'd be on his way to see Limm'ta Nax Terani, so she was pleased that he was here with her instead. She offered him a tentative smile, and he responded by opening his arms. She moved between them, wrapped her own arms around his muscular body, and felt the warmth and comfort as he encircled her.

"I'm glad you came back, Dylan," she said.

"Me too." His voice was hoarse, husky, as if he couldn't quite catch his breath. *I know how he feels*, she thought.

"Can I . . . can I talk to you? About Harper, and . . . well, today?"

"Sure," Dylan said. He released her. Suddenly there were seats behind them, and they both sat down. She looked into his handsome, clear blue eyes.

"Do you trust me?" she asked.

"Of course." No hesitation there, no hedging. A simple declarative.

"But . . . you asked Harper to double-check my results."

He favored her with a warm smile. "I just want what's best for you, Rommie," he assured her. "If there's something wrong that you can't detect, I want it fixed. That doesn't mean I don't trust you."

"Okay," she said.

"If Harper gets to be a problem," Dylan continued, "just let me know. I'll take care of him."

"Thank you, Dylan," she said.

He looked away, at the limitless expanse of black beneath their feet, and when he looked back his face was clouded, anxious.

"What is it, Dylan?" Rommie asked him, suddenly worried.

"It's . . . I've liked spending time with you, like this."

The past tense construction immediately put her on edge. What did that mean? "Me too."

"I feel like we've really gotten to know each other on a . . . on a different level. But . . . but it can't go on, Rommie."

"Why not?" If she had a heart, she thought it would break. As it was, she thought she detected a lancing pain, though it might just as easily have been Harper opening one of her access hatches and sticking his hand inside. "Is it something I've—"

"No," Dylan said quickly. "No, it's—I'm human, Rommie. I can't keep coming into your VR matrix like this. It would be too easy to get trapped here, to never want to leave. But I can't just turn away from my physical body, from the real world I have to live in."

"So that means we . . ." She couldn't bring herself to finish the thought.

"We can't continue what we've found in this world," Dylan explained. "But that doesn't mean we can't be together in mine. Your avatar is partially organic. It has senses. It feels real, to me."

"But the rules," Rommie protested. "A ship can't have a physical relationship with her captain, or with any of the crew, for that matter. It's just not—"

"The people who made those rules are long dead, Rommie," Dylan pointed out. "We live in a different universe now. The lines between human and non are thinner, more blurred than they ever were. Who's to say what's right and wrong anymore? The High Guard? I am the High Guard, Rommie. *We* are. We are the ones who set the rules now."

She could barely believe she was hearing this. She had always done her best to abide by the rules. She knew that her emotional life could never be like Dylan's, or like any human's. But she knew what emotions were, and she believed that she felt them strongly enough to affect her. To know—to really, truly know, after all this time, that Dylan felt the same way—it was just the best thing that had ever happened to her.

But she couldn't quite let herself believe it. Caution was called for, even now. Especially now. "Are you sure, Dylan? I don't want us to—"

"Rommie, we can be together. On my plane, in my reality. All it takes is for you to agree to some ground rules, a few concessions . . ."

Anything, she thought. *Anything you ask.* But she didn't want to seem too eager, so she restrained the impulse. "I'm willing to discuss them," she said.

"Okay." Dylan leaned back in his chair and crossed his arms over his chest. "Let's talk."

NINETEEN

Ashala met Cam Prezennetti where he had suggested, near the Fountain of Transcendent Victory, in Gala's Imperial Square. She had dressed conservatively, in nondescript, dark blue clothing that clung to her curves but didn't expose the flesh that made them. A yellow scarf hid her bright red hair. Even with all that fabric covering her, she looked as desirable as any woman Cam had ever met, and he felt an unexpected thrill in his heart when he saw that she had come. A light rain spattered the ground around them, steaming when it hit the flames that sprayed up from the fountain.

When he expressed his pleasure at her arrival, she gave him a funny smile. "You asked me to come," she said. "Did you think I wouldn't?"

"I didn't know for sure," he told her. "I thought probably, but . . . even when you close a sale, there's always buyer's remorse to contend with. I couldn't know you'd be here until I saw you."

"I told you, I'm the curious type."

"That's all it is? Curiosity?"

"What, do you want me to say I'm in love with you? I'm not. I'm a simple girl, Mr. Prezennetti. I've already been exposed to more strange and wonderful things than I ever dreamed I would be, growing up. But I know there's a lot more out there. I know that being with Efreld shields me, in some ways, from new experiences. I'm not sure I love him, either, but I do know that he's very good to me. When he's not too busy to pay attention." She chuckled and started to walk away from the fountain, and Cam followed. "By the way, your little scheme didn't work."

"Which scheme was that?"

She laughed, and he realized he liked the sound of it. "You're so innocent," she teased. "Efreld said it was your idea to try to kill Dylan Hunt. 'Everyone responds to a good martyr story,' he says you said. He says you figured that if Captain Hunt was brutally murdered here in the Festival system, he could call for a mourning period, and use our common sorrow as a wedge to pry open the door to Commonwealth membership. Something like that, anyway."

"Almost those exact words," Cam answered, a little surprised. He had thought the idea a small stroke of genius—the kind of genius for which he was very well compensated, although it was more often directed at the selling of products than ideas. At the same time, he realized the risky nature of the enterprise, so was taken aback to know that Havasu has shared it with Ashala. "Does he often tell you things like that?"

"We have very few secrets from each other," Ashala assured him. "Some. Just not many."

"And me?"

"You're a secret from him. So far, anyway. Until we see where curiosity takes us."

"It can take us as far as you're willing to let it," he said.

"That's pretty far," Ashala said. "You sure you're up for it?"

"I thought I was the one trying to sell you," Cam replied. "Now I'm not so certain."

"Maybe you are, maybe you're not." Ashala took his hand as they walked, and gave it a squeeze. "If you live nearby, I guess we can find out."

"I guess we can," Cam agreed, glad that his instincts had been right on the mark, as ever. "I wouldn't have suggested we meet here if it wasn't close to home."

"That's what I assumed," Ashala said. "And, by the way, I wouldn't worry too much about the situation with Captain Hunt and the Commonwealth. Efreld has some other plans in the works as well. He's a great believer in . . . what did he call it? Multiple redundancy systems, or something like that. It sounds boring, but then, he's generally a boring man."

"I'll do my best to be entertaining at all times," Cam promised.

Ashala smiled, looking at him from the corners of her eyes. "That would be a nice change of pace."

Dylan found Limm'ta Nax Terani on the Observation Deck, standing before the huge window that looked back toward where they'd been. He had seen statues and flexis of Sani Nax Rifati, and he had a pretty good idea of what the hero of the Systems Commonwealth had looked like. Limm'ta seemed to share some of those same distinctive features. Dylan remembered Rifati's strong chin, with sculpted lips usually set, at least in the images, in a firm, steady half smile. Limm'ta had that too, except that her lips were fuller, more feminine, and the smile, when she turned to greet Dylan, more vibrant. Her eyes were green and striking, widely set beneath a smooth, powerful brow that also reminded Dylan of her esteemed ancestor. Her hair fell in soft, golden waves midway down her back. With her wounds cleaned, wearing a bodysuit that clung to her lush form, its colors shifting slowly through the entire spectrum visible to human eyes, Dylan had a hard time deciding which view—the woman, or the starscape—was more lovely. *Seen a few hundred thousand starscapes, you've seen 'em all,* he decided.

"Are you feeling better?" he asked her.

"Yes, thank you, Captain Hunt," Limm'ta said. She looked at him with those bright, unblinking eyes. She spoke with a slight, unfamiliar accent and a formality that had struck Dylan as odd in the middle of a crisis, but which he now found sort of endearing. "Trance is . . . quite delightful. And I would like to thank you for coming to my aid, as well. I know it took you well out of your way."

"Not at all," Dylan said. "Well, I mean, it did take us out of our way. But we were happy to do it."

"I believe that *you* were. But I am not as sure about the rest of your crew."

"They go where the ship does," Dylan said.

"But certainly they have opinions about where it goes."

"Of course."

"Well, I would like all of them to know how appreciative I am."

"I'll make sure they get the message," Dylan said. "Is there anything else we can do for you now? Are you hungry?"

"I could eat," Limm'ta granted. "If you would join me."

"I could eat too," Dylan answered, realizing just how hungry he was only as he spoke the words.

She took a last look out the rear window. "I certainly don't mind seeing Breckenridge Drift disappearing into the far distance, I can tell you that," she said as they left the deck. "Not that I spent a lot of time there, but what happened was most unpleasant."

He led her to the Officer's Mess, a huge space that could accommodate four hundred people—though of course it no longer needed to. The two of them were alone, with the autochefs standing by to prepare whatever he and Limm'ta might have wanted. Limm'ta asked for a Panrovian spider salad, while Dylan decided to indulge a craving he'd been feeling for a traditional Vedran burger and fries.

Once they had their food, they sat together near one of the walls, with a sea of tables radiating away from them. "I need to ask you a question," Dylan said between bites. "Why hail us? Surely there were considerably closer ships that could have helped you much quicker—maybe even have saved the *Argent* in the bargain."

Limm'ta stopped with a forkful of the exotic red spider—the fleshy thorax, about half a meter in diameter, made the best meat—and looked almost shyly at him. "A couple of reasons. One, I didn't want any of Festival's ships to know our situation, for reasons which will become clear to you shortly. And two, I saw your speech, so I knew that you were in the system," she admitted. "I wanted a close-up look at you. We were headed toward you when the pirates overtook us. We transited into Slipstream twice, ending up right where they wanted us, apparently. They herded us the whole way, and then they caught us close to their own home base."

"You wanted a look at me?" Dylan wasn't sure he had heard her right.

"Of course," she said. "Hero of the new Commonwealth. Carrier of my ancestor's torch. I have heard much about your work, Captain Hunt, and I wanted to offer my support, for whatever that might be worth."

"Well . . . I consider it an honor," he said. "And I think it would be worth quite a lot."

Traces of a blush reddened Limm'ta's cheeks. "You embarrass me," she said.

Dylan was feeling a little embarrassed himself. He was incredibly complimented that a descendant of Sani Nax Rifati would seek him out for any reason, but at the same time, one of his deepest hopes was beginning to collapse. He had hoped that finding Limm'ta would provide clues to the whereabouts—if any—of Tarn-Vedra, where he had been born but which had apparently vanished during the three hundred years he'd been out of commission. If she lived within the Festival system, however, it was unlikely that she was a native of Tarn-Vedra. Still, he had to check. "You live here, in the system?"

"Yes," she answered. "In the city of Coramus, on the planet of Ishidrum."

"So, not on Tarn-Vedra," Dylan said, unable to hide his disappointment.

"Our family has not seen Tarn-Vedra for several generations," she said. Examining his face, she no doubt saw the sorrow there. "I am sorry. I know that it was the place of your birth."

"No, it's . . . it's okay. I hoped, for just a moment. But I knew it was a long shot."

"From what I have heard, Captain Hunt, you have played a number of long shots, often quite successfully."

"I've done all right in that department," he agreed. "But please, call me Dylan. And tell me about Ishidrum. Was it settled by Vedrans?"

"If you will call me Limm'ta," she replied. "In answer to your question, largely, yes. Generations ago, as I said. Several exploratory ships were sent away from Tarn-Vedra, hoping to find a new homeworld before a Nietzschean invasion eliminated all hope of escape. They were supposed to find new places to settle and then send work back to the rest of Tarn-Vedra's beleaguered inhabitants, but by the time they did, they could no longer locate Tarn-Vedra at all. The planet was occupied, but very sparsely, before our people arrived. We—not me, of course, but my ancestors, and the rest—settled most of it, and named it Ishidrum after the captain of the exploratory ship."

She set her fork down on the table and looked at Dylan with imploring eyes. "Of all the worlds in the Festival system, Ishidrum is the only one that has managed to remain independent of Festival military domination. We would very much like to maintain that status, but it grows harder every year. As the other planets—our allies, our trade partners, our friends—fall under Festival's sway, we find ourselves more and more cut off, isolated, and pressured to submit."

"But being Vedrans . . ."

"Submission is not in our nature, that's correct. My purpose in wanting to meet with you—and, frankly, to head you off, since you would only have reached us last, after all the other planets in the system—was twofold. I wanted to warn you that Festival does dominate the system, by force, and that while the leadership on some of the other worlds would no doubt claim independence, that claim would be a false one. They will do what Festival instructs them to do, no more and no less. The other reason was to beseech you to allow Ishidrum into the Restored Commonwealth separately, not as part of the Festival system. We need allies, urgently. We need some support from outside the system if we are to be able to maintain our own independence, Dylan. Festival's pressure is harder to resist every day."

Dylan was torn. He wanted to be able to do whatever was in his power for Limm'ta. If she was right—if Festival was as overwhelmingly dominant as she said—he might not want them in the Commonwealth at all. The idea was to discourage that sort of thing, after all, not to condone it, however implicitly, by allowing membership.

At the same time, he couldn't simply take her word for it. So far the one other planet he had visited seemed to bear out her description. Festival's military had definitely been in charge on Transitory Primus. But one world did not a whole system make. He was about to say as much when she cut him off.

"Dylan, I know you can't just agree to something like that without further investigation. If I could but ask you one favor, however—one favor in addition to the gigantic one you have already so kindly done me—I would ask that you take me home to Ishidrum so I can tell my people what happened to their brethren on the *Argent*. At the same time, you could get to know us a little better, and formulate your own opinion of my tale."

"I suppose that could be arranged," he said. "How far off course would it take us?"

"Hardly off course at all," she said, gracing him with what looked like a sincere smile. "In fact, Ishidrum is practically on the way back to where you came from. Perhaps you could effect your ship's repairs there, while you visit."

"That would make it easier."

"I would not expect you to stay long, or hope to keep you from visiting the other planets," she assured him. "In fact, I agree with your general plan, and think it would be most important for you to do so. I simply feel that you should do so with all the information at your disposal, instead of just what Festival and its satellites want you to have."

"And I can't argue with that reasoning," he said.

"Then it's settled?"

"Rommie!" Dylan called. Her image appeared on viewscreens all over the big room. "Please have Beka set a new course for Ishidrum."

Rommie frowned. "Ishidrum?"

"Yes. We're making another detour."

"I see," Rommie said. "Will there be anything else?"

It seemed to Dylan almost as if she was fishing for something, but he couldn't tell what. Whatever it might be, he didn't want to pursue it at this moment; he was trying to pay attention to Limm'ta. "No, that's all," he said. She threw him another frown and then vanished from the screen. He'd have to find out what that was all about sometime, but not right now.

"Thank you, Dylan. I am convinced that you will not regret this. Those pirates . . ."

"What about them?"

"I used that term, but I think that it is not entirely accurate."

Dylan found this twist intriguing. "What would you call them, then?"

"The more appropriate word would probably be something like 'privateers.'"

"The distinction being . . ."

She hesitated for a moment before answering, and worried at her spider with her fork. "Pirates tend to be freelance, out for their own interests and nothing else. Privateers work for a state, doing a government's dirty work while keeping any official presence at a safe remove."

"So these privateers, you think they were working for who, exactly?"

"I'm convinced they were working for Festival. Trying to keep us from reaching you."

Dylan started to reply, but was interrupted by Rev Bem entering the Officer's Mess. "I was told I would find you here," he said in his typically surly-sounding growl. "Am I interrupting anything? I had hoped to be able to welcome our guest."

"No," Dylan said. "It's fine, Rev, come and join us. Limm'ta Nax Terani, this is the Reverend Behemiel Far-Traveler. We call him Rev Bem."

"Trance told me there was a Magog on board," Limm'ta said, rising from her seat as Rev Bem threaded his way between the tables. "I must say, I am impressed by the diversity of this crew. A Nietzschean, a Pixie, a Magog . . . quite astounding."

"Dylan is the glue that holds us together," Rev Bem told her.

"I am learning what a remarkable man he is."

"Yes, he is that," Rev Bem said. "And welcome, lady, to *Andromeda Ascendant*. If I may be of any spiritual assistance while you're on board, please ask at any time."

"Thank you, Reverend," Limm'ta said graciously. She sat down again, though Rev Bem remained standing.

"She was just explaining that the pirates—excuse me, privateers—who attacked her ship were, in all likelihood, working for Festival."

"Is that right?" Rev Bem asked. "I can't say that it surprises me. Very little about that place would surprise me."

"I believe it to be the case, although I cannot prove it," Limm'ta said. "Festival has a reputation as a lighthearted, fun planet—a party planet, some say. And certainly that aspect of it cannot be denied. It is a destination for fun-seekers from across the galaxies. But beneath that façade, its rulers are obsessed with power, with dominance over others. If they say they want to join the Commonwealth, it is only so that they may dominate that as well."

"Nobody gets to dominate the Commonwealth," Dylan said firmly.

"I know that is your philosophy," Limm'ta said. "You have that in common with my ancestor. A pragmatic optimist, that is how I always thought of him—and you, the same. But the truth is, events have a way of swirling out of control sometimes, even when one is on one's guard. Allowing Festival into the Restored Commonwealth would, I am convinced, be a tragic mistake, with consequences you cannot begin to foresee."

"I find myself in complete agreement with the lady," Rev Bem put in. "I didn't trust those people for a second." He turned to Limm'ta. "I myself would not even set foot on that planet, even when the rest of the crew was there," he said. "From all accounts it is a wicked, wicked place where all manner of—"

Dylan cut him off. "We don't need the whole lecture, Reverend. The highlight reel is plenty. I appreciate your vote in support of Limm'ta's position, and I'll take it under advisement. We've already changed course, Rev. We're going to Limm'ta's homeworld, Ishidrum, before we visit the rest of the planets in the system. We'll keep our minds open and we'll find out as much as we can about Festival and how it works. And, Limm'ta, you have my word that if we do decide to accept Festival into the Commonwealth, it will be made extremely clear to them what the rules are, and that we will not stand for any kind of show of force against the other member worlds. The Commonwealth will be what it will be, and we won't put up with any attempt to take it over, from without or from within."

"That is everything I could possibly hope for, Dylan," Limm'ta said. Her face fairly beamed. "I am so glad you rescued me today."

Dylan remembered Harper's words when she had blown away the pirate leader. How much rescuing she had needed was yet to be determined. He found himself extremely impressed with her so far, but he knew that only meant he had to be even more on his guard at all times, keeping one eye on her and one on his own instincts.

What he had said, about the Commonwealth not putting up with anyone trying to control it, went for her just as much as it did for Festival. At least until he knew her better and found out what her agenda really was.

And the getting better acquainted part? Much more pleasant with Limm'ta than it had been with Festival's Havasu.

TWENTY

"The only thing worse than bad news is more bad news—which is, of course, the way it always happens."

—SEAMUS ZELAZNY HARPER

Rommie stood at the doorway to the Officer's Mess, looking in at Dylan. He sat across from Limm'ta Nax Terani, and was apparently enjoying the conversation a great deal. Rev Bem stood nearby, and while she wouldn't quite characterize the gathering as a party, it was clear that it wasn't really a business meeting either.

She fought down a stomach-churning sensation that she assumed must be jealousy. Dylan's tone and attitude when he'd ordered her to have Beka change course had been troubling. She wasn't sure what she had expected, but she realized that she'd been hoping for some sign, some indication of the things they had spoken of earlier. He had said their relationship could continue to grow and change in the physical world . . . but then he had talked to her as if she were merely part of the scenery.

She tried to tell herself that he was just being discreet. After all, he had been sitting with an honored guest. A beautiful female guest, but a guest just the same. Limm'ta Nax Terani was a dignified woman, a descendant of the hero of Tarn-Vedra, who meant just as much to *Andromeda*, in her way, as he did to Dylan. Without Sani Nax Rifati there would have been no High Guard, and so no Glorious Heritage class heavy cruisers. Dylan wasn't the kind of man to make googly eyes at Rommie in front of someone like that, even if he had been the kind of man—which she was sure he was not—to make googly eyes at any other time.

So he was showing discretion. He was demonstrating maturity. He was being the Dylan Hunt she prized, that she valued so highly. If he had behaved any other way, he would have been a different person, one who wouldn't hold such appeal for her.

In private—that's when he would smolder.

She was convinced of it.

Rev Bem showed Limm'ta to her cabin—there were plenty of empties from which to choose—and Dylan returned to his office to study up on whatever Rommie had been able to find out about Ishidrum. But he had barely been in there for five minutes, feet up on his desk reading through the data, when she interrupted him.

"Dylan," she announced. "You have an emergency call from Festival. From His Regency, Efreld sur Havasu."

"Let's hear it," he told her, barely glancing at her face on his viewscreen.

She didn't reply, but vanished, replaced by the less lovely visage of Havasu. "Dylan," he said with an ingratiating smile. "I understand you've had yet another nasty scrape. I do wish you would allow me to provide you with an escort."

"As you can see, Your Regency," Dylan countered, "an escort is entirely unnecessary. We're more than capable of taking care of ourselves."

"Or so you would like to think," Havasu said mysteriously.

"What does that mean?"

"Simply that you may now be in greater danger than you believe."

"Danger from what? I don't think those pirates are going to be following us anywhere."

Havasu waved a hand dismissively. "The pirates are nothing. A meaningless annoyance, and I'm glad that you dealt with them appropriately. No, I'm speaking of danger from within, Dylan," he said. "It has come to my attention that you are now ferrying a very dangerous fugitive from justice."

"A dangerous fugitive?" Dylan echoed. "You mean Limm'ta?"

"The very same," Havasu said.

"I hardly think—"

"You have known her for, what, an hour? Two? Surely you, Captain Hunt, are not unwilling to bow to the voice of experience."

"What evidence do you have of this claim?" Dylan demanded. "Of what crimes has she been convicted?"

"Convicted? None at all, Dylan. For that to happen, we would have had to have tried her in absentia, which is not Festival's way. She has avoided apprehension thus far. But of what has she been accused? And accusations, Dylan, merit serious attention, I can assure you. When she is caught, she will, without doubt, be found guilty. She stands accused of murder, conspiracy, incitement to violent acts, accessory before and after the fact to other murders and violent crimes, and various counts of fraud and robbery to fund her criminal enterprises. She is trouble, Dylan, pure and simple. Now that you have her on your ship, you should deliver her to Festival at once. I recommend locking her in the brig on the way, for once she realizes that you have changed course she's certain to give you a great deal of difficulty. But if you can keep her contained until you hand her off to us, you'll be doing yourselves, and the entire Festival system, an enormous favor. A favor which will not be forgotten."

Dylan shook his head. "That isn't happening, Your Regency."

"Dylan, I am afraid that I must insist. This is a matter of critical importance to Festival law enforcement."

"And I must insist that she is a guest of the Restored Commonwealth with all the rights and privileges thereof. I could not, in good conscience, betray a guest by delivering her someplace she hasn't asked to go."

Havasu let out a long sigh and rubbed his forehead vigorously with his left hand. "Ahh, Dylan, I had hoped it would not come to this."

"To what?"

"You are harboring a wanted fugitive," Havasu told him. "You are obstructing the path of justice. You might, for all I know, be engaging in conspiracy to obstruct justice, and possibly in other extralegal pursuits as well. I am saddened to say that you appear to be changing your own status in the Festival system from honored guest to criminal trespasser."

Dylan couldn't hold in a laugh. "You're kidding, right?"

"I am not. I am a man of good humor, but there are things about which I do not joke. This, I must tell you, is one of them."

"Your Regency, this is absurd. Even you admit that Limm'ta hasn't been convicted of anything. I don't know how Festival's system of justice works, but I'm not turning over someone who has placed herself in my hands without some pretty convincing evidence of why I should. Especially to a government that may have the goal of taking over the Commonwealth for its own ends."

"Evidence?" Havasu asked, ignoring Dylan's latter statement. "My word is not evidence enough?"

"Apparently not."

"Very well," Havasu replied. "That last time you encountered the Festival fleet, Captain Hunt, they were defending you against attackers. The next time you encounter them—and you will—the outcome will be markedly different."

Havasu broke the connection after delivering his thinly-veiled threat. That was just as well. If he hadn't Dylan would have. He didn't appreciate being played or being bullied, and Havasu had been doing both of those, it seemed. The result was that Dylan grew more stubborn, more determined. He wouldn't alter course one iota, but would make for Ishidrum with all possible speed, and worry about the rest of it when the time came.

There weren't, Harper was always pleased to tell anyone who asked, very many engineering problems that he couldn't solve. Even as a kid back on Earth, he had shown an aptitude for such things: turning cast-off machinery into a fort for a snowball fight, for instance. His team had destroyed the enemy team's fort, which was just made of packed snow, iced over with water. But when the enemy had attacked his fort and tried to kick it down, one of them had ended up with a broken foot, and they had been forced to admit defeat.

Since then, he'd learned to value warm-weather sports over cold. But it was still nice to know that if a crucial snowball fight were to come up, he could contribute in a meaningful way.

Just now, though, he himself was considering admitting defeat, except without the part where he had to break any bones. Dylan had charged him with the task of finding out what was wrong with *Andromeda*. He knew the ship's systems inside and out; knew them better, he was convinced, than anyone except those who had built her in the first place, and he was giving them the benefit of the doubt. Chances are it had been a big team effort, and no one knew a whole lot beyond his or her personal specialty.

And he could see, kind of, where the trouble was. If the ship was a person—which it wasn't, but the analogy could be made—then he had eliminated as trouble spots the skeletal, muscular, and nervous systems, and narrowed it down to the circulatory system. To be more precise, the heart, which controlled the flow of blood to the rest of the body. He had done more or less the same thing here, ruling out structural issues and electronics. The problem seemed to be in her wiring somewhere. He just couldn't trace it back to the heart of the matter for some reason.

He had tried physically following the wires, hoping to find a short or a visible break of some kind, but there were thousands of kilometers of wiring in the ship and he couldn't possibly inspect all of it visually. He'd tried plugging into the VR matrix via the dataport in his neck, but the ship had ejected him from the matrix without comment. He had tried again, and got the same unpleasant and kind of painful reaction.

So he went straight to Dylan. There was no place on the ship where Rommie couldn't eavesdrop on a conversation if she so chose, but he felt a little more comfortable talking to the captain about this in the privacy of his office. But when he went in, he found Dylan sitting at his desk with a grim expression on his face. *Terrific,* Harper thought. *He's already in a bad mood. Well, this'll make it worse.*

"What is it, Mr. Harper?" Dylan asked.

"It's the ship, Boss," he said, figuring right to the point would be more advantageous, if Dylan was in a sour frame of mind, than dancing around it. "You asked me to figure out what's wrong, and, boy genius that I am, I've made some headway. But I haven't been able to fix it quite yet."

Surprise registered on Dylan's face. Harper took that as a compliment. Dylan really did put a lot of faith in Harper's skills. "Why not?"

"I'm not sure," Harper admitted. "It's almost like . . . like she's locking me out. Keeping me from getting to where the problem is."

"That doesn't seem like *Andromeda*," Dylan said. "Are you sure about this? It's not just an excuse?"

As much as Harper had felt complimented by Dylan's earlier remark, he was wounded by this one. "Dylan, have you ever known me to make excuses? Okay, scratch that. But do you really think I'd need to, in this kind of situation? This is Seamus Harper we're talking about. *Andromeda* is a complex piece of machinery, but she's still a piece of machinery."

"I know," Dylan said. "I'm sorry, I didn't mean it like that. But . . . I just can't see *Andromeda* not cooperating."

"Exactly my point, Boss," Harper said. "But she kicked me out of VR twice. I've been trying to pinpoint a wiring issue, but she keeps refusing to show me the schematics, telling me they're not currently available."

"Do you think that's part of the problem?" Dylan asked. "The schematics aren't coming up because there's a wiring problem there?"

"That's possible," Harper said. "That's the assumption I've been working on. If I could get into the VR matrix I could confirm it, but so far, no go. In the meantime, the problems seem to be spreading, but I can't contain them because I can't isolate them. A little while ago Trance told me she's having some problems with temperature control in Hydroponics."

Dylan shook his head slowly. "This was inconvenient," he said. "But it sounds like it's moving beyond that. Let's talk to Rommie."

"Good luck with that. She's been avoiding me all day."

"Rommie!" Dylan called.

Her face appeared on his viewscreen, smiling. When she turned slightly and saw Harper sitting there, the smile vanished. "Yes, Dylan."

"Mr. Harper says you're being less than cooperative in his diagnostic check," Dylan said.

"Mr. Harper is mistaken. I've been doing everything in my power—"

"You freakin' kicked me out of the matrix!" Harper exploded. "You won't show me the schematics! How is that helping?"

"—in my power," she repeated, "to help out. Some things, I am chagrined to admit, are beyond me. Whatever malfunction is affecting my systems seems to be spreading, making it more difficult for me to allow Harper access. But for you two to accuse me of—"

"No one is making any accusations," Dylan said, wagging a hand toward her as if to emphasize the point.

"Speak for yourself," Harper groused.

"Mr. Harper, that isn't helpful," Dylan admonished him. "But Rommie, you're going to have to make a greater effort to help. We need to find out what's wrong, and we need to do it now. We're fresh out of time, and we could be looking at some serious trouble here."

"What kind of trouble, Boss?" Harper asked him.

"We seem to have wound up on Festival's bad side," Dylan said.

"They have a good side?"

"Apparently it's a small one. We were there; now we're not."

"And our week just gets better and better," Harper said.

"Rommie, you're going to work with Harper, right?"

"I will do whatever is in my power to do," Rommie promised.

"Good," Dylan said. "I guess that's all we can ask. Maybe when we reach Ishidrum we can get to the bottom of this."

"Ishidrum?" Harper asked.

"Limm'ta Nax Terani's homeworld," Dylan told him. "Our next stop. I guess I neglected to inform you."

Harper shrugged. "Hey, I'm just the engineer. No reason I should be told these things."

Dylan cocked his head and looked at Harper, and for a second Harper was sure he was going to toss out some kind of comeback. But he didn't. Harper waited another couple of seconds, and then, deciding that he had been dismissed, left the captain's office.

Obviously Dylan had more important things on his mind. All Harper was trying to do was to make sure the ship would fly.

No big.

TWENTY-ONE

> "You'll never have a quiet world till you knock the patriotism out
> of the human race."
>
> —GEORGE BERNARD SHAW

Beka was exhausted.

Piloting a ship hadn't been this wearying since the time she and
Rafe had been forced to make an emergency getaway from Bolinas
Drift in a richly-appointed pleasure yacht they had "borrowed"
from a repair facility, only to learn that it had gone into the shop in
the first place because of engine troubles that had not yet been addressed. It took every skill Beka could bring to bear—Rafe, of
course, let her do the flying—just to keep the thing from spinning
around and slamming right back into the drift.

Even with that handicap, she had managed to elude their pur-
suers, who, thanks to Rafe's habit of playing both sides against the
middle, had included both law enforcement and members of Bolinas's biggest criminal organization. But she'd been wrung out
when the chase was over, and once they were safe, she had slept for

nineteen hours straight, then had a meal and a drink and slept for another seven.

This was worse than that.

This had required two Slip jumps, which were draining enough under full power but much, much harder with a ship that couldn't quite be relied upon. It had also meant goosing every last bit of performance from *Andromeda* in normal space, especially after Dylan had alerted her that not only had they changed course, but there was every possibility that they might find themselves under attack by the Festival fleet at any time.

Normally, she would have let the ship's autopilot functions take over in normal space, but that wasn't currently an option. Autopilot was just as unreliable as most of the ship's other functions. Dylan had spelled Beka when he could, as had Trance, but with the ship in such questionable shape, she felt most comfortable when she herself was at the pilot's station, and she waved them off when she was able to remain upright. As so often happened at times like these, thoughts of Flash flitted through her mind, but she brushed them away like low-hanging cobwebs. She was determined not to repeat that mistake. The drug would keep her awake, but at too high a price.

Under normal circumstances, shooting off to rescue someone from pirates, then changing course on the way back, were not particularly exceptional activities for the ship under Dylan's command. But doing it with that ship fighting her every light-year of the way was a different matter.

Now—finally—they were in near orbit around Ishidrum, a bright blue-green ball that was so far from Festival's suns that light from only one of them actually reached the place with any kind of strength. Everyone, it seemed, had gathered on Command Deck for the approach.

"We have large-ship docking facilities on-planet," Limm'ta Nax Terani informed her. "If you'd like to take *Andromeda* down I can arrange a berth."

"I would," Beka replied. "But frankly, I don't trust the ship's controls in any kind of precise landing situation."

"It's gotten that bad?" Dylan asked.

"Dylan, it's *been* that bad. It's just that we haven't really been out where there was a lot of stuff around we could run into. If we were down near the surface we'd be like the old, blind dog my mom had when I was tiny, who would walk in any given direction until her head ran into something solid."

"Point taken," Dylan said.

"I agree," Trance chimed in. "Trying to land would be a very bad idea." Sometimes Trance got on Beka's nerves, but right now, she was glad for the backup. If Trance had actually studied the probabilities and wasn't just spouting off, then her input was valuable—especially since it supported Beka's fervent desire for a break. And even if she was just spouting off, she still buttressed Beka's position.

"I've been trying to restore the pooch's vision," Harper said. "But the best I can do at the moment is to slap some sunglasses on her and tie a white cane to her leg."

"We'll take the *Maru*," Dylan suggested, bowing to the weight of opinion. "Is there an orbital docking station we can use, Limm'ta?"

"Of course," Limm'ta answered. "That's easily arranged as well."

"I guess I'll stay on *Andromeda* and try to get her up to snuff while you guys do your thing on the surface," Harper volunteered.

"Are you sure, Mr. Harper?" Limm'ta asked him. "You might reconsider when you hear about our waves."

"You have waves?"

Limm'ta smiled. "Beyond your wildest surf dreams."

"So like I was saying, we can drydock in orbit and I can come back in a couple of days to work on *Andromeda*," Harper amended.

"Do you think we can manage the docking, Beka?" Dylan asked.

Beka wiped sweat from her brow and stifled a yawn. "Yeah," she said. She couldn't decide which she looked forward to the most—

the challenge of docking the malfunctioning ship, or the rest she could have once it was done. "I think that's doable."

"Very well," Limm'ta said. "I'll make the arrangements. As soon as we're docked we can take the *Maru* down to the surface and you can start meeting our people."

Then again, maybe a nap won't be happening after all, Beka thought.

The quality of light on Ishidrum's surface was the first thing Dylan noticed when they disembarked from the *Maru*. It was thin and pale, like a winter's afternoon back home. Festival's second sun was visible in the sky only as a tiny, flat disk, and its rays barely reached the planet at all, providing just enough extra light to brighten the shadows a touch, making even the deepest of shadows a heavy gray instead of pure black. The difference was subtle, but Dylan found his gaze moving about the landscape that greeted them, as if the light were picking out individual spots—light green leaves against the dark background of a shaded forest; the off-white of a smooth spire reaching toward the indigo sky; the arc of a ship streaking toward a landing—to highlight for the visitor's eye.

Apparently it—or something else—struck Trance favorably as well. "It's beautiful," she said with an audible gasp.

Through a stifled yawn, Beka agreed. "Nice."

"Thank you," Limm'ta said cheerfully. "Coming home is always an occasion for joy, even when I've only been away for a short while."

Dylan guessed that was probably true for most people. It hadn't been an option for him for a long time, and it never would be again. Not unless he adopted a new homeworld. *Andromeda* was the closest thing he had to a home, and while he did feel a certain comfort when he got back to the ship after being away from her, she was not simply home—she was place of work, transportation, combat machine, and more, all wrapped up in a sleek, shiny surface. She could never be *just* home.

While he could only understand Limm'ta's feelings on an intellectual level, all it took was a glance at her to know that she was not exaggerating. Her broad smile was genuine, unforced, and infectious. She had not looked this happy since he had met her—there was even a new bounce to her step, as if walking on home soil gave her a buoyancy that she didn't have in space. "Oh," she said—not a word, so much as just a small noise of pleasure, one she might have uttered while making love or having a particularly wonderful dream. Dylan followed her gaze and saw a pair of women running toward them, equally brilliant smiles on their faces.

"Friends of yours?" he asked.

"That's Anja and Yeye," Limm'ta replied. "They're my sisters."

"More descendants of Sani?"

She giggled. "Not sisters of the blood," she corrected. "Sisters of the spirit."

"I see," Dylan said. He thought maybe he did, but he wasn't sure. He wasn't about to ask Limm'ta, however, because she had already broken into a run herself. The strange, thin light caught her golden hair as she dashed to meet her sisters.

Friends, he mentally amended. *Whatever.*

Later, they sat on Limm'ta's back porch. Her home was small but comfortable and gracious. Touches of her style and her history resonated throughout the house: images of old Tarn-Vedra, including a flexi of Sani Nax Rifati that Dylan had never seen, sitting on the side of a mountain in civilian clothing, looking out over an incredible vista of peaks and forests; candles and bells and books; a swath of a rich blue fabric hanging from a corner of the ceiling like a frozen waterfall, merely because she liked the color.

The porch furniture was among the most welcoming Dylan had ever experienced. It was constructed according to some local tradition, of woven reeds and silken fabrics, and made him feel as if he was sitting on a warm, enveloping cloud. He sat in the balmy evening air with Limm'ta and her friends, watching a thousand self-illuminating insects flitting around her yard as if echoing the millions of stars overhead, their light made all the stronger, somehow, by the faintness of Ishidrum's sole moon. Rommie's avatar sat with them. Beka slept inside, while Rev Bem, Tyr, Trance, and Harper were out exploring, although they had promised to stay together and not to repeat the disaster that had happened in Gala.

"Listen to that," Dylan said to no one in particular.

"To what?" Anja asked. She and Yeye were both about Limm'ta's age. All three were fit and healthy and, Dylan had noted with appreciation, quite lovely. "All I hear are bugs and a breeze rustling the trees."

"Exactly," Dylan said happily. "On *Andromeda*—and no offense, Rommie, but it's true—there is almost never a time that you can't hear something man-made. Ticking, humming, beeping, clicking, whirring . . . there seems to always be some kind of sound everywhere you go. But this . . . this is like some kind of paradise."

"Dylan, I had no idea you were such a *kludge* at heart," Rommie said. "A neo-Luddite starship captain."

"I think it's kind of sweet," Yeye offered. "The big-time space captain really wants nothing more than to retire to the backwater planet."

"I can think of worse fates," Dylan said. "I assume there are those who would object to the characterization of Ishidrum as a backwater?"

"No one whose opinion matters to us," Anja replied.

"Do you speak for the planetary government? *Is* there even a planetary government?" Limm'ta had said she lived in the "city" of Coramus, but Dylan had been hard pressed to see anything he would have described as a city. Quiet, winding lanes led between patches of lush forest, connecting one house to another to another. Every now and then there was a shop or two, but he never saw anything that looked like a central city. The entire population of Coramus, he suspected, could have fit into a single square block of Gala. Maybe a single building.

All three women laughed at that question. "There is no planetary government here," Limm'ta explained. "There are various local governments, which sometimes get along and sometimes don't. A planetary government, however, would require a degree of cooperation that we have not yet attained."

"What is your official role, then?" Dylan queried.

The women laughed again, harder and longer this time. Dylan enjoyed their merriment, but would have liked it better if he'd gotten the joke, or known he was making one in the first place. Finally, Limm'ta came up for air, her cheeks flushed and eyes sparkling with moisture. "I guess you might say I'm an official pain in the ass," she suggested. Dylan raised an eyebrow at the crudity—surprising for someone who usually spoke with such formality. *She lets her guard down when she's among friends*, he speculated.

"I'm sure there must be a nicer word for it," Anja said when she was able to catch her breath. "Gadfly, maybe. Activist."

"You're not some kind of revolutionary?" Dylan asked. "Havasu seemed to think you were. He called you a dangerous criminal."

Yeye snorted. "He would. Limm'ta has been called the 'conscience of Coramus.' That's an appellation that I would be proud to carry, especially when it tweaks half-wits like Havasu."

Limm'ta wouldn't meet Dylan's eye, but instead watched one of the glittering insects zoom across the yard. "I try to remind people why they've chosen a particular path," she said. "When it's a good path, sometimes they need to have the reasons pointed out to them. When it's not, then they often have to have their mistakes pointed out. The latter is less often appreciated, however."

Dylan realized he should have asked her in the first place. She had spoken as if she held some official position, though, as if she represented Ishidrum's populace in some way.

Maybe she does, he decided. *Not every representative has to have a title or an office. I've dealt with worse people than consciences.*

He decided to withhold judgment, at least for now, and see what tomorrow would bring.

———

In the morning, Harper went surfing.

The night before, Rev Bem had involved them in a conversation with three portly fellows who sat in a saloon, nursing tall glasses of some violet-colored beverage that steamed just a little after every sip. They had discussed matters of the spirit, which Rev Bem had found fascinating. But right before Harper suggested to Trance and Tyr that they leave the Magog with his new friends and go look for more stimulating conversation elsewhere, the subject had somehow turned to the water just off the coast of Coramus. It had started, Harper recalled, as a metaphor that he had hardly paid attention to, but he had quickly taken an interest as it became a little more concrete.

"Each wave is perfectly sculpted," one of the men had said. "Because each is sculpted by hands that are not our own. And yet, each one is a little different. Each set is organized the same way—starting small, then building, building, building to a shattering crescendo, and then tapering off again. And yet, each set is also a little different—the tall faces of varying heights, the breaks coming in slightly different spots, the curl changing as the day goes on."

"Wait a minute," Harper had said. "Are you talking about some kinda imaginary sets—you know, out there in the oceans of spiritual grace or something?"

"No," another one answered. "Of course not. He's describing the waves here. In Coramus."

"Limm'ta mentioned waves, but I was afraid maybe she was kidding. You're not kidding, right?"

All three men chuckled at that, and probably at the look—something between excitement and confusion, no doubt—that Harper guessed crossed his face as he asked.

"There are no better waves anywhere," the first man said.

"Ever been to Waimea Bay?"

"To what?"

"Never mind," Harper said. "What time does the surf come up?"

The men had recommended that he be out on the water with his board twenty minutes after sunrise. He had yawned, already regretting not having gone to bed when Beka had. But then he might never have known where to catch the waves, so it was a fair trade-off. When morning came he had a Sparky Cola, washed it down with another one, and then went to the spot the men had described.

They were right. The waves were perfect. The water, beyond the break point, was almost glassy. And it was warm; not quite hot shower warm, but comfortable, ten degrees or so below his body temperature. He could sit out there on the board all day, waiting for the biggest waves as they came around like clockwork in those well-planned sets.

The best ones always started with the eleventh wave, he determined. He counted them down, letting the others slide by. Eleven through sixteen were the keepers. After that, they started to dwindle to twenty-one, and then a new set started.

He counted. Nine. Ten was almost a winner—it was bigger than most of the waves he'd ridden in his life. But he let it go past, and knew he'd made the right choice when eleven started to build.

He pointed the nose of his longboard toward the shore and began to paddle.

The wave built beneath him, lifting him off the surface of the water like an elevator, or a giant, invisible hand. As it took him, his speed increased exponentially. He made it to his feet, and felt the wind and spray and weak sunlight, and then he started to skid down the face of the wave, two meters, three, four. At six, he started to get a little nervous.

The top of the wave was curling in toward him, and he was still hurtling toward the shore at a speed that seemed to rival a Slip-fighter's. A second later he was jetting through a pipeline as the wave wrapped around him. But the end of the pipeline, he saw, was closing fast. He made himself as small as he could on the board. The water thundered, deafening.

Finally, the pipeline collapsed, Harper still inside it.

The board shot away from him. He tried to pound at the water, reaching for the surface, but it took him and shoved him under just as surely as if the same giant hand that had lifted him before was trying to drown him. He spun and twisted and turned, tried again to grab air, but just got a fistful of sand and rocks from the bottom, then felt more sand and rocks slamming against him as he was scraped along it.

Finally, choking, sputtering, and spewing, he broke into the air. He bled from at least a dozen spots, and though none of his bones had been broken, he knew he would wish his neck had been because then he wouldn't feel the aches and pains that would be with him for the rest of the day. Or at least until Trance hyposprayed them away.

If she felt generous.

Harper found his board and started to straggle in toward the beach, and it was only then that he saw Trance—and Dylan, Beka, Tyr, Rev Bem, Rommie, and their Ishidrumian hosts—sitting on the sand watching him. He smiled, waved, and turned crimson all at the same time. His entire extended shipboard family had observed his worst wipeout ever.

And he had loved every minute of it.

TWENTY-TWO

"Figure out what you truly want, and you'll learn what you need.
The reverse, I regret to say, doesn't work."

—HER IMPERIAL HIGH MAJESTY, QUEEN DRAKKA
IBN SALUSHIR, AT THE GROUNDBREAKING
CEREMONY FOR HER THIRTY-SECOND PALACE

Cam Prezennetti sat in his office, trying to create.

He had developed hundreds of campaigns over the years. The work came naturally to him, and he enjoyed the creative process. It wasn't enough to just come up with a catchy slogan, although he had known people who had specialized in such things. But he took a more integrated, holistic approach to a campaign. He liked to be involved in every aspect: product design, packaging, test marketing, product rollout, publicity, advertising, media placement. Others were delighted simply to see one of their slogans on an illuminated sign, but Cam wanted to watch someone buy and eat a Sticky Bar, for instance, and know that the reason the act took place at all was because of a hundred decisions he had made, going back a year or more.

That, he had long ago decided, was what separated the real professionals from the dilettantes. Cam would never be content to be a small cog in a big machine. He wanted to *be* the machine, or at least to run it. That motivation was why he was here today, working on what he had come to think of as the Commonwealth account—except that it was His Regency who was the client, and not the Commonwealth itself.

But the Commonwealth was the product, and he had made good progress. He already had a multiplanet press operation going. Journalists for media outlets across all the Festival worlds had been alerted and received regular updates, each one highlighting some particular aspect of the story Cam wanted them to tell. They learned about Dylan Hunt's history and his heroic, single-handed quest to restore the Systems Commonwealth. That was a hook on which a lot of stories could be hung. They learned about Efreld Havasu's enthusiastic reception to the idea of the Restored Commonwealth, and that was followed up by stories detailing the equally delighted responses of important figures on their own worlds. Most of those responses Cam had written himself, and the respective public figures didn't know they had uttered them until they read about them or heard them broadcast. That didn't matter, though; they would not deny having said the words, knowing their real origin.

And the ads were starting to hit, as well. Billboards, vehicle ads, broadcast ads, and more. Many featured well-known individuals from outside politics: athletes, entertainers, noted intellectuals discoursing on how fervently they believed in Commonwealth membership.

There was still much to be done, though, and Cam was finding it hard to concentrate on his immediate problems. Ashala's face kept popping up in the forefront of his thoughts. Followed closely by Ashala's equally pleasing body. The other day, after their fountain meeting, had been more than delightful—it had been, he was convinced, the singularly most perfect physical encounter he had ever had. Ashala was beautiful and sexy and oh so skilled.

As afternoon wore into evening, they had sat together in bed, sheets pulled up around their middles, and talked. By that point he was in favor of talking, too exhausted by far to do anything more strenuous. She had brought up the subject of Havasu, and he had raised a question he'd been afraid to know the answer to.

"What would His Regency do, do you suppose, if he knew that you were here with me? Like this?"

Ashala chuckled and ran a finger across the tips of her naked breasts. "Like this? I'm not sure. I don't imagine he would be delighted, though."

"I wouldn't expect delighted, either," Cam said. "But homicidal?"

She pursed her lips and looked at him before answering. "Maybe. Not so much, I think, because he would be jealous or overly possessive of me. I don't think he values me highly enough for that. But in the abstract, the idea that you were making use of something that he considered to be his property: that would disturb him, possibly enough to be homicidal."

"You don't think he values you? He thinks of you as just one more possession?"

"I'm under no illusions, Cam, about my importance to Efreld. I'm a plaything, an amusement. Easily forgotten, more easily replaced. Nothing special."

"You're very special," he argued. "Special to me."

He thought he detected a faint blush coloring her cheeks. "You're a very nice man," she said. "And a more than adequate lover. But—and I don't mean this in a bad way—you're not the kind of man who could have literally any partner on numerous planets, just by crooking a finger or saying a word. He's spoiled, and as a result, his attention span is short. I am one of many women, probably hundreds or thousands he's had. It's a miracle that I've remained in his favor this long. I certainly don't think I will for much longer."

Cam could hardly believe what she was saying. Of course, he

had known Havasu long enough to know that everything she said was true. The man had a long, well documented history.

But Ashala—she was a creature of such exquisite feminine perfection, he thought surely Havasu would never tire of her. Maybe she was selling herself short, underestimating her own appeal. She was probably basing her opinion solely on Havasu's history without taking into account her own uniqueness.

Now he tried to work on the Commonwealth campaign, but another campaign kept crowding it out of his thoughts. The two warred with each other; he couldn't have both, he was becoming increasingly sure. The Commonwealth campaign would cement his reputation and secure his fortune. When Festival had expanded its power base and Havasu ruled the entire Systems Commonwealth as he did his own local planetary system, Cam would have earned his undying friendship and support. Everything he'd spent his life dreaming of would be within his grasp.

Everything except one. Because now he knew that his goals hadn't included the most important thing; the ideal partner with which to share his successes. His previous marriages had been mere dalliances compared to how this one would be. He wanted— he needed—to be with Ashala, more than he wanted anything else. More, he was beginning to believe, than he even wanted the Commonwealth campaign to succeed.

If Havasu dominated known space, there might be no place to which Cam could escape with Ashala. But if he turned his sights away from figuring how best to sell the Commonwealth, and instead worked on a campaign to convince Ashala to go away with him, he knew that he could be poor but happy somewhere far away.

Poor but happy. A strange concept, one he'd never have believed in before.

Oddly, he thought that maybe it could work.

———

After watching Harper come out of the water—scraped, battered, and red-faced, but laughing—Trance wandered away from the others, fascinated by the scraggly trees that grew at the edge of the dunes. Their shaggy trunks were bent and twisted, their needled branches reaching inland as if blown by a ferocious wind, when in fact the breeze was light, scented with salt from the water and tart sap from the trees themselves. She picked one and approached it, letting her fingertips trace lines on its trunk, feeling the rough bark through its almost furry outer layer.

This was why she had been so discombobulated in Gala, she decided. Because there had been no plants growing there, nothing erupting from fertile earth. Her ability to read probability paths wasn't tied to nature, but her sanity was. Things that took root, that sprouted, that stretched toward sun, kept her grounded in some way.

After communing with the trees for a while, she moved on to the grasses, tall and hardy, that grew from the sandy soil. She walked among them, leaning over from time to time to caress their stalks, at other times brushing them with her tail. They ranged in color from whitish-gray to a deep, almost purplish blue, and their scent was dry and peppery. Wildflowers blooming yellow and orange and a red so intense it was hard to look at spiked up among the grasses. The thunder of the ocean was broken here by the shrill cries of leathery winged creatures hovering around the wildflowers, then darting away with a squawk whenever Trance came too near.

The beach had sloped gradually up from the water, cresting at the tree line, and then sloping down again, less gradually, into a wooded plain. Trance followed the grass and occasional trees down to where the trees grew thicker. Here they were taller, less gnarled by wind and weather, and—protected from the offshore breeze by the slope—their branches drooped more or less symmetrically all around the trunk, instead of being shoved in a single direction. Here, too, the smells of the trees themselves were stronger than the ocean's scent—pungent aromas from the sap leaking out of trunks, from the needles, from the decaying masses of trees that had fallen to the ground and now fertilized their sisters.

Trance sat on the trunk of one of the fallen trees, in a small clearing. *It must be nice to be a tree in a place like this*, she thought. The progression of life was so simple, so direct. A seed germinates, sprouting a tiny root that burrows into the ground looking for water and sustenance. A skinny trunk pushes up out of the dirt, seeking sunlight. The trunk grows, the roots spread. Eventually branches form, and leaves or needles. Finally, with maturity, the tree drops seeds to create new life and shades those new growths with the spread of its own branches. In death, it falls to the ground and the nutrients it has built up over time feed its own great grandchildren.

There were always other possibilities, other risks, she knew. A bird might eat the seed before it had a chance to sprout. Some animal might strip the sapling or uproot it. Woodcutters might chop the tree down in its prime and carry it away, depriving its offspring of its resources.

But more trees lived out their natural cycles—in this place, and others like it—than didn't. That alone made Ishidrum a more pleasant spot than Festival, in Trance's book.

She was sitting there still, lost in contemplation, when the cracking of a fallen branch brought her back into the world. Looking up, she saw Rev Bem smiling his toothy Magog grin at her. "Hi," she said, greeting him cheerfully.

"I had expected to be alone here," Rev Bem said.

"I can go somewhere else."

"No, that is not necessary," he assured her. He slowly lowered his massive bulk down onto the fallen trunk, a couple of meters from Trance. She felt it shift under his weight. "I did not mean to say that I required solitude, merely that I anticipated it."

"Oh, okay," she said.

"I completely understand why you are here," he said. "It's a wonderful spot for meditation, isn't it?"

"Yes," Trance said. "That's what I've been doing. Meditatin' my little head off."

Rev Bem chuckled, a sight that would terrify the inhabitants of at least a thousand planets, Trance knew. Jokes were not usually his long suit. "And yet it seems to still be attached," he replied. "Demonstrating the healing properties of solitude and adherence to the Way, no doubt."

"No doubt. I do like it here, though."

"As do I. This seems to be a peaceful place, where quiet is valued, and where opportunities for solitary contemplation are many."

"Yeah," Trance agreed. "Seems like. Too bad you didn't make it down to Festival, just so you'd get the full contrast."

The Magog shuddered. "Totally unnecessary, I assure you. The image of Festival I carry in my mind is more than sufficient for purposes of contrast."

"And even Transitory Primus was different," Trance went on. "More like this in terms of its setting, its natural environment. But the mood was so different. . . ."

"The overwhelming emotion on that planet was fear," Rev Bem said. "At least, that is what I noticed. Afraid of what, I cannot say with any certainty. Each other, perhaps. Certainly afraid of the Festival soldiers who were so omnipresent."

"With good reason," Trance said. "Harper and I saw them beating up one of the locals. We were going to say something about it, but by the time we caught up to the rest of you, we were all being shot at. I guess it kind of slipped our mind then."

"Gunfire has a way of focusing one's attention on the here and now," Rev Bem admitted.

"That it does. It seems like gunfire is pretty rare on Ishidrum, which is a good thing. But if Limm'ta is right, if Festival is trying to militarily dominate every planet in the system—and this is the only one they haven't taken over yet—then it would seem like Ishidrum would have the *most* to fear," Trance suggested.

"Perhaps," Rev Bem agreed. "But also the most hope, and the most to cherish. People living under the thumb of armed rule are steeped in fear, dwell in it from the moment they awaken to the time they finally drift off to troubled slumber. Here no one has to fear their own leaders, and even though they understand the possible threat from Festival, they don't obsess over it. They take steps to maintain their independence. In freedom there is peace and possibility, and that keeps people happy."

"Keeps me happy," Trance admitted. "I can see why other people would like it too."

Rev Bem sat quietly for a moment, his breathing even, his eyes closed. When Trance was starting to wonder if he had fallen asleep, he opened them again. "Now I do need a few minutes alone," he said. "I can find another spot, if you would like."

"No, that's okay," Trance answered. "You stay here. I'm going to keep wandering anyway. I saw some pink and green flowers not far away that I wanted to pay a visit to."

"Very well," Rev Bem said. "I am glad you're happy here, Trance."

"Happy's just about always better than not happy," she said, standing up from the fallen log. She tossed him a smile and headed off into the trees. This really was a world she thought she could learn to love.

Dylan and Limm'ta rested together on the beach after everyone else had left. The times in his adult life that Dylan had been able to do nothing but sit and relax—not counting the three hundred years at the edge of a black hole, because those had passed as if in the blink of an eye for him—were so rare that he could count them on his digits, probably without even having to kick off his boots. But there was something about Ishidrum, some quality to the pace of life, that encouraged such things. The crash of the waves and the warmth of the sun lulled him; the sand, ground fine by the thundering surf, was as soft and inviting as any pillow.

He was lying on his back, head cradled in his hands, Limm'ta sitting up beside him, when he broached the subject that had been on his mind since the night before. "So what's next? Where do we go from here?"

"In terms of . . . ?"

"In terms of inviting Ishidrum into the Commonwealth," he said. "That's why I'm here, right?"

Limm'ta laughed. "Of course it is. We will gather together the leaders of the various nations for a summit meeting. I can already tell you that there will be a wide range of opinions, and most likely some loud and heated arguments. But you are a very persuasive man, and I'm sure you will win them over."

"In other words, more speeches," Dylan grumbled. "More diplomacy."

"Which is what you are so good at," she said.

"People keep saying that about me. But it's a lot of wishful thinking. I've always been better at doing things than talking about them." That sense, in fact, went all the way back to Dylan's earliest memories, one of which involved him trying to persuade his parents to let him keep, as a pet, a thronic lizard that he had found in the gardens of Etashi Tarn's Imperial Museum.

His father, a groundskeeper there, was in favor of letting the boy have the lizard, as long as he promised to keep it fed and to keep its viciously sharp claws trimmed. But his mother, who as a shuttle pilot spent as much time offworld as on, disagreed. The thing would be a nuisance and a danger, she insisted, and anyway, it was a wild animal, not meant to be domesticated.

"I will take good care of him," young Dylan had moaned when she demanded the creature be removed from the house at once. "I won't let him eat anything he's not supposed to except your other pink sock, because he already ate one of them! I won't let him scratch anybody until they bleed,"—at this point, Dylan moved his own arm behind his body so she couldn't get a good look at the claw tracks on it—"and if he has babies I'll take care of them too."

Looking back, Dylan decided he should have known then that he was not cut out for diplomacy. He had lost the lizard and was punished for letting it into his mother's bedroom in the first place. Later, he'd realized that his mother had made the right call, and his father—always more open and interested in the natural world than she—should have known that a thronic lizard would make a terrible pet.

Dylan loved both his parents and considered his childhood as happy as childhood could be, but there had been a kind of constant tension between his mother, who couldn't stay put for more than a few hours without getting twitchy, and his father, who would have been content to just live in the gardens that he so carefully tended.

"I'm sure you exaggerate, Dylan," Limm'ta said. "I think you could talk just about anybody into just about anything."

"Like I said, wishful thinking."

"We shall see," she countered. "It really is the only way to proceed. No single faction on Ishidrum is powerful enough to speak for the whole. But if you can convince a plurality, then the others will come around. We value reasonableness above almost all else, and no one wants to be thought of as intransigent. But the people you will encounter do have strong beliefs about what is best for Ishidrum. My guess is that opinion is fairly evenly divided right now, with perhaps a slim margin in favor of the Commonwealth. But that would be very slim, so you will need to do some persuading."

"I'll do what I can," Dylan promised. He knew that in sheer numerical terms, it would make more sense to focus on getting the entire Festival System on board, and letting Ishidrum join or not, as it pleased. But the points Limm'ta had raised about the way Festival treated the rest of the worlds under its sway as mere satellites, to be ruled from afar with an iron fist, concerned him.

And Ishidrum, he believed, was vital for more reasons than just its own potential membership. He'd been mulling over an idea for a while, ever since meeting Limm'ta, in fact, and he decided that the time had come to bring it up.

"There might be something you can do, too," he began.

"What is that?"

"As a descendant of Sani Nax Rifati," he said, "your word would carry a lot of weight in my mission. You speaking out about the Commonwealth would almost legitimize it in a way that nobody else possibly could. When you get right down to it, I'm nothing. I'm just a High Guard officer with a big ship and a nostalgia for the way things were when I was a young man. But do I bring any real intellectual weight to the argument, or any emotional resonance? Maybe a little, because of my long snooze. Makes a good story, anyway. But you . . . the emotional impact alone of you making a pro-Commonwealth pitch would be enormous. What do you think—travel the galaxies, see lots of pretty sights, and help further your ancestor's dream at the same time? Sound good?"

Limm'ta didn't answer right away. That was for the best—if she had, he wouldn't have believed she had given the question proper consideration. Instead, she drew designs in the sand with her finger. Finally, she looked at Dylan. "I have given that very idea a great deal of thought," she admitted. "Ever since I heard about you and what you were trying to accomplish. It has a huge appeal to me, for many reasons."

She drew in a deep breath, blew it out in a sigh. "But I don't think I can. No, that's not right. I don't think I *should*."

The degree of disappointment Dylan felt surprised him. He hadn't thought he was pinning a lot of hopes on what was admittedly a half-baked idea, but maybe he had been just the same. "Why not?"

"I . . . I think that I am needed here, on Ishidrum. I feel that my impact is greatest here, where I am known and have achieved some measure of respect. I need to maintain my focus, to keep my goals practical and attainable. If I were to join you I fear that I would be forced into a kind of symbolic role, a figurehead. But in so doing, I would become just a small part of a big effort. I would lose myself."

"That's not necessarily true," Dylan objected.

"No, not necessarily. But probably. Knowing myself as I do, it seems to be the likeliest result. I like to get my hands dirty, Dylan, to dig in the muck of conflict. I like to go to politicians, to knock on their doors and make them listen to me. I would not have that luxury anymore."

"I've knocked on plenty of doors," Dylan insisted. "Knocked a few of them down, too."

"I am sure that you have. But I . . . I like to know when I knock that whoever answers it knows who I am—not what I stand for, but who I truly am. If that person knows I am someone of consequence, someone who is serious and whose word is her bond, then my argument is met with proper consideration."

"I'm sure your word is highly regarded every place," Dylan said.

"Only here on Ishidrum. To the rest of the universe, Limm'ta Nax Terani is a nonentity. Unlike Dylan Hunt, whose fame is widespread."

Dylan wanted to object, but in fact, she had a point. He had never heard of her until her distress call from the *Argent*. In spite of his own meager notoriety, and his well-known admiration of her famous ancestor, no one had ever told him of her existence. He supposed that just buttressed her contention; by working here on Ishidrum, she was able to make a significant difference, but her impact might be diffused if she tried to expand the range of her influence.

"Not a nonentity," he said at last. "Simply someone they haven't had the pleasure of encountering yet."

"Pleasure?" she repeated. "Are you sure?"

"Absolutely," Dylan answered. He realized suddenly how close their faces had become, without him even noticing, as if they had been drawn together magnetically. The rest of the world had receded into the far distance; the rush of the surf, the rustle of the ocean breeze through the trees, the warmth of the day were all deep background, and only Limm'ta filled his senses. Limm'ta's eyes were half shut, her full lips moist and parted slightly. Pretty sure that she would not object, he gently pressed his own against them.

She did not, in fact, object.

TWENTY-THREE

> "To vacation someplace that you'd like to live, or live someplace
> that you'd like to vacation, is sure to invite disappointment all
> the way around."
>
> —CORNELIUS T. BARKE, "LIFE'S LESSONS
> LEARNED," CY 6774

Tyr was not especially surprised that Harper, Trance, and Rev
Bem loved this planet so much, because he *hated* it.

Even when he had been a slave, toiling away in the diamond
mines of Xochityl—though the work had been brutally hard,
mindless, backbreaking labor—he had never been so bored. Nothing happened here, it seemed.

Ever.

The only possible advantage this place had was that there were
precious few threats to one's survival—unless the phrase "deadly
dull" was, in fact, not a cliché but a genuine possibility. Since they
had landed here, no one had fired at him, swung a fist or shot a
tentacle at him, or otherwise made any attempt to cause him bodily harm. He had eaten well, had helped himself to a variety of
beverages, had taken long walks and sat on the beach and eaves-
dropped on conversations about a vast number of different topics.

Lots of conversations.

No action.

He tried to tell himself that it was a welcome respite from always having someone trying to kill him. And in a way, it was. But there was no one, at least so far as he could see, trying to do much of anything. To anyone. A lot of chatting, a lot of quiet alone time, and not much else. He was pretty sure even Harper was getting tired of surfing perfect waves. If not, there was more wrong with that *kludge* of an engineer than Tyr had previously believed. Only someone like Rev Bem—or perhaps Trance—could possibly be content in a place like this for more than a week.

As for himself, if they stayed here that long, he would certainly go insane.

And when he did, then things would start to happen. A berserk Nietzschean was just what they needed around here to spice things up a bit. Hell, bring in half a dozen berserk Nietzscheans and the place would become interesting enough to stick around for a while.

To be honest, one of the conversations he'd found himself involved in had at least been somewhat interesting. He had been in a small café with Harper and Beka, and they'd been chatting with the folks at the next table over, and somehow the talk had turned to Festival's dominion over all the other worlds in this system except for Ishidrum. Tyr had wondered if those living on the dominated planets understood their situation, and if people on Ishidrum valued their freedom from it.

"Definitely," the woman sitting there had said. Two men and a woman occupied that table, and they'd been sitting there before the group from *Andromeda* had come in. The woman had long silver hair, and wore a blue satin dress with threads of silver that might have come from her own head woven through it. "At least, definitely for our part. I've never traveled to the other planets, so I can't say for sure if they feel like they live in occupied territory, or if it's just the way it's always been for them. But here, we're grateful every day for our freedom."

"One thing confuses me," Tyr said. "I have not seen much i the way of defensive capability here. Why has Festival not simpl moved in with overwhelming force and taken the planet over, i they are as determinedly imperialist as you all seem to believe?"

"I can answer that," one of the men said. He was a heavy fellov carrying the weight of at least two of Harper around on his frame and his face was flushed. "They just haven't got around to it ye We're far away, we're small, we're barely significant to them. won't be unless we make a fuss that they'll make the effort."

"So you're, like, not raising your hand in class, and hoping th teacher doesn't notice you didn't do your homework?" Harper asked

"Crude, but essentially appropriate," the woman replied.

"That's our Harper," Beka put in. "Especially the crude par Not so much the appropriate, but it does happen once in a while.

"Seems like an unpleasant way to live," Tyr observed. "Like a Anakaran field mouse cowering in fear, hoping a winged predato flies past without stopping for him."

"Why is that analogy better than mine?" Harper queried.

"Because it is," Tyr offered.

"I don't think it's quite that way," the second man argued. Thi one was leaner than the first, and probably a few years older, hi skin covered with a patina of tiny lines, like parchment. "We valu our freedom, but that doesn't mean we live in fear."

"But if you don't take measures to guarantee your freedom, Beka suggested, "isn't that almost a guarantee that it will be taker from you?"

"I'm sure measures are taken," the woman said. "We just don know what they are."

"For your sake, you had better hope the same is not being saic by everybody else on the planet," Tyr said. "Or you will all fin yourself taken by surprise someday."

The conversation had turned to more mundane matters afte that, and Tyr had found himself quickly growing bored with it Bored, as he had been for so much of their brief stay on Ishidrum

Now he stood by the edge of the sea and fumed. He picked up a smooth, flat stone, and hurled it into the water, where it skipped nine times before it sank. Nine—that was an improvement of two over the last seven rocks he had thrown. When he hit an even dozen, he would knock off and find something else to pass the time.

He hated this place.

To Rommie, it seemed like Dylan and Limm'ta were spending an awful lot of time together. She didn't want to spy on him—well, she *wanted* to, but he was her captain and she was an honorable warship and she wouldn't, unless she felt that she really, really had to. But she was concerned, and because feelings like jealousy were still relatively new to her, she decided to seek advice from the only female she could think of who was somewhat emotionally stable and not a flighty purple Pixie.

She found Beka sitting on Limm'ta's back porch with a book. It was the old-fashioned kind, with pages that one turned by hand as one read the words. Beka had her idiosyncrasies, Rommie realized—she loved her old CDs of ancient Earth music, and she was even willing to indulge in such an antiquarian pastime as reading books.

Rommie pasted a carefully prepared smile on her face and sat down next to Beka.

"Hi, Rommie."

"Hello, Beka," she said.

"What's shakin'?"

Rommie glanced about quickly, in case Beka was speaking literally and not just using the old idiomatic expression. "I was wondering if you could give me some advice," she said.

Beka shrugged. "Don't ever believe anything my brother Rafe tells you. Don't use Flash. Don't try to negotiate Slipstream with your eyes closed, or under the influence of Castalian ale."

"I meant about something a little more specific," Rommie said. "But thanks. Did you—that part about the Slipstream?"

Beka shut her eyes as if she was afraid of seeing it again. "Yeah," she said. "Horrendously bad idea."

"That was on the *Maru*," Rommie guessed.

"No. *Andromeda*."

Rommie felt a little shiver of terror run up her spine. "I didn't know—"

"I didn't want you to," Beka told her. "Anyway, it worked out okay. I kept it under control. It was just . . . kind of stupid. But you know how it is. Liquid courage. Drink just enough to make you think you can do anything, when in fact your response time, reactions, and judgment are all seriously impaired. Or maybe you don't know how it is. But trust me. Actually, I did both of those at once—when I realized what a bad idea it was to try to fly with that stuff in me, I closed my eyes. Very scary."

"I'm sure it was," Rommie said. "And I think I have an idea of how you felt, given that my systems are all impaired as well. We need to get Harper off his surfboard and back up to the ship so he can keep working on me."

"That would be an excellent idea," Beka agreed. "We can't stay here forever. Limm'ta doesn't have enough books to last me more than a couple of months."

"It is . . . peaceful here, isn't it? But that's not what I came to ask you about."

Beka inserted a bookmark between the pages and closed her book carefully. It must have been centuries old, Rommie knew, but had been maintained in good condition. "What, then?" Beka asked.

Rommie couldn't think of a subtle way to phrase it, so she just blurted it out. "Do you think Dylan is spending too much time with Limm'ta Nax Terani?"

"Too much time?" A smile slowly spread across Beka's face. "You're jealous?"

"No. I am a Glorious Heritage class heavy cruiser, Beka. I don't get jealous."

"You're also a highly advanced artificial intelligence," Beka reminded her. "Constantly growing, changing, and evolving, just like people do. Who's to say that doesn't also affect your . . . emotional life? Leading to things like jealousy."

"That's absurd," Rommie insisted.

"Is it? Your emotions are just as real as any other part of you, Rommie. You can't deny them. Anyway, weren't you and Dylan—I thought you two were—"

"That's equally absurd," Rommie said, getting what Beka was driving at. "First of all, he is my captain. Fraternization in that way is strictly forbidden by High Guard rules and regulations. I can, of course, quote chapter and verse if you'd like me to."

"That's not necessary," Beka said, waving her off. "But I was pretty sure . . ."

"Dylan and I have a very close working relationship," Rommie admitted. "We have, over time, become good friends. Nothing more than that is allowable or acceptable."

"So if he offered, you wouldn't—"

"He would not offer!" Rommie declared. She wondered if she was pushing back too hard, since Beka had already floated this theory once. Her memory banks recalled plenty of references to those who protested too much. She lowered her voice, speaking less emphatically. "And no, I would not accept. I am simply concerned that—"

"That Dylan is spending too much time with an attractive young lady," Beka finished.

"That Dylan is putting the overall mission on hold for a dalliance with this local person," Rommie corrected her. "That he's letting Harper surf while he should be working on repairs. My maintenance nanobots are doing what they can, but there's only so much they can accomplish. I need Harper on a lot of it. And I'm concerned that we are whiling away our time here when we should be continuing our visits to the other planets in the Festival system."

"Have you asked him about it?"

"I haven't," Rommie admitted. "I don't know how to bring it up without risking the same kind of response I just got from you. I don't want him to think it's jealousy that's motivating me, or—"

"Well," Beka interrupted, "then you'd better make damn sure it's not."

"Beka, I—"

"Remember who you're talking to, Rommie. I'm not Harper or Tyr. I notice the kinds of things they might miss. It's been obvious for a long time that you have kind of a thing for Dylan. There's nothing wrong with that. He's maybe not my type, but he is a nice guy, good looking, strong, healthy, funny, accomplished, great hair . . . okay, maybe he is my type. Except that I usually seem to go for the bad boys, who usually break my heart because that's what bad boys do. But I can understand why you would feel the way you do."

"The way you believe I do," Rommie corrected. "I haven't agreed to any part of your theory."

Beka shrugged. "You don't need to. I know what I see."

"Beka, the point is, we're wasting time here. Festival has already alerted us that they consider Limm'ta a criminal, and by associating with her, we are earning their displeasure. Dylan might be blind to this, or he may just not care, but the longer we stay here the more he's putting everyone's life in danger."

"You might have a point there," Beka agreed. "If Festival wants to attack us, they could be using this time to mass their ships along the route we'll have to take when we leave. If it was me, that's what I'd be doing, anyway. Either closing in on Ishidrum, which seems somewhat defenseless, or setting up an ambush somewhere nearby."

"Yes, exactly," Rommie said. She had become so caught up in denying what she had come to talk about in the first place that she couldn't see a path back to that subject.

"So you think we should tell Dylan it's time to move on."

"Someone should," Rommie replied. "He probably would listen best if it came from you."

"You think?"

"Of course," Rommie assured her. "You're second in command. You have a lot of influence over him."

"But maybe not as much as Limm'ta."

"Well, that's the challenge, isn't it?" Rommie asked. "That's what we have to overcome."

Limm'ta in bed was every bit as accomplished, graceful, and beautiful as Limm'ta out of bed, and the slightest bit intimidating because of it all. Dylan knew that it would be easy to be too impressed by this woman—and that some of his feelings were certainly a response to who she was, who her ancestor was, rather than just to what she had shown him of herself. At the same time, he was pretty sure that even if she had no family history at all, and was just someone he'd met, he still would have been mightily affected by her.

It had all happened very quickly. He supposed that was partly due to his own time constraints. He couldn't afford to linger too long on Ishidrum, as he still had most of a solar system to visit—if Festival's fleet would let him, now that he'd earned Havasu's displeasure. The kiss on the beach had come on their first full day planetside. They had spent the rest of the evening together, and then the night. Now morning dawned again, their second day here, and he was sitting up in bed looking at her slumbering form and remembering how soft and sure her caresses had been.

As if his gaze had physical weight, she shifted under it, then opened the eye that he could see. Seeing him there, she smiled and turned over, sitting up beside him. The sheet fell away and her unadorned beauty stirred him again.

"Good morning," she said sleepily.

"Good morning," he agreed. "Very good."

"Yes, you are. Did you sleep well?"

"Like a baby," Dylan said. "Thanks."

"I'm glad," she said. "Because you have a busy day ahead of you."

"I do?" This was the first he had heard of that.

"You do. Today's the day you meet with the members of our summit. Did you forget?"

"I knew we were planning to have a summit," Dylan said. "I didn't know it would happen so fast."

"Didn't you want it to? I thought you were in somewhat of a hurry."

"Well, yes. I just . . . didn't know bureaucracy could function so quickly."

"We are not a very bureaucratic society," Limm'ta pointed out. "I know what you mean—in some places, I'm sure, there would have had to be meetings held about where the meeting to plan the summit meeting would be held. Not here. Anja and Yeye made some inquiries, and today representatives of every nation will be here to listen to your presentation."

What presentation? Dylan thought. He would have liked a little advance notice so he could have put something together. Presumably, if he really was meeting with decision makers, they would have seen the speech that had been broadcast out to all of the Festival system's planets. Limm'ta had seen it, after all. Which meant that he couldn't just repeat that, but had to come up with a pitch that was a little more tailored to Ishidrum's particular situation.

Which would be tricky, because Ishidrum seemed to be on the outs with the rest of the system. All in all, this would have been a challenging speech to write and deliver even if he'd had a few days to work on it. With only a few hours available, he would just have to wing it.

"I guess I can throw something together," he said. "How much time do I have?"

"Oh, plenty of time," Limm'ta answered. "They aren't gathering for another hour. What would you like for breakfast?"

Dylan frowned, a distinct sense of déjà vu overtaking him. Why did people always give him so little notice when they wanted him to speak? And what made them think he'd want anything to do with breakfast beforehand?

Next time someone wanted him to give a speech, he would make sure it took place at night. And before dinner.

That didn't seem like too much to ask.

TWENTY-FOUR

"In unity, there is strength, it has been said. That is backward,
however. The truth is, in strength, there is unity."

—NIETZSCHEAN PROVERB

The summit was held in an outside amphitheater, not far from the
beach where Harper had surfed. Dylan didn't know much about
local standards of behavior or attire, but from the looks of things,
Limm'ta had been correct when she'd said that hers was not a very
rigidly bureaucratic society. Even though she spoke with studied
formality in public, most of the two dozen or so leaders gathered
in the amphitheater were decidedly informal. They lounged on the
massive stone blocks that comprised the amphitheater's sides, chatting casually, joking with one another, at times shouting insults and
wisecracks back and forth across the open space. Dylan, who leaned
toward informality himself, wasn't sure how best to bring up a serious subject with this crowd. He caught himself wishing he remembered some of Havasu's stock salesman's jokes.

Limm'ta gave him a quick lesson when she got up to introduce
him. She went down to the center of the amphitheater, on its low-

est level. As she spoke, she turned occasionally, making sure, with nonchalant ease, that she looked at everyone in the place. Dylan noted also that as soon as she reached the center, all conversation ceased. She really did command the respect of these world leaders, it seemed.

"I am here today to introduce to you a most august personage," she said, her sometimes-surprising formality coming to the fore again. "Captain Dylan Hunt of the Restored Commonwealth. Most of you, I am certain, saw Captain Hunt's address from Festival recently, and I can only implore you not to judge him based on that. He was new here in our neighborhood and did not have the advantage of knowing our neighbors from Festival as well as we do."

This earned her a roar of laughter and a smattering of applause. Dylan noticed, however, that a few of the assembled leaders did not respond favorably to her jibe, so he guessed that not everyone on Ishidrum hated Festival with the same passion that she did. Made sense—few consuming hatreds, he had found, were universally shared or completely reasonable.

"At any rate," she continued, "Captain Hunt is here to discuss with us his dream of a Restored Systems Commonwealth, and the prospects for Ishidrum's involvement in such an organization. I personally would like to thank Captain Hunt for making this journey to see us—and, for that matter, for rescuing me when I ran into a bit of trouble on my way to fetch him—and I trust that you will all do your best to make him feel welcome as well."

More applause, and then Limm'ta took her seat beside Dylan. "Your turn," she whispered, letting her hand brush against his outer thigh as she sat. He glanced at *Andromeda*'s crew, gathered on the steps around him, and rose. After a light breakfast, bathing, and donning his dress uniform, Dylan hadn't had any time remaining for such things as preparing his remarks. Which made it pretty much the same as the last speech he'd had to give.

He walked down to the center of the amphitheater, knowing he would have to improvise the whole thing: play off the mood of his audience and hope he could hold their interest and maybe sway them. Trouble was, he didn't quite know what it was he was supposed to sway them to. He wanted them to join the Commonwealth, of course. But according to Limm'ta, if Festival ended up joining as well, Ishidrum might well quit. His own personal credibility might take a hit if that happened.

No more time to think about it, he told himself. He had reached the spot from which Limm'ta made her remarks. He was on.

"In the last day or so, I've learned a little bit about Ishidrum," he began. "It's a beautiful place, and I'd love to stay longer and learn more. But the thing is, I'm kind of busy these days. As Limm'ta pointed out to you, I'm doing a lot of traveling, and a little bit of speaking, about a subject that is very important to me. I do appreciate all of you making the effort to come here and let me talk to you, and I wish I had prepared a speech for you. But I didn't, so I'm kind of flying by the seat of my pants here. I'll try to keep it brief, for your sakes as well as my own.

"I've been privileged, as a High Guard officer and as captain of the *Andromeda Ascendant*, to be able to travel to many different places and meet a huge variety of individuals in those places. In that time, in those travels—and with a historical perspective that I've got to think is pretty unique—I've come to some conclusions that I'd like to share with you. First is that people—sentient beings of every type, as far as I can tell—are drawn to one another. Drawn to the idea of community. Discounting a very few complete hermits, here and there, I think pretty much if you drop two people down on an empty planet, they'll find each other and they'll be more comfortable in each other's presence. Drop down two more and they'll start a community. Drop ten more and you'll get a town. That's just how we're wired: we would rather stand together than alone."

Dylan paused, looking out at the faces: old, young, male, female, most recognizably humanoid but some not. They watched

him with polite attention, their clowning and private conversations
set aside for the time being. As he looked at them, he tried to collect his thoughts. For a moment he had known what would come
second, after the "first" he'd already detailed, but then it had vanished. Realizing he was letting the silence go on too long, he struggled to fill it.

"And second is . . . second, there have been, at various times
throughout recorded history, dark ages. Some planetary, some interplanetary, but every civilization has endured them from time to
time. They come, they pass, we move on. In the overall time line
of our history they usually don't last all that long, but they are
clearly disruptive. They put an end to progress, they interrupt civilization, they set us off course and it takes a long time to pick up
the pieces—no, sorry, that's a terribly mixed metaphor. It takes a
long time to find the right path again.

"But the thing is, sentient beings everywhere, even in the dark-
est part of those dark ages, find themselves lighting their candles
against the darkness. We are drawn to community, and we are
drawn to the light. We can't—we *refuse* to live in darkness. Each
time the shadows descend, we take it upon ourselves to rediscover
fire. We reinvent electricity. We relocate the sun."

Dylan allowed himself a brief smile. He was getting on a roll, he
thought. Pretty soon he might actually make some degree of
sense. Or was that too much to hope for?

"I'm going to start sounding like a mathematics instructor in a
moment, because I'm going to be adding my numbered points together to reach some kind of answer. Certainly, I know that I'm
generalizing, that we don't all respond to anything in the same way,
that there are those who prefer the darkness and the solitude and
would be perfectly happy with a planet all to themselves. But they
are the flukes, the oddballs; they are not the norm. The norm, in
my experience, is those who are drawn to community, drawn to the
light.

"What does this have to do with the Systems Commonwealth?

The Commonwealth is the community—the greater community of sentient beings, made up of the populations of inhabited planets everywhere. At least, that's what it was once, before the last dark age. And that's what it will be again. The Commonwealth is the candle against the darkness, the light for which we reach. The Commonwealth's credo is that no one should be alone who doesn't want to be alone. No world should have to function in solitude, set apart from the rest. We prefer to stand together. In unity we find strength, we find companionship, we find power, we find freedom, we find decency, and we find mutual respect. And we find those things because the Commonwealth stands for them.

"The Commonwealth believes that none of us are free until all of us are. The Commonwealth holds that none of us has economic security unless we all do. The Commonwealth insists that unless all its member worlds are kept from harm at the hands of those who would do us violence, none of us are safe.

"By banding together, by seeking unity, by finding community, we can make these things happen. We can extend the hand of friendship to others, we can lift up those who need some help, we can judge ourselves by how we treat those who have the least. We sometimes ask for sacrifices to be made for the greater good, but when we do, you will know that those sacrifices are being made by all, not just by those too powerless to resist.

"The Commonwealth—and this is the beauty of it, really, if you're bored by what I'm saying, at least listen to this—we know that our success isn't complete if one child goes to bed hungry on one distant planet, so even though we have these high-sounding goals, and sometimes we seem to have achieved them, we keep trying. There will never be a point at which the Systems Commonwealth says, 'Okay, we have all the good planets—the wealthy ones, the militarily powerful ones, the ones everybody knows the names of, so we can stop, we can close the ranks and not let anyone else in.'

"The Commonwealth keeps trying. It isn't perfect. It was never perfect the first time around, and I can damn well guarantee you that it won't be this time. That's the thing: it's an evolving, organic process. We know perfection is an unattainable state, but we keep working toward it. Because it's just that important.

"I hope you will give serious consideration to joining the Systems Commonwealth—not necessarily because it's good for Ishidrum, although it will be, but because it might give Ishidrum the chance to do good for someone else. Thank you for your time."

Dylan stopped and began to head back to his seat. A single pair of hands came together in a clap. *Great*, he thought, *I made a complete ass of myself and some joker wants to make sure I know it.* But the hands drew together a second time, and a third, and on the third one they were joined by more. Before Dylan had taken five steps, the entire amphitheater was clapping, on their feet, their approval almost lifting Dylan up like a wave and carrying him to his place at Limm'ta's side.

When he reached her, she was beaming, and she took his hand in hers. "Well done," she said quietly.

Harper clapped his shoulders. "Good job, Boss. You sounded like you almost knew what you were saying." The others were smiling, too, and clapping along with Ishidrum's national leaders. Rommie looked a little distracted, but Dylan figured she was probably still trying to diagnose her various malfunctions.

"Thanks," Dylan said happily, relieved that it was over. "I guess it went okay, huh?"

"You should think about staying here, Dylan," Limm'ta said. After the meeting, they and *Andromeda*'s crew and a few of Limm'ta's friends had gone to a restaurant for a big, celebratory lunch. Now, a couple of hours later, Limm'ta's friends had taken the others to show them more of Coramus, leaving Limm'ta and Dylan alone at the restaurant. Their table stood in an outside courtyard, its stone walls covered in a tangle of flowering vines. Each table was round,

with a hole cut out of the center, and more flowers grew up out o
the hole, spilling over onto the tabletops. The food had been out
standing, and now they lingered over coffee that was the best Dy
lan could remember having consumed in ages. One of the greates
inventions of ancient Earth, coffee. He'd be forever indebted to
Harper's home planet for that one.

"Stay here in Coramus?" he asked.

"At least on Ishidrum. You're an instant celebrity. And you
opinion would be highly valued. Unlike myself, you could cer
tainly find yourself in a leadership position somewhere."

Dylan had been thinking along similar lines. Ishidrum was defi
nitely a place he could see living happily. But not any time soon
He had a lot of parsecs to cover before he would be able to settle
down. Someday, though—if he didn't manage to get himself kille
first—he would, he supposed, be ready to retire. When that da
came, he could do a lot worse than Ishidrum. He explained his rea
soning to Limm'ta.

"But I don't want to wait that long to have you as a neighbor,"
she said. With a blunt fingernail, she traced a pattern on the bacl
of his hand. "I like having you around."

"I like it too," he said. "And the truth is, once the Common
wealth is up and running, they won't need a relic like me gumming
up the works. So it might not be as long as you think."

"My guess is that, after today, you'll have one more member
world," Limm'ta speculated. "I know there were some who op
posed it, and others on the fence. But I'd be willing to wager tha
you moved them off the fence and probably gathered a majority to
your side."

"I hope so," Dylan said. "And I hope they won't jump back over
it if Festival joins too."

She drew her hand away and her face turned pale. "You're no
still thinking of allowing them? Festival is not suited to join any
organization of civilized planets—they're barbarous, vicious, vio
lent people. They're the enemy of freedom."

"I think I have to," Dylan said. He had just reached that conclu-
on this morning, swayed in part by his own extemporaneous
peech. "For precisely those reasons you mention. What good
oes it do to cut them off from the community of peace-loving,
ivilized worlds? That would only serve to isolate them, to con-
ince them that they are right to continue on their present course.
hey would have no incentive to release the worlds that they have
nder their control now, and every reason to hold them all the
ghter."

"But . . . by inviting them into the Commonwealth, don't you
ıst condone what they've done?" Limm'ta asked.

"By inviting them into the Commonwealth, we give them a rea-
on to change," Dylan replied. "And we give the greater commu-
ity of worlds some degree of influence over them that otherwise
ouldn't exist. The Commonwealth gives us the opportunity to
ntice them to behave better. What, after all, is a more important
unction for a community than that?"

"I see what you're getting at," Limm'ta accepted. "But I'm not
ure that it will work in this case. You don't know Festival like I do.
he extent of their evil—and I don't use that word lightly—runs
ar deeper than I think you understand. They will not be easily di-
erted from their course, and they will use Commonwealth mem-
ership as a means to amass more power and wealth."

"They can try," Dylan argued. "But they won't succeed. They'll
nd that the Systems Commonwealth is used to dealing with
yrants, and has had a great deal of success putting them in their
lace."

Limm'ta sipped from her cup while he spoke, and then set it
own on the table, empty. "I wish you would reconsider, Dylan,"
he said. "They cannot be trusted, not even for a moment."

Dylan found himself a little surprised at the forcefulness with
vhich she addressed the issue of Festival's membership. He had
elieved that her main goal was to get Ishidrum accepted as a
ıember world, independently of what the Festival system did as a

whole. Having achieved that, he thought she would be satisfie
Now it looked as though she wouldn't be happy unless Ishidru
was a member but Festival was not.

Was she playing him in some way, he wondered? The flirtatio
the physical intimacy, the flattery . . . was it all designed just to ge
her way? Her friends had said she was remarkably successful as a
activist here on Ishidrum, and if she was so willing to use any c
the tools in her toolbox, including those, that could explain why.

He was about to ask her flat out what her agenda really wa
when Rommie rushed into the restaurant, frowning. She looke
worse than Dylan had ever seen her—harried and distraugh
"What is it?" he asked, standing up from the table.

"Dylan," Rommie said, her voice cracking. "We . . . we have
problem. A big one."

"What is it?" he repeated. "Rommie, what?"

"I'm . . . the ship is preparing to launch kinetic missiles
Ishidrum," she said urgently. "And I can't stop it."

TWENTY-FIVE

> "The best political weapon is the weapon of terror. Cruelty commands respect. Men may hate us. But, we don't ask for their love; only for their fear."
>
> —HEINRICH HIMMLER

"What do you mean, you can't stop it?" Dylan demanded. "You've got to!"

"Dylan, I can't," Rommie said. She looked like she was ready to cry. Dylan didn't blame her. Kinetic missiles could tear Ishidrum apart. There would be no tears shed if that happened, but only because there would be no one left to cry. "I can't get control of any of my systems."

"How can that—where's Harper?" he asked. "And the others?"

"They're not far behind," Rommie said. "I ran—I couldn't even raise you on your subcutaneous commlink, because that routes through the ship as well. I'm completely cut off."

Making her feel worse about the situation wouldn't help, Dylan knew. Nor would trying to assign blame. Right now, what he needed was to set things right. And it needed to be done before they found themselves in far more trouble than they could handle.

A situation that seemed to be just moments away.

"Dylan," Limm'ta said anxiously. "I hope this isn't some kind of . . . I don't know, negotiating tactic?"

"Of course not!" Dylan snapped, amazed that she would even suggest such a thing. "This is serious. We need to get back to the *Maru* immediately."

"I'll see that it's ready to go," Limm'ta said.

Dylan put his arms around Rommie, trying to comfort her. "Rommie, it'll be okay. You keep trying to reach *Andromeda*. We'll take the *Maru* and we'll get to her as soon as we can, and we'll manually override the missile launch."

"I don't know if we have that much time," she answered.

"How do you know the launch sequence has been initiated?"

"I—we were out walking," she explained. "And I felt—weird. Like someone was stepping on my wiring. Only not really—I can't quite describe it. I turned around and started to come back here, to tell you, as soon as I realized I couldn't raise you on the comm. Then the weird feeling got worse. It was like I was being shut out, system by system. Before I was totally closed out, I became aware that the kinetic missiles were being prepared for launch, and I knew what the target was. That was when I really started to panic, and I ran all the way back here. But by the time I found you, my disconnect was complete. Now I don't know what's going on at all."

Dylan was about to respond when he saw Tyr loping toward them, followed by Trance, then Beka and Harper. Rev Bem brought up the rear. They all looked concerned, but obviously didn't know the seriousness of the situation. Rommie had sought Dylan out, told him first.

He stepped out of the courtyard and went to meet them at the restaurant's entrance. "We're going back to *Andromeda*," he said. "There's a problem."

"No way. A problem?" Harper asked sarcastically. "That never happens to us. Is it a bad one?"

"Only if you think blowing Ishidrum into little tiny smoking pieces is a bad one," Dylan answered. "Personally, I'm not in favor of it."

"There are other places I'd blow up first," Beka offered.

"Agreed," Tyr said. "Not many, but a few."

"Then let's go," Dylan urged. "We may not have much time left."

Andromeda seemed to be working fine when they reached her. The AG and environmental systems were running, and the automated defensive systems recognized the *Eureka Maru* and let her land without incident. But when they disembarked from the *Maru* and tried to take control of *Andromeda*, the ship refused them access.

"Rommie . . ." Dylan began.

"I'm trying, Dylan," Rommie said. "I can't get through to my AI or my holographic avatar."

"I'll go see what I can find out, Dylan," Harper offered.

"You do that," Dylan affirmed. "Our first priority has to be shutting down that missile launch." He looked at one of the flatscreens as if it would spring to life. "*Andromeda*, offensive weapons status, please."

Andromeda's face appeared on the screen. "Kinetic missiles firing in six minutes, twenty-seven seconds, and counting."

They had arrived just in time. "Abort firing sequence," Dylan ordered.

Andromeda's face winked out.

"*Andromeda*, abort firing sequence!"

No response.

"*Andromeda*!"

"She isn't listening to you, Dylan," Beka said.

"I can see that."

A single one of the ship's OM-5 kinetic kill missiles could destroy a small planet like Ishidrum. *Andromeda* had used the plural, and she wasn't prone to exaggeration. Multiple missiles would not only destroy the planet, they would scatter its ashes across half of the Festival system.

"*Andromeda*, respond."

"That isn't helping, Dylan," Rommie said, her face pained.

"I'm jacking in," Harper announced over shipwide comm. "Figure I can do more good in there than out here."

The virtual reality matrix. *Good idea*, Dylan thought. "Go for it, Harper."

"Going for it, Boss." There was silence for a few moments, and then Harper's voice sounded again, an unpleasant whine in it this time. "Owww. That hurt."

"What, Harper?"

"She kicked me out," Harper complained. "On my ass."

"Literally?"

"Well, virtually, at least."

"Rommie?"

"I can't explain any of it, Dylan. I can't get in either."

"Who's in command of this ship?"

"Officially, you," she said. "Of course."

That was what he had wanted to hear. "Then I'm going in." Entering the VR matrix was a more complicated process for Dylan, since he didn't have a neural interface built into him as Harper did. But it wasn't impossible—it just required slightly more complex headgear. He jacked a cable into the necessary goggles and put those on over his eyes.

"Status report, offensive weapons!" he shouted.

Andromeda appeared on the screens again. "Kinetic missiles firing in four minutes, thirty-two seconds, and counting."

"Abort!" Dylan ordered.

She vanished.

Dylan put his hand down on the control pad, making the required connections.

And he was on his way.

There was always a moment of serious vertigo when he went

into the VR matrix. It was almost like entering Slipstream, only in microcosm. A chaotic rushing sensation, colors and lights whipping past him as he hurtled down the serpentine path into the ship's inner being. When he landed he was dizzy and disoriented, his stomach churning. Harper was more used to it—even seemed to enjoy it sometimes. Dylan was pretty sure if he was ever going to learn to like it, he would have done so long ago. As it was, he tolerated it, barely.

None of the rules of physics that he knew seemed to work quite the same way here. He walked on something that was like the ground, in the sense that it had solidity beneath his feet and kept him from falling, but it was as much an illusion as everything else. All around him—up, down, stretching infinitely far on every side, lights and visible circuitry created something that looked like a complex cityscape, but abandoned, lifeless. Dylan kept going, through the flashing and blinking and strobing, through pitch black and blinding white.

He was looking for Andromeda. Her android body was one thing, her holographic avatar something else, but this was where she really lived, where the consciousness, to use the closest available term, resided. She had to be here somewhere.

At least she hadn't thrown him out like she had Harper. But then, Dylan was the ship's captain. As far as a malfunctioning *Andromeda* might be concerned, Harper would have no authority whatsoever. He wasn't High Guard. Captain Dylan Hunt was. Dylan was in charge, and it seemed that even his broken ship knew it.

When he finally found her, he had to look for a moment because he had never actually seen Rommie in precisely this way. She more or less faced him, but much of her was blocked by someone else—Dylan saw a broad, muscular shirtless back, a shock of light brown hair—whom she clutched in passionate embrace. Mercifully, whoever it was still had his pants on. But Rommie saw Dylan and her eyes widened, and she pulled away from the embrace, and the man she was with began to turn to see what she was looking at.

And as he did, Dylan saw himself.

"Dylan?" Rommie said, and in her voice there was the tremor that Dylan would have associated with a straying lover, caught in the act. But where was the betrayal, here? He didn't understand what he was seeing, didn't understand how he could be looking at himself, in Rommie's arms.

"What's going on, Rommie? What is this?"

The other Dylan released her and turned fully to Dylan. On his face was a look that Dylan fervently hoped he never wore: a kind of antagonistic smirk, like someone looking at a hated enemy who was barely deserving of the attention.

"What's going on is that she's with me," the non-Dylan said. "And she doesn't need you."

"Dylan, I don't understand. . . ." Rommie began.

"I don't either," Dylan assured her. "But I think maybe he does."

"I understand fine," the faux-Dylan said. "She does what I tell her to now."

"You're the one who initiated the launch sequence," Dylan realized. "Rommie, stop it. Abort the missile launch."

"I . . ."

"Ignore him, Rommie. We're launching those missiles."

"Weapons status, Rommie," Dylan ordered.

"Kinetic missiles firing in two minutes, eleven seconds, and counting."

"Abort, Rommie."

"Dylan . . ."

"Don't pay any attention to him," Dylan's shirtless version said. "He's nothing in here. He's only real out there, where it doesn't count."

"I've had just about enough of you," Dylan said angrily.

The fake Dylan tossed him a dismissive sneer. "You think you can back that up?"

"I'm pretty sure I can," Dylan said, his anger boiling toward rage at the idea that this . . . this electronic imposter was in here, pretending to be him, and trying to take over his ship.

Trying, and maybe succeeding.

Dylan knew he had less than two minutes to wrap this up before Ishidrum was obliterated. If beating the nonexistent stuffing out of a collection of electronic impulses was what it took, then he would be happy to oblige.

The other Dylan stepped away from Rommie, and Dylan moved around him in a semicircle, his legs bent slightly at the knees for balance and to be ready to jump in any direction that might become necessary, arms tensed at his sides, hands open.

Fake-Dylan feinted toward Dylan's left. Dylan recognized the move, and turned toward his own left to meet the real assault head-on. He caught the other's shoulders. As they grappled, he realized that he'd been expecting his fake duplicate to feel somehow unreal, insubstantial. Instead, he felt just as much like flesh and muscle and bone as Dylan himself did.

And, not surprisingly, he was just as strong.

The two men held each other, pushing, grunting with exertion as they tested one another. It didn't take long—and he didn't have long, anyway—for Dylan to realize that this was not the way to win the battle. He couldn't outmuscle himself, so he'd have to out-think himself.

So he released fake-Dylan's left shoulder, giving a shove as he did, and dropped his hand, bunching it into a fist at the same time. While fake-Dylan was still reacting to the shove Dylan pistoned his fist twice into fake-Dylan's midsection. Fake-Dylan bent forward at the waist. Dylan followed up by bringing both hands down on the back of fake Dylan's head, driving it even lower, and slamming his knee up into fake-Dylan's jaw.

Fake-Dylan staggered, and Dylan allowed himself a quick glance at Rommie. She watched the whole struggle with horror. Dylan knew that he was looking at a ticking clock. If she didn't get a grip in a minute or so, it would be all over for everyone down on the planet.

The momentary lapse of concentration was all fake-Dylan needed to recover from the battering and charge into Dylan like a football linebacker. They both went down in a pile of fists and elbows and knees. Fake-Dylan pummeled Dylan, and vice versa. Dylan felt blood spray from his nose, and a blow over his left eye split the skin there, temporarily blinding him. He got in a few good shots, too, tearing flesh, feeling teeth crumble under his fists. Fake-Dylan spat blood and tooth matter onto the ground and kept up his assault. Dylan struck again, his fist rending the electronic version's skin, exposing gristle and the white of his cheekbone.

But nothing seemed to slow down his opponent for long. Fake-Dylan maneuvered so that he was on top of Dylan, whose back was pressed against the not-ground, fists raining into his face. He tasted blood, felt it filling his throat, choked on it.

Time was running out. It was obvious now that the fake Dylan knew the virtual environment better than the real one, fought here with more skill than flesh-and-blood Dylan could muster. Dylan tried to push off the ground, but it wasn't really solid, wasn't really anything except information, bits of digitally processed data, and he wasn't able to make it respond the way it should. Fake-Dylan's wounds were no more real than any other part of him, and he thought his own punches were losing their effect while fake-Dylan's wore at him.

Then, through battered and bloody eyes, he saw a shadow behind fake-Dylan. Rommie. Come to watch her lover finish him off?

Instead, with a grim, sorrowful expression on her pretty face, she held her hands out on either side of fake-Dylan's head. He was still pounding away at Dylan, unaware that she was behind him until her fingers spiked into his skull from both sides.

Fake-Dylan froze, his eyeballs rolling up in his head, and then he began to shiver, as though from electrocution. His body spasmed uncontrollably. Dylan took advantage of the chance to squeeze out from underneath him, and he forced himself to his feet, legs shaking and weak. Rommie's eyes were blank now, and after a moment she removed her hands from fake-Dylan's head, dropping him like an empty husk.

Dylan moved toward her, but some powerful, invisible force hurled him away.

His last thought, as he spun through inner space, was, *Too late, then.*

TWENTY-SIX

"Trust you? What, do I *look* stupid to you?"

—GERENTEX, IN A BUSINESS NEGOTIATION

Everything was ready.

Ashala would meet Cam at the fountain again, the same one they had met at the first time they had been really together. From there they'd go to the space elevator and up to the orbital docking station, where a ship was ready. The nearest Slip point wasn't far away. Within a day, they would be beyond the long reach of Havasu's influence. Within a week they would be someplace he could never find them.

Cam knew it meant giving up a lot. All his dreams of stardom, of being at the absolute peak of his career.

He had thought those dreams were the most important thing in life, the only things that could possibly matter.

Now, suddenly, he had other dreams. These hadn't built up over a lifetime—at least, he was not aware that they had—but had, instead, taken just a matter of days to claim their place at the top of his list of priorities.

But they had, and that's what mattered. Cam felt like a new man. He had never thought of himself as someone who would put the love of a woman above career advancement or financial gain. Especially now, when his plans—and Havasu's, he was happy to admit, since they dovetailed together so nicely—were so close to reaching fruition. The fact that he would take such steps, shift his priorities so drastically, took him by surprise. But it was a happy surprise, he thought. It meant that he was growing as a person. Putting aside material considerations, matters of pride, for something as ethereal as love. *That's a good thing, right?* he thought. *That's a sign of wisdom, of decency.*

Both were adjectives he had never thought to apply to himself before.

He believed there was a new spring in his step, a foolish but unshakeable smile on his face, when he approached the fountain. There were quite a few people milling about it, enjoying the view of the liquid fire that splashed in it. Around the Imperial Square there were even more, some looking up at the lighted signs he had written and caused to be placed here. The professional satisfaction he would ordinarily have felt at that hardly phased him.

But his smile vanished.

She wasn't here.

Cam was ready to leave, to walk away from his home, his career, everything he had built over the years. This was the moment he had been waiting for since the idea had occurred to him. When he had told Ashala about it, she had responded positively, enthusiastically, and their lovemaking had been even more explosive than before.

He pressed through the crowd around the fountain. He just couldn't see her, that was all. She was sitting on the steps someplace. Or waiting in the shadows, making sure the way was clear. That was like her, careful, considering all the possible consequences of her actions. Cautious, calculating Cam had become the impulsive one.

He saw tourists from a dozen different planets, and from every nation on Festival itself—the fountain of liquid fire was famous far and wide, and was listed in every travel guide. He saw locals, Gala residents who came to admire it, or to eat their lunches in its glow, or maybe to rob the tourists while they beheld the fountain in amazement and left their pockets unguarded.

He didn't see Ashala.

A knot formed at his throat, and he couldn't swallow around it. He started to feel dizzy. *Where is she?* he wondered. *She has to be here someplace.*

For a moment he decided that she must have worn a disguise, to make slipping away from Havasu easier. But he knew there was no disguise that could hide her from him, no clothing that could hide her exceptional figure, could conceal her breathtaking face.

Slowly, a horrific realization dawned on him.

She hadn't come.

She had been leading him on, playing with him. Using him to pass the time, as she accused Havasu of doing with her. Perhaps it was equally true in both cases. Cam had been—what was the word she had used? An amusement. A diversion.

When he started to take things too seriously, to get too attached, she had needed a way out of it.

This was that way. The message was unmistakable, and she hadn't had to tell him in person, hadn't had to be part of an unpleasant scene. By simply not showing up when she was expected, she had made her feelings crystal clear. If he followed up, if he went to her and demanded an explanation, then he would be acting the fool, and they both knew it.

Cam hated to be made a fool of, but more than that he hated to publicly demonstrate what a fool he was. Ashala had been able to tell that about him, so had chosen to make her statement this way, knowing that he would simply let her go.

Anyway, there wasn't much else he could do. He couldn't go to her and make a fuss. That would alert Havasu, and then he would surely lose her just the same. But he would lose his job, his livelihood, at the same time. Possibly his life, as well.

He was stuck. She had played the game better than he had. There was nothing he could do but accept it, no way he could change the outcome. The best he could possibly hope for was that Havasu would remain ignorant, and he could keep the Commonwealth campaign, keep his place on the pecking order of the sales world. Perhaps one day, in time, he could forget Ashala, forget the way she smelled, the way she moved beneath him, the way she looked up at him and smiled.

He knew it wouldn't be easy.

But it wasn't as if he had a choice.

The spring was gone from his walk, the smile vanished from his face. He turned, shoulders slumped, feet shuffling, to walk home. He had gone, in the space of a few minutes, from someone who had it all to someone who had nothing. He might, from time to time, find moments of satisfaction, even pleasure, from his career. But he would never again know the ultimate happiness that had been snatched from his grasp.

He was almost out of the square when a hand clapped him on the shoulder. For a brief moment, hoped flared in him. *She is here, after all.*

"Mr. Prezennetti?" Not her. A man, instead. He wore no uniform but his bearing was military—back ramrod straight, shoulders squared, eyes clear and alert.

"Yes," Cam admitted. "What is it?"

"I'm going to have to ask you to come with us," the man said. Cam noticed that he wasn't alone—there were three others, forming a kind of ring around him.

"Why?" he asked.

"Don't ask any questions, please," the man replied. "We can't give you any answers. But all will become clear, soon enough."

"Is this about—" Cam began. But the man shook his head, and Cam let the question die unasked. He didn't want to say her name in this man's presence. And if it wasn't about Ashala, he didn't want to risk drawing attention to what he'd had with her. Better to just go along, find out in due course who these men were.

"Very well," Cam said. The man who had spoken indicated that Cam should follow him, and started up the nearest road. Cam went along without argument or complaint.

He had nothing left that anyone could take away from him, he knew.

Nothing that mattered, anyway.

"Launch sequence aborted."

Dylan opened his eyes. Rommie's android avatar stood before him. The VR goggles lay on the control panel in front of him. His head throbbed, as did every muscle in his body, but he could see fine and he no longer tasted blood. Maybe a faint aftertaste, but that might have been imaginary. The damage done to him had just been done in virtual reality, then, and he would only carry the pains mentally for awhile.

"Rommie?"

"Dylan, I don't know how to . . ."

"Somebody mind tellin' me what the hell's goin' on around here?" Harper demanded. "Because I am, like, freakin' lost. And I'm a genius, so everyone else has got to be completely in the dark."

Dylan shrugged—gingerly, wincing as he did. All in his head, maybe, but it still felt as if he'd been through a brawl. "You'd have to ask her. You're sure the missiles aren't going, Rommie?"

"I said I aborted the launch sequence," she replied crisply.

"Thank goodness for that," Tyr said. "That would have been a terrible waste of some very expensive weaponry."

"Rommie, what happened?" Dylan asked.

"It . . . it embarrasses me to talk about here, in front of everyone," Rommie said. "But I am, after all, just an artificial intelligence. Emotions are simply a particular combination of electrical currents running through my systems—"

"As they are for all of us," Rev Bem pointed out.

She ignored his comment. "—so I should set my embarrassment aside and just tell you what I've learned."

"That would be an excellent idea," Dylan said. He rubbed his eyes, still a little surprised that his hands didn't come away bloody. *It was so real.* . . .

"Dylan—the other Dylan, I should say—was nothing more than a virus. I was infected with him—with it—while I was in orbit around Festival, by officers from the Festival fleet who boarded me while you were all on the surface."

"Except me," Rev Bem brought up. "I remained here. I should have seen something."

"It's a big ship," Beka reminded him. "You can't be everywhere. And you were working on your memoirs, right? You were probably focused on that."

Rev Bem waved a dismissive paw at her. "I've given up on that project," he said. "I realized I need to live a little before I have anything to say that'll be of interest to the younger generations. I haven't seen nearly enough of the universe yet. I was working on it then, but it should not have distracted me."

"*I* should have seen something," Rommie admitted. "And I did. But as soon as I was infected with the virus, I was ordered to forget what I had seen. None of you were within communication range of the ship, and by the time you returned, I had, in fact, followed the orders and had forgotten."

Dylan was beginning to understand, though he almost wished he didn't. He touched his finger to his lips. "And this virus took the form of . . ."

"Of you, Dylan," Rommie said, shamefacedly. "It took your form. It came to me, from time to time. It seemed like you came to me, or at least that's what I believed. You became romantic, pas-

sionate. I knew that it was wrong, that it was a violation of all my
programming, and of High Guard regulations. I knew it, but . .
but I wasn't myself. The virus was altering my responses. It was
making me . . . making me fall in love with you, I think is how you
would put it. Only it wasn't me, it was a virally-infected me, and it
wasn't you, but that—that construct that resembled you. He . . . it
the virus . . . was responsible for all my systems malfunctions. It
was taking over control of my systems, locking me out of them, little by little taking command of the entire ship.

"At the end, when you were fighting him in the VR matrix, I
knew—even despite the effects of the virus—that the real Dylan
Hunt would never be fighting to end people's lives, but only to save
them. That was what it took to bring me out of it enough to tap
into him, and when I did that, then I learned the rest of the story. I
am . . . I feel humiliated, that I let my emotions get the better of
me, that I believed that you and I were falling in love, but . . ."

"But it wasn't you," Dylan assured her. "It was the virus making
you think that."

"Yes," Rommie answered quickly. "It was the virus. That's all it
was. The virus."

Dylan knew better than to push it. He was close to Rommie
and vice versa, and he had thought, now and again while they'd
been together, that she had a kind of crush on him. It was possible
that the virus had only been effective because it had sought out her
weaknesses and capitalized on them. But he didn't say anything,
didn't want to rub salt in whatever psychic wounds she might bear
as a result of this whole incident.

"You're certain it was the Festival fleet that infected you?" he
asked her.

"Definitely," she replied. "When I tapped into the virus I was
able to extract all my memories. I can play them for you, if you'd
like."

"That won't be necessary," Dylan said. "But I guess 'His Regency' is going to have to answer to the *Andromeda Ascendant*, then.

First we need to return to Ishidrum, though, to let them know everything is okay, and to formally accept them as members of the Restored Systems Commonwealth." He turned to Beka. "Is the *Maru* ready to make the trip again?"

"The *Maru*'s always ready," Beka said with a smile. "She's *my* ship."

"Ummm, Dylan?" Dylan hated it when Trance spoke with that hesitant tone—it was never good news. He turned to her, and saw that her cute purple face was frowning.

"What is it, Trance?"

"Before we go back, there's something you should know."

"Yes?"

She paused before answering—clearly, this was something she would rather not have to bring up. "I had a . . . a hunch. And Limm'ta left some of her bloody clothes on board, after we took her from Breckenridge Drift. So I . . . I kind of ran some tests, while you were otherwise occupied."

"What kind of tests?" Dylan asked.

"DNA, mostly. You know, like that. And then I compared the results to *Andromeda*'s databanks. *Andromeda* has really good records about Commonwealth history, you know—really fascinating reading, sometimes, and—"

"There is a point to this, Trance?"

"Of course."

"Would you mind closing in on it sometime?"

Trance rubbed her hands together and curled her tail. "Limm'ta Nax Terani is no relation to Sani Nax Rifati. I mean, maybe one of her extended family married into his family or something, somewhere down the line. But that's not what she says. She claims to be a blood descendant, and she isn't."

Dylan was stunned by her disclosure. "You're saying she lied to me?"

"I'm just saying she is not related by blood to Sani Nax Rifati. There is no direct lineage between their DNAs."

He was in no mood for semantic games. "She's been lying to me. To us. All along. Is she even Vedran?"

"She may well be," Trance admitted. "I don't know, I wasn't testing for that. Just comparing her to him."

"And it's not possible that *Andromeda*'s databanks are mistaken?"

"They're not, Dylan," Rommie reported. "Sani Nax Rifati is the reason I even exist. My databanks contain massive amounts of information about him, including his entire DNA sequence."

"Those memory banks weren't affected by the virus?"

"They were not. Just to be sure, I've rechecked Trance's results while we've been talking, since eliminating the virus. Her results are accurate and definitive."

"I see. Thank you, Trance. Rommie. I . . . I'll be in my office for a while."

TWENTY-SEVEN

"There are more than a million worlds of which we are aware, and on those worlds, individuals by the billions. Yet there was a time, on each of those worlds, when their population believed—no, *knew*—that they were alone in the universe, the only sentient race that could possibly exist, anywhere. We never know what we know until we find out what we don't know, and the latter list is always far longer than the former."

—SANI NAX RIFATI, IN CONVERSATION WITH
SUCHARITKUL, CY 4280

Beka was surprised—like everyone else, she guessed—by the extent of Festival's treachery. She hadn't liked the place, though she had admired some of the people there. Well, one of them anyway. She thought about Fyodor Tennyson, about her first look at him, standing beside the bar, unaware that he was being watched. He'd been so handsome, so sure of himself, so physically impressive, it was no wonder she had been drawn to him. But then he had turned out to be so *nice*, too.

That part had been unexpected. He had helped her look for Harper and Trance, using up most of his night even after it became obvious that it wasn't going to get him anywhere with Beka. He had helped keep her safe in a dangerous landscape, and he'd done it all with a smile. If Festival could produce men like that, the planet couldn't be all bad, in spite of Rev Bem's certainty that it was.

She felt a little sorry for Dylan. It had become clear to her that he and Limm'ta had sort of a thing going on. Infected Rommie had, according to Rommie's warped perceptions at the time, been right to be jealous. But now for Dylan to find out that the whole relationship had been based on lies? Beka knew he wouldn't stand for that. Whatever he had been building with Limm'ta was over, unless somehow Trance and Rommie were both wrong—not the likeliest eventuality she'd ever heard of. Dylan would leave Ishidrum behind for good, and he'd carry a grudge about it for a while. He would still accept it into the Commonwealth, because that was the kind of guy he was. But he would not accept Limm'ta back into his life, into his heart.

In a way, he would be leaving Ishidrum the same way she had left Festival: regretfully, wondering what she might have been able to have if she had stayed behind. Wondering if the person remaining down on the planet's surface was *the* one, or just *a* one.

But you're a pilot, she told herself. *First and foremost, that's what you do and what you are. You've gotta fly.* Chaining herself to a planet, or to a single person, would be slow death. Mobility was key. Moving on gave her a fresh start every day, the chance to invent herself all over again, as easily as shaking her head to change the color of her hair. Tying herself down wasn't the way she wanted to live her life, not as long as there was a pilot's station in front of her and a billion parsecs of space waiting to be seen.

She had a powerful feeling this trip down to Ishidrum would be a short one. No need to pack. She went to the *Maru* and started running through preflight checks. It would feel good to be under way again.

Being very nearly blown into tiny pieces and scattered to the stars tends to clear one's head, Tyr thought. If Rommie had been delayed in reaching Dylan, or if Dylan hadn't taken the threat seriously enough, if the *Eureka Maru* had been sabotaged as well . . . there were too many ways that things might have ended badly, for Ishidrum and for all of them.

Ishidrum had been a quiet, peaceful place, the kind of place where, if one could learn to live with the boredom, it would seem that survival to a ripe old age was virtually assured. He knew nothing was that certain. There was still the matter of how the people planned to prevent Festival from annexing them by force, and if that happened things would become decidedly more dangerous. And if it wasn't Festival, it might be someone else—Magog, or Nietzschean raiders, or some other visitor with less than friendly intent.

But the idea of an Ishidrum-like home, someplace where combat wasn't a daily activity, where a pride could live in peace, where the Nietzschean urge to survive could be satisfied—that had started to hold some appeal to Tyr. He supposed he was just in a questioning state of mind, looking at options, considering possibilities.

He had almost been sold on the virtues of joining an organized military operation like Festival's, but in retrospect, he realized how counter that ran to his instincts. The purpose of a military was to fight, and the purpose of fighting was to kill or be killed. The best way to guarantee an early death was to take part in something like that. The Nietzschean life span was a hundred and fifty years, and he had not achieved half that yet. He had a lot of years left, and he wanted to make sure he saw them all.

So short of finding a planet like Ishidrum, only with genuine security—and now that he knew they might exist, he would certainly keep his eyes open for it—maybe staying on the *Andromeda* was the best place for him. Dylan's goal, after all, was peace. Peace meant nobody shooting at anyone, which was a good first step toward a long life. Obviously, it was a goal that was still beyond Dylan's grasp, but every day, he came a little bit closer.

And as long as they were moving, he could keep looking for that planet, for that last best place where he could live the rest of his years in safety.

That was the best argument of all.

Anyway, it was good enough for him.

———

Dylan sat on a couch in his office and tried to put together a plan of action. Part of him wanted to just speed away, to let Limm'ta figure out that Ishidrum wasn't going to be blown up when the missiles didn't come. Probably she had already reached that conclusion—she was a lot of things, he was finding out, but stupid wasn't one of them.

Dishonest, yes. Also concerned, vital, passionate, beautiful, and strong. The kind of woman he could find himself settling down with someday, except for that first part. The dishonest part.

Dylan hated lies, and he hated liars. Havasu had lied to him and sabotaged his ship. Dylan wouldn't forgive that easily. But weren't the things Limm'ta had done nearly as bad? She had lied from the very first. She had distracted them from their mission, pulled them far off course, involved them in conflict with pirates—all with a damaged ship, not functioning at full capacity. Of course, she hadn't known that part—not unless she was in league with Havasu, and that didn't make any sense. Still, she had risked all their lives, and then having done so—and having persuaded Dylan to risk incurring the wrath of Havasu's fleet—she kept them from completing their mission. He wondered if he had accepted her invitation, and decided to stay on Ishidrum, if she ever would have told him the truth. Or would she let him go to his grave believing that she really was descended from his lifelong hero? He decided that he could forgive Limm'ta no more easily than he could Festival.

But there was still a big difference between the two worlds. Limm'ta didn't speak for Ishidrum, didn't represent the planet in any official way. And Ishidrum seemed to be a peaceful world, for the most part, not interested in attacking its neighbors.

Festival, though, was another story. Havasu was its undisputed leader, and under his command it was intent on military domination, on taking by force whatever it couldn't acquire through economic dominance. When Havasu betrayed Dylan, the whole world betrayed him. But when Limm'ta did, that was an individual betrayal, not a governmental one.

In a way, that made it hurt all the more. But he knew he needed to set his personal feelings about her betrayal aside, and keep his mind on what was important for the mission. He was glad he had achieved that realization, because the distinction was an important one. It paved the way for what he had to do next.

"You lied to me," Dylan said.

Limm'ta blanched. "Dylan, I . . ."

"Don't try to deny it, Limm'ta. You'll only make things worse."

They were standing on her back porch—the place where Dylan had spent one of the most pleasant evenings he could remember in a very long time, talking and laughing with Limm'ta and her friends.

There was no laughter now, though. Just he and Limm'ta, standing there facing each other, both tense. A frown marred Limm'ta's lovely features, furrowing her forehead and drawing her lips down. She looked away from him. "Yes," she said at length. "Yes, Dylan. I lied and lied, and then I lied some more. I admit it."

"Why?"

She met his gaze again, as if surprised he would even have to ask. "Isn't it obvious? I wanted Ishidrum to join the Commonwealth. I believe in your goal, Dylan. I believe in the Systems Commonwealth. I have studied the original one, and I think that, in spite of its faults, its flaws, it is still the best model of interplanetary cooperation out there. It's the right thing—the right thing for Ishidrum, and the right thing for the known universe as a whole. There should be a million member worlds, Dylan, and I believe you can make it happen. I just wanted us to be a part of it."

"But you could have made that case without lying, without claiming to be someone you're not. Is your name even Limm'ta Nax Terani?"

"Of course it is," Limm'ta said sharply. As if the lie about her name would somehow have been worse than all the others she had told. Her fists were clenched so tightly that her knuckles were white. Dylan wondered who she wanted to hit. Herself? Him? Maybe she should; maybe the memory of her blow would remind him to be more careful about who he trusted in the future.

"Ever since I heard the first rumor of your survival, Dylan, and of what you are trying to accomplish, I knew that it was a wonderful thing. I wanted to help you, but most of all I wanted to bring Ishidrum into the fold. I love my planet, Dylan, and want the best for it. I believe with all my heart that Commonwealth membership is that—the best.

"But I had no particular power here, no influence beyond a single raised voice, and maybe some sway over a few friends. So I traded on the coincidence of my name, and a passing resemblance. I invented the story that I was related to Sani Nax Rifati. There was no one here who could disprove it, even if they doubted. And I never gave them reason to doubt. I had read enough of his works to know his life and his ideals very well—as well as you, I would venture to say."

"Maybe better," Dylan admitted sourly. "I've been just a little on the busy side, and I might be a bit behind in my reading."

"Yes, maybe better. When I spoke—after I came up with the story, and word got out that I was a descendant—people took me more seriously. My influence grew. I was invited to other cities, other countries, to meet their leaders, and I found an audience for my ideas. For *our* ideas, Dylan, yours as well as my own."

"Please don't lump us together, Limm'ta," Dylan said. "We're not the same."

"We cannot be separated," Limm'ta argued. "Not intellectually. We are both dedicated to the cause of the Systems Commonwealth. We are both firm believers in the ideals elaborated by . . . by the man who is not my ancestor, but who I fervently wish was. Surely you can see that."

Dylan didn't want to accept it, but to deny it would have been just as dishonest as her claims of her lineage. "All right," he said finally. "I grant you that. You are a believer in the Commonwealth. But still, you could have argued for it without lying."

"I could have. And I could have been ignored, and been shut out, and been sent away. I could never have had anywhere near the impact here that I have. Not nearly. It's like . . . how far do you think you'd have gotten, if you were just some guy who put on an old High Guard uniform and found an abandoned ship? If *Andromeda Ascendant* were empty, and Harper or Beka decided to wear a uniform they'd found in one of its closets? It's your story that sways people, Dylan. They see a man who was in suspended animation for three hundred years, who lost everyone he ever loved, but whose devotion to a cause is so great that he carries on in the face of virtually insurmountable odds. That's a story, Dylan, that's an attention-getter. I didn't have a story like that. I just had a name. So I went with what I had. I'd do it again, too."

"I'm sorry to hear that," Dylan said. He didn't know what he had hoped—that she'd throw herself at him, maybe? Beg forgiveness? Swear never to let it happen again? Whatever he had wanted, it wasn't this—a defiant insistence that her lies had been worth it, that the ends she pursued justified the means by which she achieved them.

And still . . . and still he couldn't quite bring himself to think she was wrong. Sometimes maybe the end result was what mattered. Sometimes putting one's own personality, one's own history aside in the service of a greater good, was a valuable contribution. Living with her lies must have been hellish, but she had soldiered on because she believed the cause was just.

It sounded almost like something he would do, if the circumstances had been reversed.

"Dylan, you mustn't . . ."

"Mustn't what, Limm'ta? I do understand what you were trying to do. I can't approve of the way you went about it. And I can't stay here any longer. I can't run the risk that you'll keep lying to me, and I don't think I can trust you again."

Her eyes filled with tears. "Dylan," she said pleadingly. "Dylan, I . . . I just wanted . . ."

"I know what you wanted," he said. "And you can have it. I'm leaving—*Andromeda* is leaving this system. Hopefully for good. Festival will not be accepted into the Restored Commonwealth, but Ishidrum will be. If the world's leaders agree that they want to join, they can formally submit their application and I will accept it. But I'll need to hear it from an official representative of the planetary council, not from you."

The tears were flowing now, rolling down Limm'ta's cheeks. She nodded her assent. "I understand," she said. "I . . . I can only say that I'm sorry I caused you any pain, Dylan. I wish it had not happened this way."

"But it did."

"Yes, it did."

Dylan turned away from her, opened her back door and walked out through the house. He looked at the books and candles and historical objects, at the flexi of Sani Nax Rifati on the mountain's edge, presiding over the home of someone to whom he was not, in fact, related, and he swallowed his own emotions, fought back his own bitter sorrow. He hated to leave here like this, hated that Limm'ta was standing on her back porch, weeping, hated that his own loyalty to the Commonwealth required that he always put the mission first, above whatever needs his own personal happiness might have had.

The Commonwealth is worth it, he thought.

It had damn well better be.

TWENTY-EIGHT

"Each ending a new beginning, each death another birth, the
cycle goes around, the wheel turns, and turns again."

—ANONYMOUS, *A FATHER'S COMMON BOOK*, CY 3411

When they reached *Andromeda* again, the ship was surrounded.

As Beka threaded the *Eureka Maru* between the huge silver warships, Dylan recognized the markings on them. Festival fleet.
None of the ships made any attempt to impede their progress, and
shortly they were safely on board *Andromeda*.

Holographic Rommie met them as soon as they climbed out of
the *Maru*. "Festival ships, Dylan. Dozens of them. We are completely outgunned, and we're hemmed in."

"I can see that, Rommie," Dylan said, walking toward Command. "When were you planning to tell me?"

"I just told you."

"I mean . . . why wait till now? You could have alerted me before
we arrived."

"We were assured that the *Maru* would not be attacked," Rommie explained as they hurried up a corridor. "So we decided that

you didn't need to worry about this situation until you had finished dealing with the one down on Ishidrum."

"That's very considerate of you," Dylan said. "Although it might have occurred to someone to mention it earlier, in case Beka and I might have wanted to know that we'd been offered safe passage. Or if maybe we suspected they might not just be waiting until we were all in the same place so they could kill us all more efficiently."

"I see your point," android Rommie said, meeting them in the hall. Holographic Rommie blinked out. "I apologize."

I'm getting a lot of apologies lately, Dylan thought. *I'd rather just be told things that were true in the first place and not have to worry about accepting apologies for things that aren't.* Going off on her wouldn't be helpful, though. Her systems had been stressed lately, just as everyone's had. Instead, he asked, "Have they made any demands?"

"His Regency has been waiting for you to be available."

They reached Command Deck. Everyone was at battle stations, Dylan noted with some satisfaction. "It looks like I'm available now," he said.

"Shall I hail him?"

"Hold off a second," Dylan instructed. "What's our situation? How much trouble are we in if I tell him what I really think of him?"

"Very serious trouble indeed, I should say," Tyr answered from his weapons station. "We are well armed, point defense lasers are fully charged, missile tubes one through forty ready for launch. Some of the enemy ships may even be close enough for Tweedledum and Tweedledee to see action. But we are vastly outnumbered and they have had time to take offensive positions."

"Ready with evasive maneuvers, Dylan," Beka announced.

"All systems are at A plus plus," Harper chimed in.

"Probability of survival . . ." Trance began. "Well, I'd rather not say."

"So pretty much standard operating procedure," Dylan said.

"Pretty much," Beka agreed. She wore the smile she usually did when the odds weren't in her favor but she was committed to action anyway. Dylan was a big fan of that smile.

"That said, Dylan," Tyr put in, "I do so love it when you tell self-important gasbags what you really think of them."

"Then stick around," Dylan promised. "I'll try not to disappoint. Rommie, put him through."

A few moments later, Havasu's face appeared on Dylan's viewscreen. He looked, in Tyr's words, every inch the "self-important gasbag" that he was. His little eyes were almost lost in his ruddy face, his mouth curled and twitched like something that had crawled onto his face and was dying there.

"You've got my ship surrounded, Havasu," Dylan said, dispensing with the formal title for a change.

"Yes, that seems to be the case," Havasu agreed.

"Why?"

"Because I am a man of my word," Havasu answered. "I told you that if you took up with that—that provocateur, that you would be forcing me to take drastic action. Believe me, it is not what I wanted, not at all. But you left me no choice."

"There's almost always a choice," Dylan said. "In this instance, you have the choice to back off and not lose a bunch of ships and soldiers."

Havasu twisted his face into an approximation of a smile. "Is that a threat?"

"You decide," Dylan answered. "I just don't like being strong-armed. It doesn't sit well with me."

"I hardly think it's fair to say you're being strong-armed, Dylan. It isn't as if I didn't give you every opportunity."

"It's not?" Dylan shot back. "Then why did you sabotage my ship in the very beginning—while I was on your planet, supposedly enjoying your hospitality?"

Havasu made a move that might have been a shrug. Or maybe

he just had an itch. "Oh, that. I was simply covering all my bases. Anyone would do the same. You do have, after all, a bit of a reputation, Dylan."

"I have a reputation as a chump?"

"Your word, not mine. I would say, do-gooder, perhaps?"

"Since when is there something wrong with doing good?"

"It depends on where one stands, doesn't it?" Havasu asked. "Your definition of good might not be the same as mine."

"So you sabotaged my ship," Dylan said again.

"The way I see it, my only mistake was in not taking full control of it earlier," Havasu replied. There was something behind Havasu that Dylan couldn't quite make out—something moving. Havasu was in his big office, standing near his desk, with huge windows as a backdrop, but in the middle ground was some activity. Havasu seemed to be paying it no mind, so Dylan tried to ignore it, to focus on the regent's words. "Since you did exactly as I feared you might. That planet—Ishidrum—is a pox upon the Festival system. If I could pick it up bodily and hurl it into some other galaxy, I would do so. As it is, it sits there, taunting the other planets in the system, trying to foment revolt against Festival."

"Because it's a bad thing to try to get slaves to rise up against their masters?" Dylan asked.

"You exaggerate, Dylan. Ishidrum is doing nothing of the sort."

"Just by existing, Havasu, it's pointing out a better way."

"It very nearly didn't exist. I have plenty of ships around it now and I can still accomplish what *Andromeda* did not. I just won't get the political mileage out of it that I would have if things had gone according to plan."

"I'm sure not. So I guess the assassination attempt on Transitory Primus—that was your idea too? Try to get us out of the way, and if it didn't work, blame the attack on more of your so-called revolutionaries? All because you knew that if we visited very planet in the system, we would eventually get to Ishirum?"

Havasu rubbed his thin lips with the fingers of both hands. "I suppose there's no harm in admitting it now. It was not, in fact, my idea—not originally. It was his." He gestured over his shoulder, and the camera refocused enough for Dylan to see what was going on back there. He recognized the sales guy—Cam something, he remembered. But he barely recognized him, because there were hooks spiking through his flesh in a couple of dozen spots, and the hooks were attached to chains, and the chains were all taut, being slowly drawn in different directions. He was still alive, for the moment, conscious, and absolutely terrified of what the next few minutes would bring.

Dylan didn't blame him a bit.

"It was one of his better ideas, too," Havasu continued. "One of his worse ideas is what you see the results of behind me here. But the Transitory Primus one—I don't mind saying, I liked that one a great deal. If something tragic had happened to you, the other six worlds you have already accepted into the Commonwealth would still, I believed, continue their alliance. The word of our martyrdom would spread quickly, and more would join. With you martyred because you had refused my protection, I would have been just devastated, personally, and no alliance of planets would have turned down my request to join in honor of the dear, departed Dylan Hunt."

"You make it all sound so sensible," Dylan said. "When in fact, it's insane. You're not a fit partner for the Systems Commonwealth, Havasu, and the Festival system is not going to be accepted into it. The other worlds of the Commonwealth have already been alerted, by the way, so 'martyring' us now would have no impact on this decision."

No message had been transmitted, of course—it hadn't occurred to him until just now. But he nodded at Rommie, who re-

turned the gesture, and he knew that she would start transmitti
such a message immediately.

"I don't believe you, Dylan," Havasu said.

"Believe what you like. If you'd care to monitor our outgoi
communications stream, you can view it for yourself."

Havasu chuckled. "Can I tell you that you disappoint and i
press with the same breath? You are quite the antagonist, Capta
Dylan Hunt. I should have had greater respect for you from t
beginning."

"You should have greater respect for the worlds you try to crus
under your thumb," Dylan countered. "They won't put up with
forever. And another message that will be transmitted momenta
ily, to those worlds, is that they will be accepted into the Restore
Commonwealth if they throw off Festival's yoke. They have
make up their own minds to do so, though. Oppressed people ca
be shown the path to freedom, but they have to choose to take t
first step."

"I shall tremble in anticipation," Havasu said smugly.

"I'd give serious consideration to trembling if I were you," D
lan warned him. "They might not have given much consideratic
to any other way of doing things. But with the example of t
Commonwealth, and of Ishidrum, you may well see them chang
ing their minds in the near future."

"What makes you think Ishidrum will survive to see anoth
dawn?" Havasu asked. His florid face turned even more red wi
anger. "Our ships have kinetic missiles too, you know, and you'
not leaving me with much reason to contain my impulses."

"Ishidrum had better not suffer as a result of this," Dylan to
him. He had hoped that Havasu would have seen the uselessne
of such action, but it was looking like Havasu was not the mo
graceful of losers. He realized even as he answered that wi
leaders like Havasu out there, and planets like Festival, the Con
monwealth was needed more than ever. He felt a little bett

about having left Limm'ta behind—his own personal needs would have to wait until he could live in a universe where peace and cooperation were prized by most, if not all. "They have not yet formally applied to the Commonwealth, but I can assure you that an attack on them, from any quarter, would be considered an attack on the Commonwealth as a whole, and would be dealt with as such. And you do not want to bring the Commonwealth down on your head."

"I could start by taking out one of her flagships," Havasu suggested.

Dylan tensed. If it came to a fight, they'd give as good as they got. His crew would see to that. But in the end they would be beaten. There were just too many of the Festival ships, and as Tyr had pointed out, the overwhelming force would carry the day. "I would advise against it," he said. Suddenly the salesman's name came back to him. "If Mr. Prezennetti is still with you—ask for his input. I think he'll tell you that public opinion can be a powerful weapon, and if you attack us you forfeit that battle automatically."

"I have no need to ask Cam anything," Havasu grumped. "I know that he would agree with you. At any rate, I think it's a little too late to involve him in the conversation."

"That's most unfortunate," Dylan said, mentally adding the salesman's murder to his growing catalog of crimes for which Havasu would have to answer one day. "If he agrees with me, he's obviously a smart guy. Which I used to think you were, Havasu, but you're persuading me otherwise. Let's not let things get any worse than they are, though. Call off your fleet—now—and we'll be on our way."

Havasu glared at Dylan, furious and impotent at the same time. His mouth worked, but no sound came out. His fingers twitched. Dylan knew he was on the verge of ordering *Andromeda*'s immediate obliteration, just because he was so enraged.

But then his face collapsed, all the tension rushing out of it. His jowls drooped, his brow lowered, and he suddenly looked much older than he ever had before, as if all his despicable actions had registered on it at once.

"Very well," he sad sadly. "Go, Captain Hunt. I would not come back to the Festival system if I were you, not for a very long time. Another three hundred years might be sufficient, but if you return before that time, you will find that you are not welcome here."

"Believe me when I say that I have no interest in coming back here," Dylan assured him. "Unless I absolutely have to. If I do, I'll be leading a Commonwealth fleet."

"I imagine you will. Go quickly, now, before I change my mind."

"Beka?" Dylan asked.

"Ready to roll, Captain," the pilot said.

"All right, then. All forward. And Havasu?"

Havasu just stared at him, gnashing at his lower lip.

"A message from Tyr Anasazi. He wants me to tell you that you're a self-important gasbag. *Andromeda* out."

He broke the connection as the Command Deck exploded in laughter. When he could speak again, Tyr said, "I like the way you make enemies for me, Dylan."

"Figured you don't have time to tick off everyone in the universe by yourself, Tyr," Dylan said. "So I thought I'd help out."

Tyr laughed again, a full-throated, infectious sound. "Thank you, Captain Hunt. And if I might offer a personal comment—I cannot think of a better officer to serve under."

Dylan accepted the compliment graciously, but he wasn't quite sure where it had come from. Had Tyr been giving thought to changing his loyalties again? Dylan knew that Tyr's allegiance had been, for a long time, somewhat . . . fluid. But he had thought that was behind them, and that Tyr was on board for the long haul now. Maybe he needed to pay closer attention to his crew. He knew he could trust them. But he hadn't always paid close enough attention to their problems, their emotional lives, so wrapped up was he in the mission that he believed in. He thought they believed in it too. But it wouldn't hurt to check in from time to time.

He caught Rommie looking at him, but then, when she noticed, she turned away. *Maybe not such close attention to some*, he decided.

But he could not think of a better crew to serve with.

ABOUT THE AUTHOR

Jeff Mariotte has written many novels, including the original horror epic *The Slab*, and the teen horror series Witch Season, as well as some set in the universes of *Buffy the Vampire Slayer*, *Angel*, *Charmed*, and *Star Trek*™. He is also the author of more comic books than he has time to count, some of which have been nominated for Stoker and International Horror Guild awards. With his wife, Maryelizabeth Hart, and partner Terry Gilman, he co-owns Mysterious Galaxy, a bookstore specializing in science fiction, fantasy, mystery, and horror. He lives in the American Southwest with his family and pets in a home filled with books, music, toys, and other examples of American pop culture. Find out more at www.jeffmariotte.com.